The Almanac Branch

"Grace's story is compelling....[S]tylish, sinister portrait of a woman on the edge."

—*Seattle Times*

"*The Almanac Branch* is a riveting, superbly written, dark novel of familial intrigue."

—Water Abish

"The story is intriguing and richly complex."

—*Los Angeles Times*

"There's a lot of fine, introspective writing about families in this book, and Bradford Morrow shows himself capable of creating bizarre, yet believable characters.... Twenty pages [into *The Almanac Branch*] the reader wouldn't put it down if it were on fire."

—*Kansas City Star*

"Subtle, crafty, witty, vivid, as well as disturbing and haunting, Bradford Morrow's second novel is a Woolfian triumph....Here is a major author, of palpable style and impenitent mind."

—Paul West

"Bradford Morrow's new book is a joy. Beautifully constructed and flawlessly paced, its subtle unities, vivid prose, and riveting story yield the best and richest sorts of pleasure."

—Patrick McGrath

"*The Almanac Branch* is imaginative and quite often breathtaking; it is a dark novel of insight and mystery."

—*San Francisco Chronicle*

Available in Norton Paperback Fiction

Richard Bausch, *The Fireman's Wife and Other Stories*
Simone de Beauvoir, *All Men Are Mortal*
The Mandarins
She Came to Stay
Heinrich Böll, *The Casualty*
Anthony Burgess, *A Clockwork Orange*
Mary Caponegro, *The Star Cafe*
Robert Coover, *The Origin of the Brunists*
Rick DeMarinis, *The Coming Triumph of the Free World*
Sharon Dilworth, *The Long White*
Leslie Epstein, *Pinto and Sons*
Montserrat Fontes, *First Confession*
Mavis Gallant, *Overhead in a Balloon: Twelve Stories of Paris*
Francine du Plessix Gray, *Lovers and Tyrants*
Ron Hansen, *Desperadoes*
The Assassination of Jesse James by the Coward Robert Ford
Janette Turner Hospital, *Dislocations*
Ward Just, *In the City of Fear*
Ivan Klíma, *My First Loves*
R. M. Koster, *The Dissertation*
Mandragon
The Prince
Thomas Mallon, *Aurora 7*
Bradford Morrow, *The Almanac Branch*
John Nichols, *A Ghost in the Music*
The Sterile Cuckoo
The Wizard of Loneliness
Anthony Powell, *The Fisher King*
Jean Rhys, *Collected Short Stories*
Good Morning, Midnight
Wide Sargasso Sea
Joanna Scott, *Arrogance*
Josef Skvorecky, *Dvorak in Love*
The Miracle Game
Daniel Stern, *Twice Told Tales*

THE

ALMANAC
BRANCH

A NOVEL

BRADFORD MORROW

W. W. Norton & Company
New York London

First published as a Norton paperback 1992.
Reprinted by permission of Linden Press/Simon & Schuster.

Printed in the United States of America

First Edition

Library of Congress Cataloging-in-Publication Data

Morrow, Bradford, 1951–
    The almanac branch : a novel / Bradford Morrow.
        p.   cm.
    I. Title.
PS3563.08754A79 1992
813'.54—dc20   92-20230

ISBN 0-393-30921-5

W.W. Norton & Company, Inc., 500 Fifth Avenue, New York, N.Y. 10110
W.W. Norton & Company Ltd., 10 Coptic Street, London WC1A 1PU
1 2 3 4 5 6 7 8 9 0

The author would like to express his gratitude to Karen Kelly for allowing him a glimpse at a migrainous childhood, to Tom Cugliani for his memories of Shelter Island in the sixties, and to Donna Fish for gaining him access to the medical library at Mt. Sinai and helping him to understand what he read there.

For Susan

and in memory of
Suibne Geilt

List, O my friend, unto the tale of love,
  and God forbid that I should speak and
  that thy heart to hearken should not feign!
As 'twere El Asmai himself, of passion
  I discourse Fancies rare and marvelous,
  linked in an endless chain.

—*Arabian Nights,*
Tale of Hasan of Bassorah, 822nd Night

PART I

HOW THE RAVISHMENTS BEGAN

They spoke in light, when they felt like speaking. They spoke only to her, they said. When she asked them what they wanted, they retreated into the bark of their tree, and the night turned back to black. Sometimes she just watched them where they congregated in that old ailanthus outside her window, and didn't ask them questions. They would do as they pleased, whispering in hostile tendrils of crackling light words she often couldn't understand, or tracing curious cartoon figures on the pane with mercury and yellow sparks, or bursting into a cloud of crystals when at last she told them to go away. She alone knew them in the beginning, though she hadn't known them well enough to be able to say, in her child's voice, "Such and such took place." But now, because of what she had done, and after they had warned her not to, others would know they were there, and that meant there was going to be a problem.

It was late when the knocking was heard. Her father found her in her room standing at the third story window, slapping her palm against the glass, which was luminous with the light that came from a window across the back yard. Her face was dappled by shadows thrown through the wet limbs and the errant snow drifting down between them; and her father's wonder at how she had gotten herself so worked up, and what kind of dream could have left her in such a state—naked and shaking—was only overwhelmed by what formed on the girl's lips once he got a blanket around her and lifted her into his arms.

"They come in off the branch," she said, rubbing her eyes.

"Who, Grace?"

"They did, out there."

He looked over her head into the night where winter

smoke had settled with the snow over everything, peered down in the courtyard at the brick walls veined with ivy and dangling cables. A silhouette of some intruder, which he always hoped for, something to substantiate these events, was nowhere to be seen. He lifted the window a little, as her room was warm, and heard the music of the pianist who lived across the way, echoing against the brick. The city, someone always awake—couldn't that guy learn something else, all those crowded arpeggios flying every which way, and the piano out of tune through every note.

"They're gone now," he assured his daughter, setting her down and running his hand over her damp hair. The room had cooled, and he pulled the window shut.

"They want in."

The man heard her brothers talking in the hall—small voices of complaint about this middle of the night stuff going on again—and he shouted over his shoulder at them to go back to bed, and hearing their footsteps retreating down the corridor, asked her, quietly as he could, "Grace, who wants in?"

"Right there, them light people," she pointed to where they were still, out there pulsing and pushing, sending out their white razor flame. They weren't happy about being tattled on, was what the small one with the electric zigzag tongue told her. Hey, that girl was going to pay for her indiscretion. Her father was saying something to her but she couldn't quite make out his words given what an angry din the intensified lights had raised. They never really said they wanted to be her friends, but on the other hand they didn't think they had done anything to her that would provoke such treachery. She opened her mouth to apologize but they weren't interested in listening to apologies. They reminded her that she could have come out onto the branch and joined them whenever she wanted. Hadn't some of them been beckoning? Her father put her back to bed, and read to her for a while. The music from across the walled yard stopped, and the tree dimmed and was silent.

Just before Christmas, two nights later, a static voice came to her and said, Hey Grace? you want to see a trick?

"No."

Watch this, watch this, you won't believe it.

She went to the window, her fingers gathered to her chest, her quilt wrapped like a shawl around her as she stood there and again watched the light show. The flare man—the only one of the light people Grace felt was a friend—was alone, and had on a shell-pink tuxedo through which you could see his skeleton. Across his face, a crisp fuchsia smile.

Don't look down, girl, just watch this, he said.

Grace was afraid to call for her father, in part for fear she might awaken the small one who had threatened to sting her with that zigzag tongue of his, and in part because she didn't want her brothers to say anything about her light people, especially Berg, who made fun of her, and them, whenever he got the chance.

Everybody ready?

Sheepishly, she shook her head yes.

It was an astonishing display. It made her smile back at him, despite her terror. The flare man had gathered himself into a small ball of voltage, about the size of a baby, and then ran lightning snakes down and up and out, winding their way around every branch and limb of the tree so that the tree burst bright into bloom, and this ailanthus, this glorious urban weed—this botanical survivor, which sprouted between subway tracks, survived in pitch-dark cellars, in ventilation shafts, which sent down roots into fissures in the streets, where they strangled pipes and needled the bedrock—which was called, for all its love of darkness, the Tree of Heaven, wore for a moment its full garland of summer leaves, right here at the beginning of winter. The leaves nodded, cordial and companionable. Each leaf was impeccable in shape and contour, each was composed of humming, blue light.

Grace clapped and laughed, until the force of a flash

against the casement knocked her backwards into her bureau.

❖

Shelter Island. How appropriate the name must have seemed. Seasoned a traveler though he was, my father, whom I have called Faw as far back as I can remember, had never been there, and for all he knew, the island was nothing but a hump of granite, with patches of bitter grass cropped by stinking unshorn sheep, or a mud flat furred with pampas and populated by birds and scuttling crabs. But he liked the way it looked on the map, cradled between two earthly arms of the north and south forks of Long Island. I can still see him settling his lanky body into a library chair and putting his lean, intent face down close to the map. I can see how he imagined Peconic Bay flowing outward toward the east, Gardiners Bay flowing in from the open waters, how all the coves and inlets of the island swirled in their wash. Together they suggested renewal to him, my renewal. They hinted of absolution and health. And though there have been people in my life who have tried to convince me that a man as self-absorbed as my father could only have removed me and the rest of us to the island to reduce the distraction of raising a family—to hide behind mine his own need for renewal, or a darker need to be left alone—I have refused to believe it. Even now I know that it's never been quite that simple.

My father was an atlas man. He trusted maps more than the land itself. He lived by them, and the names people had given to the rivers and towns on them. While he was not what you would call a religious person—we children were never exposed to the sepulchral interior of a church, or any lessons about virgin births and miracles and so forth (except somehow I knew that St. Peter was crucified upside down, which I thought was pretty wild)—he was superstitious to a fault. My father would trust the most important decision to what most people would consider trivial, a word, a number, a color. So when my night visions got "completely out of hand"—these were Mother's words the morning after the flare man's show, words not meant to be overheard by me who never felt the night visions to be visions, as such—he went to his map case. Out came his compass. I watched him, my muscular yet delicate Faw, as he pinned its metal tip into the paper at the point where we lived, pulled the pencil leg out, and described a circle. Half the area inside the circle was light blue, the ocean. He let his finger wander over the map as if it were a Ouija board, then his intuition (yes; for though he was superstitious, he was willful in his way) tempted him out along the length of the burnt umber body of Long Island. He smiled at me, and it was one of those moments in which I couldn't tell whether we were experiencing something together and I was supposed to offer a conspiratorial smile in return, or whether he was enjoying himself while mildly teasing me—something he loved to do from time to time. With his free hand he gathered me over against him and showed me where we were going.

Shelter, I read.

Did I know what that meant?

He explained. All of it seemed so innocent at the time, and rather than feeling used, I felt grateful, rather than feeling apprehensive about what my father was about to do to himself, and the rest of us, I felt elevated by the warmth of his affection toward me.

Thirty years I have tried to piece together what happened to me, to all of us that crucial winter. It's been a task that I've taken up, and dropped, and then taken up again, and dropped again. Only now I realize that I must reconstruct all this, because it's no longer a matter of curiosity, but survival—this time, in fact, not merely my own. Crises have a habit of engendering more of their kind, just as do healthy organisms, emotions. My family's early catastrophes brought on the later ones, and we have had a time of

it trying to break the trend. You get used to things that
came before coming again, you even get to where you not
only expect but secretly want to see more of the same
trouble you've already gone through—"If it wasn't for bad
luck I wouldn't have no luck at all."

It happens because you become familiar with a certain
way of living, so that living perversely feels natural and
comfortable. Health has become foreign to you, and frightening, and far away, so far away as to appear unreachable—
no matter how you define it. For me, health means having
a conscience and living by it with as much energy as is
available to you, it means having a discipline. And health
has always seemed distant to me, far more distant than any
island, until recently. Catastrophes have had a way of taking me down so far and, given that I've been a faithful and
willing traveler, may now have brought me, whether I like
it or not, to a place of—and I use the term reluctantly,
because it's a word that smacks of religion and I'd argue
that none of this has to do with religion—redemption. On
the other hand, as my older brother Berg insists, now that
he has an adult stake in such matters, redemption "is something that only happens in the movies, and it happens because audiences demand the happy ending, they insist on
deliverance, even when they know that everything is point-
ing in just the opposite direction." A filmmaker and, until
this most recent project he's got himself entangled with, in
business to make money, Berg has always been one to believe in providing his audience its dose of generic, feel-good
resolution. Give them what they need, take from them
what you want. I, in my role of recovering cynic, and as
someone who now must finally face up to, even go up
against Berg, who is about to ruin himself, along with the
rest of us—through inadvertence as much as greed—cannot
speak for others, can only speak for myself, can only address my own redemption, such as it is, or might be.

Of New York, where I was born, in April 1957, and lived

until my seventh birthday, I can remember a few fragments.

There was a sailboat pattern on my bedroom curtains, with tall brown mountains that ringed the tan water in which the boats rode. The wrought-iron in front of our townhouse near the park up in Harlem was strong, and the smell of summer garbage along the streets was strong. The nocturnal visits of the light people and the aphotic bouts with my head were often followed by my father's reading to me from *The Arabian Nights*. Those ribbons of Sir Richard's words, his translation of the epic in lush and honeyed sentences—how they wrap my memory even today. And Shahrazad, my heroine and mentor, liar for the ages, was the sister I never had. My mother, Erin, was a pale, blue-eyed woman of medium height, with a tall brow and angular, honest cheekbones, fine manly hands whose veins were very prominent. Her hair, auburn shot through with scotch, was to my eye so flowing, as flowing as any Pre-Raphaelite's but without the usual *douleur*, and far more Irish. (People sometimes said that when I got older she and I would look like sisters, as we shared these features—except my eyes were green.) My mother often smelled of potpourri, which was an obsession of hers, an eccentric one I always thought, wresting petals off cut flowers, roses mostly, and drying them on the kitchen counter spread with dish towels. These are clear, unblocked memories, and they're the only ones I have got, because what my life was before we emigrated to the island seems to blend into an indistinction that is as familiar as the perfume from those cloisonné bowls of potpourri, and as impossible to distinguish as the scent of one flower from another.

My migraines, which were alluded to as seldom as possible in our family, as if they were leprosy or madness, were referred to by us with the amiable old name of "megrim"—which sounded to me like "my grim," an accurate-enough homonym. They were the source, it was agreed by the

several doctors to whom I'd been taken, of my visions
. . . psychotic ecstasies, as one of the specialists—whom Faw
loathed—called them; auras was Dr. Trudeau's word. Everyone was always more upset, and perhaps awed by the
sheer phenomenological peculiarity of the visions than I,
and as a result tended to ignore the migraine itself. For me,
the auras, the whispering lights and fantastical occurrences, were indeed enthralling and even ecstatic, whereas
the megrims that led to them were just weighty and dead-
ening. During the megrims all I wanted was for my senses
to stop receiving signals from the world, and for everything to come to an end. The megrims backed me into a
dark wet quiet which, unlike the darkness my jolly haunted
ailanthus tree thrived in, forbade growth. It is common for
us to speak of St. Hildegard's sublime visions, when we
speak of such things, and to marvel at her mystical stars and
her descriptions of the city of God and the Fall of the
Angels and all that stuff, but seldom do we think of her as
just a pitiful girl racked by pains she didn't understand, and
which to this day medicine has neither explained nor been
able to cure. Rarely have I rued the fact we weren't religious. But when I have, I've fantasized what my so-called
visions might have meant to me if we were. I could have
been a saint, instead of Grace Brush. But some of the things
I've done in life as a result of not believing I wouldn't give
up for anything, let alone a martyr's seat up in big bad
boring heaven. Let others retire in celestial peace and walk
the Elysian fields—which I picture as being a kind of golf
course, pristine and manicured, with paths of raked star-
dust. For myself, give me my earthly weeds and I'll go my
own direction.

I didn't like, and still don't, people feeling sorry for me,
so as often as not I did my best to mask what was going on.
The flare man I can see in my mind's eye as clearly as if it
had been yesterday, rather than a quarter of a century ago.
If I hadn't lived in a migrainous world would I remember
more about—and thus be able to better record—what our

family was like before we left for the island? I'd like to think that I would have sharper memories of my brother Desmond. As it is, I do not.

There were other houses on the island that dated from the same period as Scrub Farm, mid–nineteenth century. Families lived on and on in them, passing them down to children who married some cousin or another, in the island tradition. There they settled, just as their ancestors had, and stayed put, rather than to risk launching themselves like sea-battered coracles out toward the world beyond their shores. Like most islanders, they preferred to live among their own kind, and together survived all the hardships that poverty and ignorance and bad weather brought their way.

But while Scrub Farm's owners got through the Depression, the widow Merriam outlived every relative she ever had, and died heirless at the beginning of the new year, 1964. Scrub Farm was hardly a farm. For one, there wasn't much land to cultivate. The wind had for centuries blown across its stony fields, bending the trees, drying the soil. Whenever a storm came in off the ocean, Scrub Farm would have been the first to be hit, set as it was at the foremost edge of the island.

The house hadn't been kept up, and it attracted on the day of the bank auction no bidders except Faw, who bought it over the phone, having seen a photograph of it. He acquired the house and all its contents for less than five thousand dollars. "As is," was the phrase used by the auctioneer. Within a week of closing—early March then—he made arrangements and out from the city we came, the Brush family, in a borrowed truck stacked high with our belongings.

Never give up a known for an unknown, who said that? Still, the way we piled into the front of the truck made for a kind of physical, animal togetherness that shadowed the currents of anger that were running, especially between my parents, in a binding way—the same way a prisoner's

striped pajamas bind him with the prospect of being in his
barred cell.

Dr. Trudeau's idea was coming to pass and at least in the
beginning Mother was willing to play her role in it, because of me, and because she was so surprised that Faw had
decided to take the advice of one of my doctors, something
he had never done in the past. She had doubts, to say the
least, however. If I didn't improve, would she be stuck out
there with all those inbreds and fishermen, hated by the
natives as a summer person who got it in mind to live there
year-round? Mother never liked even leaving our neighborhood in Manhattan, thrived in her way on the city's chaos,
loved nothing better than to look out from the roof of our
building, on summer nights, into the steamy black of Central Park limned with lamplight down its lanes and at its
borders. Was she to be not just exiled to this island, but to
a remote part of it as well, there at the end of a causeway?
She had looked at the photograph of Scrub Farm—that
Polaroid glazed with streaks dark as the skin of the egg-
plant she sliced for our last supper, boxes stacked high in
every room of the apartment, the place oppressive with
that combination of melancholy and anticipation which
fills rooms about to be vacated.

The photograph showed a weathered exterior of
bleached-out, sun-cupped clapboard. Two stories with a
filigreed widow's walk dangling like a tottery derrick, or
one of Gumby's ant-enemies, from the peak. A carriage
house, fuzzy in the background behind a row of decrepit
trees. A single bayberry bush caught in a moment of shivering in the low scampering air. A yellow cactus clung to the
stony soil. It didn't look like such a place could be in New
York State, it looked foreign. Everything appeared dilapi-
dated, bare, and, but for the house on the slight rise and the
sizable cherry tree next to it, low—no doubt from aeons of
sea and wind working away at it. She hadn't liked what she
saw. Aside from the thin green trace of horizon, and the
blue line of ocean, which reminded her of the blue line the

police barricade makes along the avenue and the green line they paint on the pavement when they're going to have a St. Patrick's parade, the very thought of which cheered her flagging spirits, everything in the image felt prehistoric and desolate to her, and wholly untenable.

I heard my parents talking that last night, when I couldn't sleep, when I stood there at my window trying my best to ask the light people to come out to say good-bye, knowing that since I didn't have a megrim there was little chance they'd be conjured. I heard her ask him why she had to leave home and he didn't. She said, "I hate the country, I hate the idea of having to water trees" (to which he answered, "For chrissake you don't water trees, Erin")—and so forth. I do remember her reminding him, and about in these words, "You've always preached to the children that you've got to stand square and fight your demons"—so wasn't this exodus to Shelter Island just the supreme example of how not to face problems? And could he deny her the claim—she was crying, then, and it made me afraid, how hysterical her voice sounded—that he was all for this island move because it would leave him free to spend his time in town, building "your goddamn Geiger," while the family moldered, safely out from under his feet, in bucolic isolation? I didn't know what bucolic meant, but I can remember the word because it was said when the flare man came out, much to my delight, for just an instant.

What gives, girl?

I have the distinct sense that he may have invited me to crawl out onto the ledge and give him a farewell kiss, but that doesn't sound very flare-man to me, now. That is to say, he wasn't much of a sentimentalist, more of a performer—so if he did, it would have been in the cause of showmanship, or else to murder me.

What gives?

"We're going away."

Want to see a trick, real neat one?

My mother's voice came pushing in toward my room,

and I did my best to close it and her off, then looked at the flare man again, who tonight was a mustard yellow. "I said we're going away, didn't you hear me?"

Well, do you want to see, or not?

"You want to come, too?"

Grace, he said, impatient.

I still don't understand how imagination works, what it is, what its relation to the body is, because the flare man was so sophisticated, and I, who (surely must have) created him there on his ailanthus branch, so young to have invented this. He flipped himself over onto one skeletal finger of one hand and balanced on the branch, then filliped himself to a twig, still aloft on the finger. A wiggly tongue of yellow light streamed from his navel, and he slowly lifted his finger up so that he was perched on the yellow stream, which just barely touched the twig. Arms and legs extended, he turned his face toward mine and a wry smile began to curl across his lips, a wry and yet loving smile. He didn't say anything, though usually, in my experience with him, he would have said something at about this point during one of his exhibitions, something like, Can you believe this, or, Check this out, or, Am I amazing or am I amazing? Rather, he winked, and seemed to concentrate, and then he did something I never thought was possible for him to do. He pulled the yellow light back into his skeleton belly, and turned his head in order to look at me full in the face. He was floating.

I stood there in awe. He knew that I'd seen him do some fantastic tricks before, but never abandon the tree itself. He didn't brag, though. What he said was this. He said, Open your eyes wide, girl.

"Why?"

Open them, go on.

I opened my eyes.

Then he said, Have you ever cried backwards, Grace?

"Huh?"

Cried backwards, listen, it's great. Open your eyes wide,

and don't move. It's great, it's a great way to cry, because nobody can see that you're crying, just so good to know how to do it, in case you need to do it in the future sometime. So just be still, and what we're going to do, it'll be really neat.

And he did, he came over, floated to the window, and I was looking straight at him he couldn't have been more than a few feet away from me (he seemed smaller the closer he got) and he reached out with the tip of his finger toward my eyelid—my eyes were closed, I couldn't keep them open, and yet I still could see him—and a stream of light came into the pupil of my eye. My mouth began to fill with liquid light, and he said, Swallow, and I swallowed, it was acrid, and I gulped it down.

See you around, Grace, and I was still gulping when he swam back into the bark of the tree. I felt almost rapturous at having been allowed to commune with my friend without having had to pay the usual dues. My parents' room was quiet, when I listened against the panel of my door. They were all asleep.

We arrived on Shelter Island midafternoon. Gray clouds bore into the slate sky above. The ferry wake hypnotized a flow of gulls, and we stared down into the churning, engine-chafed water and watched the loading dock recede. The farmhouse was out past not one but two causeways, on Rams Island, as it was called, along a sparsely built beach road, and faced out to the white ocean. A mild breeze tripped across the flat, and I pulled my hair out of my mouth—there were always to be mist and air moving across the flat of the island here, buffeting the surface of Coecles Inlet and Shanty Bay. Faw and the boys unloaded, while Mother fidgeted with her wavy masses of hair. She touched the back of her sturdy hand to her lips, and caught her breath—having rummaged in her purse she realized she'd lost the keys. We stood before the front door on the deep green porch. It didn't matter about the keys, the door swung open when I pushed against the handle.

Inside the front room were shimmery cobwebs jeweled with flecks of sandy dust. Mrs. Merriam's possessions were draped with sheets. The first-floor bedroom had been used by squatters. A boot missing its tongue lay at the foot of the stairs. Throughout there were signs of trespass and of trespassers' lovemaking. A display of nature's own encroachment took the form of a bald vine that had crept up from the cellar—imitating, it seemed to me, my ailanthus back in New York. It grasped at the maple-snipped sun in the oriel window. What was dingy melded with mystery in my darting mind.

"I like it here," I said.

When I broke away to run upstairs and look out from the balcony to the sea, she said, "Grace, be careful," and the way she said it made me realize that it was she who was afraid, and so I came back to her, looked at her, and saw she wasn't able to look at me, so I followed her through the front room toward the kitchen.

Here things were in no better shape. The faux-oriental kitchen linoleum was curling up around its appliances, the appliances were themselves in different states of disrepair—the impertinent Norge stove wheezing gas, the racks in the refrigerator hung with green, tobaccolike beards. The doors to the downstairs rooms would not stay closed, the silver "American"-emblazoned radiators banged and hissed. Even when it seemed like too much, there was more. The upstairs windows, where she went, me still gliding behind, whistled when she opened them, and their sun-grayed lace shook out the dust of who knew how many years of neglect.

"My God," or something like that—and I said, "Mom, you'll see, everything will be all right."

The place was, in a word, uninhabitable, "uninhabitable," she said, "Scrub Farm my eyes!" What else was the poor woman going to say? We have no guarantee of Grace's improving in a funhouse like this, Charles, she might have said—and it would have been a logical response to the state

of the place, its spinning spiders and beguiling noises—but
she decided to keep her own counsel as best she could, and
draw a curtain across her own thoughts, so that neither I
nor any of the others would be able to scrutinize her. Looking back, I can see how it would be possible for her to have
made up her mind that very first day, to leave us behind,
all of us, for the shackles we had become on her. Sure, it
is true she always worked hard to paint scenes of perfect
motherhood on that curtain, so I, her daughter, and the
boys would admire her, which we did. Lord knows, she
must have told herself, for our sake, my dear stoic mom,
doors can be fixed, windows can be refitted. But when she
and I stood there alone in the kitchen, and she pulled back
her hair, caught her breath, then pressed the knuckles of
one hand tight upon her lips, the very tone of her being was
changed. I saw it. She drew herself in, withdrew, retracted.
She looked the same, but had become a different woman.
When she—we—emerged onto the back porch, and she
said, "Have you seen what this, don't those auction people
from the government have some responsibility—" I could
hear that it was something she said because it was something she was expected to say, and no more. She might as
well have kept on walking, left the porch, left the house,
taken herself down the beach road then and there, as go
through those ludicrous (that's too harsh, call them pathetic, or better: overwrought) motions.

Faw knew none of this, of course. "What?" he said, and
it was the kind of "what" that means, Spare me, I don't
want to hear it, as he strained to lift trunks and chairs and
mattresses down off the truck through the tangle of half-
untied lashings.

Berg and Desmond were distracted. I wanted to find out
if the sea-worn apples in the orchard, wrinkly as those
pony's balls we saw in Central Park last year, tasted any
good after a winter of dangling on the crooked limbs, and
Desmond wanted to come, and so did Berg, but they helped
their father anyway, because he had announced that "this

is where you boys are going to become men, and you know
what men are?"

"Grown up," Desmond guessed.

"Men are responsible people, you know what responsibility is?"

"Jesus H. Christ," Berg talked back, like he did sometimes, even then, and Faw heard him and told Desmond,
"Did you hear what your brother said?"

"Yes," Desmond replied; he hated it when Faw did this,
held him up to Berg as some behavior model, when in fact
he didn't want to be either a good boy or bad.

"That's not what responsibility is."

"Yes, sir," with tardy half-closed eyes.

"And Burke?"

Burke, whom we called Berg because his fingers and toes
had poor circulation and were icy to the touch, was twelve
that year. He was trying to grow his moustache. He wore
his shirts backward for a time, making me button them up
for him. It was a look. As narrow-shouldered, narrow-
waisted, and narrow-wristed as he was—all this made him
appear, at a glance, a wispy bit of defiance—Berg was
strong and limber. Buttoning his shirt on backward (he'd
scissored slits in the front seams at the arm to allow for
mobility) was one of the few things he allowed me to do
with him. I was just his sister, and fully understood I didn't
count for much. Why should I? How could I?

"Can we go back home now?" obnoxious as he could
manage.

"Thank you for showing Desmond how men don't act."

"Go to," and Faw, who held the bulk of a rayon-shiny,
unwieldy mattress, pushed Berg, who tripped over the
path rocks shoving back against him. Was it because Berg
was a man he didn't fall down?

Mother went back inside. She disappeared upstairs for
an hour, and no one bothered her. Berg went over to the
shore by himself, and so Desmond and I worked hard with
Faw. By the time the large ocean stars burned between the

running clouds that carried brief squalls of tough, short
sprinkles, we had, after our own fashion, moved into Scrub
Farm.

One footnote, about that first night, learned by me years
later, in a letter from my mother. Rain as fine as pencil lead
had begun to mark the yard. Mother was in front of the
kitchen fire, too exhausted to eat dinner with the rest of us,
her feet resting on the brick hearth. From where she sat she
noticed a draft along the floor through the room, got up and
walked toward the source of this damp, streaming air.
What she discovered was that the glass in the mudroom
door was broken. No one had gone in that room yet, a small
cul-de-sac of a side room off the pantry. She came back into
the kitchen, saying nothing, and gathered some sheets of
crumpled paper from the heaps that lay everywhere from
unpacking, and left, thinking to tape a sheet over the
breach in the glass. She took the flashlight with her, as there
was no bulb in the overhead light. Seeing the flashlight,
Faw or Desmond or one of us asked if she needed help, but
she said she didn't. Maybe she wanted to be alone again, we
thought. When she entered the mudroom, and ran the
beam of light over the walls and floor, she saw what had
caused the glass to break. At her feet lay the carcass of an
enormous bird—a heron, a black-backed gull, perhaps even
an osprey, she wasn't sure—broken on the brick floor, its
wings askew and its neck twisted, the sheen of life gone
from its feathers.

The poor creature had been dead so long that the flesh
beneath its feathers was decomposed and its death-scent
was gone. She stood there, serene and silent. The reason
she had said nothing was that she didn't want me to see.
There would be no end to the nightmares it would set off,
she had reasoned, not, knowing how little such a sight
would have affected me. But what was behind her serenity
she couldn't fathom, her letter explained. She spread sheets
of newspaper over it, trying her best neither to touch it nor
to assign it much meaning—though it was her nature, just

as it was Faw's, to assign every little thing meaning. She later put us children to bed, and went to bed herself after listening for a while to her husband, downstairs, in another of the unexplored places of the house, talking to someone on the telephone in his clumsy, confident German.

And, oh—about those orchard apples. They did look from afar like pony balls, but up close resembled the shrunken head that Faw brought back from Brazil once, only bald and without a bone through the nose. They were delicious.

❖

Sometimes you believe everyone is a sphinx without a riddle, except perhaps someone you love, or strive to love, whom you view not as sphinx, because you know him and he speaks to you in ways you feel you can understand. The one you love says something, and you lean into it, and you try to understand, and if you can't you let it go at that, appreciating the riddle for what it is—the action of love itself—and not forcing on it the need for a solution. My father was surely full of riddle. Early morning, after we arrived, having gone to bed long after all of us had, he was back on the telephone. I could hear him, again in the German, and I guessed he was about to convert into one of his riddle phases.

I was right. Awake just in time, I heard him drive away. By afternoon he had flown to Munich.

"Dear Grace, poor Grace," Mother might say—and she would not be wrong—and talk to the wall about the fact that here was Faw, all obsessed with this newest doctor's opinions about the megrims and the auras and getting us out of the city to somewhere quiet, and then, like that, he up and runs to Europe as if nothing were amiss, what kind of man is that? By what fricking design of distractedness or permutability could he tell himself that anything of the sort was fair or decent, she wondered aloud, walking back and forth down in the kitchen—wondering perhaps not in those exact words, moving around through the rooms with me following behind, and Desmond trailing behind both of us, getting the meaning through her tones and the way she flung her mane.

"It's okay," I assured her, thinking Don't drag me into it. I didn't want her to believe that I minded, because I didn't.

What I thought then, in the childish terms that were available to me, is what I think now: his disappearances, which came often and often went unexplained, were the result not of distraction, but of absolute, untrammeled focus, of pure enthusiasm for the moment and what should be done just within its energy pool. Something on the order of, "The hell with long-range plans, the hell with tomorrow, just hone in hard on the paroxysm of the minute, whatever it might be, and count on the big picture to work itself out later."

You should know I am not being charitable, or daughterly slash overdevoted, to assert that there was value in his methods, as he did have a way of making things work. The more unlikely, the more implausible it was, the more interested he would get in a project. He had built from scratch, with his own hands and head, the latter used as much for butting as reasoning, the vast entity of Geiger—referred to by us, who had to have special names it seems for so many things, as the Sprawl—and tended to its multiplying small subsidiaries as if he were pure radiant heat burning over a benign, creative, and corporate virus. Geiger was a masterpiece of sorts. Its own history was a history of the penumbra of that great dark shadow we cast across our land in the name of popular culture. It was a constellation of all those little unlikely and implausible ideas that become companies. The Sprawl produced everything from plastic boxing gloves to edible Halloween masks, from commemorative beer steins to limited-edition porcelain Presidents' Busts. The glowing yoyo, GloYo, was his—I still have one in its original cellophane package. Paper swimwear, see-in-the-dark playing cards, talking seashells, the last with draw-string and a small recorder planted in the conch and secured with glue; you would pull the string and the shell would sing Happy Birthday or Auld Lang Syne. The Pet Rock was an idea he considered genius and always wished had been his own; he was involved with packaging frag-ments of the Berlin Wall last year. Someone once called him the trinket king, and while that moniker fails, and miserably, to reveal him as the truly distinguished, compli-cated, impassioned, resolute individual I know, he would be the first to admit he adored trinkets, not for himself—he himself was quite ascetic, and loathed clutter—but for his customers. He still claims, although I have never seen any evidence to prove it (nor, it must be added, to deny), that back in the earliest days, when the company was spread to its thinnest and widest proportions, Geiger had a research and development man working on a program in plant and pet psychiatry, and another that might link up weight loss with astral projection. The thought was that if something, anything, could be cobbled up into a product that would satisfy FDA and FCC standards in either of these fields, they could take it out and market it. Market what? one might ask. Market anything. It could have been a manual of sayings you would memorize and then repeat while rub-bing a special ointment onto your forehead, or on the leaves of your dying potted plant. It could have been an alumi-num pyramid you balanced on top of your head for twenty minutes a day, seated in lotus, if somebody else hadn't got to that idea first. The point is, Geiger's range of products and ventures was wider than it was deep, was more whim-sical than its profits would have led one to believe, and that was just the way Faw had wanted it to be organized, to spread the odds. Like the island starfish that Desmond and Berg and I would find in the foaming surf, the Sprawl had a way of self-generating new limbs with such ease that its very nature invited breakage, and multiplication. Indeed,

whatever problem there had been in Munich he resolved,
I would surmise, by splitting the company into branches,
pruning it, thinning it, disentangling the disputers as he
sliced away, putting Cato's maxim to work in such a way
that everyone involved in being divided and conquered was
grateful to have been of service. I know this because I have
seen him do it any number of times since.

"Men," he advised Berg, whom despite all his rebellious
behavior Faw hoped to polish into a protégé, "are very
often just like Grace's starfish"—I began to collect the starfish during my walks on the beach, bring them home to dry,
four legs or five it didn't matter so much to me, and shellac.
"They float around, walk around, cling to this and that, and
hope for the best. It's when something goes wrong, they—
men and starfish—react in different ways. The starfish
never wants to lose his arm. He never wants to come under
attack by a big ravenous sea snake, or a big greasy eel, say.
But men, you'll see when you get older, a lot of them go out
of their way to lose their arm."

"Yeah?"—Berg was always more attentive when Faw
resorted to this type of imagery to illustrate his points.

"And why?"

"Why?"

"I'll tell you why. The starfish grows his arm back, he
has no choice. Maybe he even likes it better with four arms
instead of five. Maybe he thinks, Hey this is better for
walking around on the coral, or whatever. But his genes tell
the wound to grow back the arm, because starfish are supposed to have five arms, and starfish do what nature wants
them to do. Men? They don't play by the same rules. Men
are not simple servants of Nature, but servants of their own
will as well. Sometimes they go in and let themselves be
attacked by the sea snake just so they'll lose that arm, just
to see whether they have the ability to grow it back."

"That's a pretty dumb reason to lose your arm."

"You're right. And as often as not they can't do it, and
mope around for the rest of their lives with a stub for an

arm. It all has to do with ideals, rather than goals. You set a goal, you get there, or you don't. If you don't, you move on to the next goal. You set for yourself an ideal, you set yourself up for frustration. There's nothing like idealism to send somebody down the path of foolish risk. You should remember that." Faw, I still contend, was a man of goals who tried to veer Berg away from precisely what he's become—a man of fool-hearted idealism.

After Munich came West Berlin, and after that South America and the Philippines to make arrangements for importing folkloric art—baskets, fabrics, bows and arrows, masks. His gewgaws kept him moving. Distribution, and the knowledge that it worked best through personal contact, through a physical being who shows up every now and then to check out how things are going, was the element in Geiger that seemed to be paramount in its prosperity; that, and the conventional buy-low sell-dear equation, which was very much a part of Geiger's philosophy, modified perhaps to buy-for-nearly-nothing sell-low.

These were the reasons we so seldom saw my father. He would never let someone else do something that he could do better, was rather bad at delegation of responsibility, but supremely good at showing others how to do something efficiently. I don't know, to this day, how he kept up the pace of these sorties.

❖

"Things to do on the beach in winter," I wrote in my big round script, for the rain turned into sleet and the winds shifted toward the south that month when we were all trying to find our way in the new surroundings, and brought down a chill from Canada, forcing us out into its gales of romantic and ominous clouds, ironically, by pushing us indoors at first, toward each other, where things were even less comfortable.

"Things to do on the beach in winter.

"Wonder why the tide pools don't freeze. Look at the dead fish and junk that's been washed up after the big storm. Skip stones. Listen to the foghorn. Listen to the buoy bells clang. Pop seaweed bulbs under foot. Admire the shagbirds and gulls who don't shiver in the snow that is coming down to sit on the water. Notice how the sand feels like cement under your rubber boots when you walk the shore. See no sailboats. Set bonfires out on Pomps point. Roast marshmallows and melt down the chocolate bars to put between graham crackers to make S'mores. Fly a Chinese dragon kite and lose it when the string breaks. Watch it drift and drift away until it drops like a snowflake, into the waves. Not get sunburns. Get windburns. Be freezing your heiny off but not want to go home. Be talked to by your mother for being cold but not wanting to obey her and go home. Sulk. Be sent home. Go home. Sulk. Be in pain from the windburn. Have a windburn vision at dinner. Think about the dragon, how brave it was fluttering down into the icy whitecaps. Wonder where it was now. In Connecticut, in Africa? Does paper float, do dragons float? Think about whether you should have written a message on it in case it drifted to a foreign shore, like they do when they put messages in bottles.

"Wonder when Faw is coming home."

Mostly, stay away from the beach in the winter and, yes, often wonder when Father was coming home.

❖

Then, wintry spring gave way to real spring. The light that reigns in memory of that first island year was the morning light, which was sometimes one color, sometimes another, but often was the color, out on the water, of my favorite ice cream—butter brickle—as the sun grew wider and wider and lulled over the scrub (whence Scrub Farm) pine dunes, or was swept under a clean sheet of squall cloud, or dotted by sails and noisy, fearless gulls.

Mother seemed to settle in, and I began to wonder
whether my initial interpretation of how she acted in the
kitchen on the first afternoon was wrong. I'd been tired,
she had been tired. Maybe, I thought, I got it all wrong,
because now she seemed to like the thought of taking us
children down to the water. She would even slip out of her
sun dress and have her cream-brown suit with the ruffled
skirt on underneath and get out into it with us, being
buoyed up in the swells with me in her arms, or Desmond,
though Desmond didn't like to do that when Berg was
around because he was getting too old to put up with that
kind of mothering. She was so pale she was the same color
as the sand, and the sun had not much effect on her. Her
arms would get a little rosy, and her forehead would
freckle. She had the same figure as Berg, almost. It was hard
to believe she'd had three children, she seemed so much like
a young girl, or boy, herself.

But, wishful thinker, I would come to know that I'd not
been wrong. Not in the last analysis. There must have been
enough going on, at least to interest me, that her actual
pulling away from us, or else just simply her daily absences, went, I should be ashamed to admit—especially in
light of my earlier intuition—unnoticed. Faw's absences,
too, while noted, were so much part and parcel of our
existence that we became accustomed to his not being
there. That we were becoming well-loved orphans seemed
not to register in our waking lives; if anyone had asked us,
we would all have agreed at the time that our parents were
good parents, adored us, were affectionate and, yes, attentive within the limits of their outside interests. Even Berg
would not have abided the term "orphan" as descriptive of
us Brush children, though it could be said that, in the last
analysis, he may have suffered the most from these depriva-
tions.

Day to day life on an island is usually a chronicle of
boredom punctuated by moments of great pleasure, or
pain—what soldiers report being in war is like. But we

children were not so easily bored as your usual ship-
wrecked mariners, whom we saw in television movies, fitfully asleep amid piles of coconuts they'd chopped in half
with their big cutlasses, now and then staring up into the
merciless Caribbean sun and dreaming up mirages of
home, seeing oases surrounded by palm trees and dancing
girls offering papayas to the mad who'd failed to find fresh
spring water and had begun to drink the standing ocean
brine in the mangroves, which as everyone knows makes
sailors crazy as monkeys.

When the men who were working on the house came,
there was at the farm a sense of progress, and shaping, and
building. We were each, in our own ways, I think, caught
up in it, though Berg was as ever distant, and Mother was
less interested in the details than I, and Desmond. There
is no sound I had ever heard that was more poignantly
powerful than the great, beautiful bass note made by a floor
sander—it was a thousand of those Tibetan monks who can
sing a chord of three notes at the same time all chanting the
deepest tones in their collective register, and had the same
richness and spirituality. To watch them tear down a wall,
it was to me magisterial. There was hardly anything they
did, these builders, that I wasn't enamored of. Four, five,
on a special day even six of them at the house, working
together, playing on a portable plastic radio country music
or rock, sometimes working hard, sometimes lazing, dig-
ging into their paper sack lunches at noon, young, old, such
different personalities. They asked me questions and I answered.

They asked, "Grace, would you bring a glass of water?"
And I would run with such excitement to fulfill that important request. They asked, "Grace, would you go find your
mother?" "What do you need?" I might answer. "Don't
need anything, just I have a question for your mother about
a problem here we better talk to her before we go ahead."

"You can ask me," I would try, but they smiled and lit
their cigarettes, and shifted back and forth in their large,

reputable workmen's bodies, which I beheld with the same awe I might a lion, or locomotive.

The pantry floor was spongy and one man—a boy, really—had got down into the crawl space under the house, with his pocket lighter, cursing about how silted up it was under there, and it turned out the joists (all these new words) and beams supporting the subfloor were rotted. His voice, tiny, rose up through the stone-hard maple saying, "Footing's all dry-rotted to hell too."

"What does that mean?" I asked, still resisting going to get Mother, proud to be so favored by the men that they had no fear of using words like "hell" in my presence. Ernest pulled a mock-long frown. "Well, we got to rip this here floor up is what, we got to pour a new footing, scab in some pressure-treated along whatever beams there are down there that are any good yet, level her up, insulate, knock in a new subfloor, and floor it out, don't know why they ever built out on Ram, just too exposed to the elements for a building to stay of a piece." "Well," I said, "whatever you think," which drove Ernest and the others into laughter hoarse from cigarettes. I knew, as he smiled his appeasing smile of broken teeth and crow's feet, that he wanted to be able to say something like, Yes, all right, Grace, you're the boss, but had to say instead, "You had better get your mother."

They were obliged to go to her because I wasn't grown up yet, but I was aware that she didn't really want to hear about problems with the house and in the end all she said was what I had said, "Go ahead, I don't care."

I, of course, cared desperately, from my more humble vantage of having to listen from behind her skirt.

She added, on her way out, "If Grace gets in your way just chase her off."

"She's no problem," he answered without hesitation; I suppose it is fair to say that fifty-sixty-year-old Ernest Dresser was my first love besides Desmond—whom I loved more than anyone, and about whom I will have things to

say—and, of course, my father. Ernest wore the same
clothes every day, brown plaid faded shirt, blue jeans faded
also, with a work belt of thick, worn leather from which his
tools dangled, and the heaviest, gunbluing-black boots I
have ever seen. What girl could resist a gentleman who
carried his hammer from room to room with that kind of
tender, ingenuous authority?

And when Ernest and the others finished the pantry
floor and put down new pine trim along the baseboard and
crown molding to match, the room looked so good to me—
that is, so stable and solid. "Came out better than it had any
right to," was what he said about every project he finished
at Scrub Farm. I knew that whatever he touched would last
for hundreds of years, would be standing long after we all
were gone. I was sorry when they finished and were ready
to go to their next job. I kept trying to find other things
wrong with the house that required their attention, and
actually did manage to stretch their stay another few days
by discovering that a section of rain gutter outside my
window needed to be refastened, where the branch of the
cherry tree had knocked against it during storms. They
wound up pulling off the entire green-copper length along
that side of the house, and replacing it with new aluminum,
which looked much uglier.

But then, one day, quite abruptly it felt like to me, the
carpenters were gone, and I had to turn my attentions
elsewhere.

Besides Ernest, I became attached to Djuna Cobbetts.
She had a ruddy brow, and bluestone eyes, and a benign
oval face sheathed in whorly gray hair, which was always
pulled back into a tight bun. Short and softly rectangular,
Djuna moved into the carriage house at the end of the
drive, surrounded by ruined crab apples and bayberries.
Whenever Berg took off over the dunes with Desmond to
fight with driftwood swords, or hunt fiddler crabs and darting tiny fish that were trapped in tide pools in the rocks,
she would be my companion.

Ernest knew Djuna and they enjoyed an easy friendship, the kind of friendship I surmised was the best that could be had, one which carried over the course of a lifetime, one which when I saw how they acted toward each other—with the most natural affection—I knew I would want for myself. Djuna, as it turned out, I saw more than Mother. And Ernest, for those several months, more than Faw. By autumn, I'd begun to think of them as if they were married, as if they were surrogate parents. And through the school year, through winter, even through that awkward, desolate string of weeks that come between winter and spring, when all the trees are still nude, and the causeway stones are wrapped in ice, I always hoped Ernest might have to come by to fix something.

That anniversary at Scrub Farm, when the ocean mellowed from its grays into brash, deep blues, was a silent, uncelebrated affair. My diversions eliminated, all that wonderful swirl of activity fell into an unwanted, unwonted calm. It was as if the focus had suddenly been turned again on the family, and the spell of carpentering and restoration was broken and we had to begin making the choices ourselves of what to do with our lives next. In my father's perpetual and mother's increasing absence, Djuna and Desmond became half of my discourse, and the great magic console, the television that sat in the corner of the library, became the other half.

Should I feel embarrassed to admit to such an addiction? Well, insofar as the television does not finally submit to discourse, as such, or dialogue, but simply states its piece, and allows for no rebuttal or objection, relies on its own beauties to bring the viewer back and back again into its sphere of influence, I suppose I should be ashamed of my relation with and eventual dependence upon it. It was and always will be a nasty device, a drug, a disease. You accept the box, or you turn it off. And I, understanding all this even then, accepted it, indeed I embraced it like a friend.

It was like a genie's lamp to me, I rubbed its abundant blank glass belly (Faw told me that's what made it work, and though I think Berg knew the better of it, they allowed me to make a fool of myself every time I turned it on, by rubbing it with my palm in circles), pushed in a button, stood back, and waited, until soon enough there would come over its creative face another world, a world we never had back in the city—because we didn't own a television then—a world more funny, more miraculous, and often more engaging than our own.

Outside, the wind whistled across the white sun, seeming to bemoan Faw's absence, and the absence of my brothers, who had biked over to the ferry to fish eels, or porgies, and it whistled for my mother, who was off somewhere; and I understood that nothing made me feel warmer or more peaceful than to sit, cross-legged like the Red Men did in Westerns, and stare.

The day the television was introduced into Scrub Farm was a rite of passage day. There can be no overstating its importance to the spiritual ecology of the place. From the first moment it glowed and blared in the library (so called, though few books were in it), Shahrazad's tales were in a competition for my attention. Faw would still read to me when he was around, but I knew that there were other stories, too, the black and white picture stories.

I suspect that some of the principles I hold dear can be traced back directly to these afternoons spent in the library. A grown woman, I still believe there was some ineffable value in the way Elizabeth Montgomery stood in her middle-class house, in her Jackie Kennedy sleeveless dress, and closed her eyes and twitched her pert nose to project herself into a different time and space—wherever she wanted to be, whenever she wanted to freeze situations until she could figure them out, or fiddle with the future as she saw fit. She was transcendental, she was Shahrazad's own boon sister. So was Jeannie, the hieratic Jeannie, the

busty and sensuous "I dream of" Jeannie. She crossed her
arms out before her, closed her eyes, nodded her head, and
just like that, moved herself into a different world.

Different worlds, I knew from the box, existed. I finally
had corroboration. Shahrazad had not been lying, and I was
not crazy. Here were real women, I thought. They remain
real to me even now.

Theirs were the maps I learned how to read. They became the rule by which I measured things around me.
Samantha, the witch, for instance, I compared, and con-
trasted, to myself, and Darrin, her husband, to Faw. How
I wanted to be like her, a quiet power. A woman with
secrets, with a sweet exterior and a soul of certain fire. She
was my ideal, and whenever she put her foot down—which
sometimes she was forced to do, transcending the laws of
nature with the same ease a baker makes bread—the earth
and air moved in accordance with her wishes. Yet however
much I idolized her I could never comprehend her taste in
mortal men. I never understood how she could put up with
Darrin, and his job, his boss, all of his worries and interests.
I looked at my own life, and thought that as supernaturally
powerless as I might have been I had some strengths
around me upon which I might rely. Faw, to wit. Faw was
strong, Darrin weak. Darrin was the furthest thing from
Faw that there was on earth. Darrin's was a square jaw,
Faw's was pointed; Darrin's body was encased in bourgeois
musculature, just fit and trim enough to look passable in
plaid shorts and a white shirt. I have never seen my father's
body, since even when he accompanied us to the beach he
wore long trousers and a long-sleeved shirt, but I know that
he was a man whose litheness and powerful will carried
him through anything. My love for Faw made sense to me,
Samantha's for Darrin did not, except insofar as it gave me
the first inkling of how distorting an emotion love could be.
It was all so useful. Surely, I thought, it was love that kept
her there with him, and allowed her to be able to sleep with
him every night secure in the knowledge that if he did

something to her that she really didn't like, say he got
carried away a bit, had a bit too much of his favorite poison
at the office party, she would be able to twitch her nose, and
rematerialize him in the closet, perhaps, having turned him
into a giraffe the height of a fire hydrant. I always wished
that she would do something like this. Why not turn him
into a hobnail boot and walk him through a dump site?
There had to be girls in the audience besides myself who
saw the drawbacks of this man. But whenever she did
freeze him, leave him standing in the room with an insipid
grimace on his face while she figured out her next move,
no matter what she made up her mind to do he'd come out
of the spell scratching his head and still thinking he was the
boss. I knew I'd never freeze Charles Brush.

But Darrin, fastidious Darrin, saucer-eyed at the slightest thing, mind-boggled at every turn—how at home he
will look in heaven, walking its courses, proceeding from
tee to infinite tee, shooting nothing but holes in one. Part
of me must have tolerated him because of his obvious love
of her. Love of Samantha and her magical power was something he and I shared. Not to mention how much I still
admire Jeannie for how she, too, kept her household in
order, ruling it from her genie's bottle. There was no way
her astronaut captor could keep his hands off that Aladdin's
lamp or whatever it was once he'd found out who was
inside. Those were the days when a little flesh on the belly
of a woman was considered a good thing, those were the
days when America was feeding on the same innocent
Wonder Bread that Jeannie made her peanut butter sand-
wiches with, and got that jelly belly with. So, yes, Jeannie
looked fine in her bikini top with those low-waisted pantaloons, she had style, and wasn't the slightest bit embarrassed by a life that consisted of keeping the astronaut
happy. She even kept his fey psychiatrist friend in check,
and never let him discover what he suspected: that Jeannie
was a genie and had powers far beyond anything he had
ever read about in his textbooks.

"Master," she called her man all the time. "Oh, Master," she'd intone, and then proceed to do whatever she wanted to do, and he, very much like Darrin, had to take whatever she got it in her head to conjure up. This, that, whatever it was he had to like it, ultimately, because hidden under the surface of their relationship was a mutual understanding that it was she who wielded the final authority, she who wore the pants. She never did him any serious dirt, though. In the end, they were all happy, after their half an hour of crisis.

I sat and delighted at how Samantha and Jeannie and Darrin and the astronaut got into trouble all the time, delighted in how things inevitably got resolved, week after week after week, and problem after problem. It was better than any junk you could find in the Bible. Okay, so problems came up, and these television people worried, got themselves into seemingly inexorable jams, sad but so-funny predicaments, and their enemies began to rub the palms of their hands together thinking that this was going to be it, and they were going to get caught off base doing something that would disgrace them forever. But with the shake of a head, the wrinkling of a nose, everything was set right, and the bad guys were foiled. Spirits and magic and common sense were put to the test. This was better than religion, this was the way things should work.

Jeannie and Samantha could do nothing wrong in their men's eyes, or in mine. No matter what they did, they did it in such a way that their men were able to maintain a sense of being the man, and not merely a man but *the* man, the boss, the transcendent hero of a clearly ridiculous, clearly delusory drama of male predominance. Jeannie slept in a bottle, Samantha was reclusive for fear she might twitch her nose by mistake and manufacture a disaster. Both were hidden from the world not because they were ugly, or stupid, but because they were beautiful and unique and clever, because, above all, they had real powers against which a man possessed neither defense nor even a strong

argument. They had powers like I thought I might someday like to have, as I lay there curled on the floor like a cat.

❖

Trudeau I saw every other week. Faw and Mother would
drive me in, leaving the boys in Djuna's charge. It would
be a sultry morning, with the drear heat already sitting on
the road, and the commuters looking harried behind the
wheels of their cars. Manhattan would finally start showing itself, in its pinnacles and the tops of its towers, here
and there between Queens overpasses and billboards.
Through the tunnel, and already I'd begin saying, "Do we
have to go?" and my mother would say, yes I had to go.
Trudeau had hours at Mount Sinai, and that was close to
the old neighborhood, which made me feel an ambivalence,
happy to be near the light people, uneasy to be near them,
too, because I had tried—as Djuna recommended—to forget about them, forget everything I could, and being there
forced me to realize how utterly I'd failed at doing that.

"Meaning what?" Faw would ask.

"As I've said before," she (Trudeau was a woman) said,
"the icicles are something more common in postadoles-
cents, as Grace has described the blind spot in the center
of her visual field—"

"It's not a blind spot." I was fussy about the details, if
only because I knew them so intimately.

"Well, what is it, Grace?" Faw asked.

"There's nothing there, inside the icicles."

"Well, that's what she just said."

"No, she said it was a blind spot."

Trudeau said, "There isn't supposed to be anything
there, it isn't that you can't see it, whatever would be in the
blind spot, it's that there isn't anything to see, is that what
you mean, Grace?"

"Yes."

As my episodes dated to when I got my braces, the tradi-

tional Brush braces—canted front teeth ran in the family—
Faw had some theory about the braces being the cause of
all my troubles. My brothers teased me about my silvery
mouth ("Maybe we should melt Grace down, silver's worth
a lot more than—") but what was of interest to Trudeau
was my appetite—the braces certainly didn't stop me from
eating. Faw noted I was "quite the pig," though I was thin
as a birch limb, my arms and legs strong and spidery under
the colorful frocks I liked to wear.

Said Dr. Trudeau, "My presumptive diagnosis would
still be" (at this medicalese my father was always seen to
roll his eyes) "that her migraines—"

"Megrims," interrupted Mother, trying to be helpful.

"—are congenital, and not the result of an injury to the
brain, or progressive dementia, or a tumor—looking
through these materials, by the way at some point I'd like
to find out from you why it is she's been through so many
analyses without getting on a single program before this.
Grace is, or has the model physiognomy for this, reddish-
blonde hair believe it or not is common in migrainous
females, as is Grace's appetite coupled with the fact that she
is—"

"She is awfully thin," Erin said.

"I'm not too worried about that, but some of these other
things are more unusual. For instance, that these phos-
phenes precede her full scotoma, well . . . Grace, you're a
rather extraordinary girl, whether you like it or not."

I smiled, liking it that I was extraordinary.

"And it hasn't the least thing to do with teeth"—which
meant, of course, upon Faw's hearing that it was still all his
fault, just as the "goddamned crooked teeth" had been
(there'd been no crooked teeth in Mother's family, as she
pointed out to the doctor, from where she sat in the chair
near the door, her already narrow and pale face appearing
thinner, whiter, under the fluorescents of the office). When
Faw mentioned to Dr. Trudeau he sensed he should feel
responsible somehow about her condition, Trudeau's re-

sponse was that, no, that while "the gene pool doesn't lie," megrims don't seem to run down family trees.

At the end of the fourth or fifth visit with us Trudeau got some insight into why and how the case had gone through so many hands. She had prescribed ergotamine, a "paso-constrictor," which sounded like a kind of big murderous African snake, and recommended that to prevent hyperventilation I breathe into a paper bag, which I should always keep nearby. I wondered at her masculine face, which I thought was handsome, but not as handsome as either my father's, or Desmond's, "Like under my pillow?"

Dr. Trudeau straightened the chart papers on her desk and smiled. "Under your pillow would be fine."

"Like, where the sandman lives?" and as I said it I noticed a rod of light flowered upside down through the clinic office.

"And breathe in, out, in, out, as deeply as you can, into the bag. Just think of the bag as your friend," and turning to my father catching him just as he was about to interrupt again, "once learned never forgotten, like swimming, there are precursors to this, and if inductions are ferreted out, like in her case this additional structure of fear which induces hyperventilation, and from what she's said and what I can piece together I believe that even mild circumoral paraesthesia—"

Faw frowned. "Excuse me, but at the risk of sounding coarse I've got a lot to do still today. It's not these headaches, but the flare man stuff that—"

"Migraines are not headaches, Mr. Brush."

"I like the flare man okay."

"She needs quiet, support, understanding—it's the only way to help her to be rid of her fears."

I protested, "I'm not afraid."

"Grace has nothing on earth to be afraid of," Mother said, and straightened her back; how was it these doctors always made her feel defensive? "She has a family that loves her she's got that lassie apso, lasso—"

"That was Damsel, Bung is a beagle."

Dr. Trudeau continued, "Grace. This dog, is this the dog you said your brother—is it Burke is his name?—dropped out the apartment window?"

"What did, did Grace tell you that?"

"Is that true?"

As I said, "Yes," Faw said, "Christ almighty that's not the way, that's not what happened, totally fallacious, that dog was constantly getting himself into one jam after another, did you tell the doctor about how Midge ran him in the clothes dryer, she heard the barking so he didn't go through the whole cycle but he had plenty of time to cough up all over the laundry before she could turn it off and get him out of there, so that's not accurate about my son throwing him out the window."

"Did you get her, that is to say did you replace—all that concerns us here is whether this symptom complex, because this isn't a disease, you remember my telling you about the variant familial hemiplegic migraine, because I don't think this stops here—"

"I mean he died—"

"Damsel was a she and she went to heaven, really a darling she was more darling than Bung is although Bung is a darling, too."

"Right, see?, Bung, another one of the same—"

"No, Damsel was a lasso apso." I smoothed down my skirt over my thighs, straightening every fold in every pleat.

"Dr. Trudeau? Listen. I respect you, I love Grace, I have a schedule this afternoon that will not allow, what, if you'll pardon me, do dogs have to do with anything?"

"Anything, as you well must know in business, may have anything to do with anything. As Blau has suggested, as different as grand and petit mal, incidents of an epileptic nature—"

"This isn't epilepsy."

"I never said it was, if you'll hear me through—"

And I interrupted, "Those horny toads died, they dried all up."

"What?"

Trudeau proceeded, holding my father's eye as best she could, "When Grace—and Grace you should be listening to what I'm saying, too, dear—when you find yourself hyperventilating, which means you're finding it hard to slow down your breathing, the simplest way for you to regain a regular breathing pace is for you to breathe into a paper bag, all right?"

"Okay," what that again?

"In and out, and Grace you must concentrate on breathing slowly and regularly, just like counting sheep."

But I said, thinking of the orchard apples, "They looked like the shrunk head Desmond got from India," and the doctor reprimanded, "Grace, listen to me," but Faw corrected me, "Brazil, Grace, it's Brazil," and explaining to Trudeau, "I was down there on business, brought the children something from Brazil."

"Those shrunk heads was gross," I concluded.

"Neither of you is hearing a word I'm saying," as she glanced at her watch.

I looked up at the panels in the dropped ceiling. We were back to square one. Eggshell white crawling with half-paralyzed worms. They stayed in place, and they smelled like rock candy, smelled of nothing. Which was to say they didn't carry the scent of apricot, which was the smell I most often associated with my visions. They didn't slither much like any of the worms I'd ever seen on television, just boring worms I would step on if I could get my foot up there to the ceiling. Except no, I thought, then the bottom of my foot would be gooshed-up with boring worm juice—

"So now, let's just to conclude: what you recommend, let me understand exactly, what you recommend as antidote to all this, her face disappearing, these flare people"—and I would have sighed here with loving exasperation, and wouldn't have corrected him, but would feel kind of sorry for having to put him and Mother and all of them through this—"waving to her in the tree, peach smells—"

"It's apricot," Mother asserted from her chair, and I smiled back over my shoulder at her. She looked white as the bald white paint of the wall.

"—is to stick her head in a bag." As he spoke he'd slipped on his jacket, which had lain in his lap, rather neatly folded as Dr. Trudeau had noticed. I now stared at Dr. Trudeau's shoes, tidy matte leather pumps, delicate for work shoes, pointed and with some extra heel. I liked Dr. Trudeau, and I worry as I write this that I err on the side of burlesque in the way I report such painful and profoundly embarrassing times. I wished that Faw got along better with her; I thought that because the doctor was a woman she somehow understood how that worked when the hole in the middle of my icicle hair came to be. I wanted to ask her whether she'd ever seen such a thing herself, because she seemed to know about it, but if she hadn't she figured Faw might get mad, and march off to yet another doctor, which I didn't want. Trudeau was speaking, and I found myself looking at her eyes, which were now quite amber, and very glowing, and I thought, "Her eyes are in upside down." I dropped one of my shoulders down, lay my head to one side, bent over, and got a good look at her face from this different perspective. I was right. Her eyes would look much more regular if she were suspended from the ceiling.

"Grace?"

I nodded from my cocked-head position.

Trudeau moved close, put her hand on my shoulder. Her grasp was firm, confident, "Grace, can I tell you what I think? I think you're doing much better. I think we were right when we thought that flare men weren't able to leave their trees. That's where they live. And they have to stay where they live. And since he wasn't able to follow you out to the island, you've been doing better. Isn't that right?"

Well, that was all fine, but, I wondered, getting back to Dr. Trudeau's eyes, which were so close now and how for sure they were in upside down, and how they would look right if she were hung from the ceiling, I couldn't help but wonder, would the wiggly worms up there be able to eat their way through the lashings tied around her feet, and make her fall straight down on her head?

❖

Berg drifted, like a jellyfish can drift in rough waters, but was pulled in by Faw from time to time. Over the protests of his teachers at school, Faw, having decided it was time that his eldest son learn something about how the world of commerce worked, announced that he was taking the boy with him to an island in the French West Indies. There he had intentions of setting up an extension of a foundation he had established the year before in Cape Hatteras, the Gulf Stream Trust. We none of us understood what such a project was about, nor what this Gulf Stream Trust meant, nor even where Cape Hatteras was, and when he attempted to explain any of it to us it only became more obscure. There was something about a church for drowned sailors; there was something about Columbus's younger brother Bartholomew; there was something about a woman there who burned a candle every night, all night, for the mariners who had been lost at sea—something about how their souls could find their way across the dark waters to the safety of the church by following the candle that she'd set in the window on the side of a hill. It all sounded very mysterious (churches and Faw, as I have said, never having been attractive to one another).

No matter what it was, both Desmond and I knew we were supposed to be envious of Berg's new status. Mother did not throw a tantrum. She was anything but hysterical. She even seemed to be in favor of the idea, a response that surprised each of us in different ways. Speaking for myself, I was confused at first. Here Faw was doing something with Berg that he'd never done with Mother, taking his son to this exotic faraway place—it seemed unfair. Her disaffection quelled quickly what jealousy I might have felt on her behalf, and began to make me think once more about what I'd noticed that first day in her. Of course, I thought. She must want him out of here, and then she could do whatever pleased her. Was she that far gone? I wondered. Looking back, I think that she was. I also think she sensed I was watching her.

When they returned, Berg more than ever distanced himself from us younger children; the transition in him that Faw had been looking to midwife seemed to have been accomplished. While the dinner at which Berg was invited by Faw to sit with the guests, while Desmond and I were told to play as quietly as possible in my room, may have signaled that this reconstruction of the hierarchy—as I viewed it—was to be permanent, later events would show that it would not turn out as my father might have hoped.

Things were changing, nevertheless, in the family. Balances were being reweighed and reweighted. Faw and Berg were over there, Desmond and I over here, Mother elsewhere on her own. And what was I to think, before the guests arrived, when I overheard Faw telling Desmond, "Your brother is a scrapper, a fighter, and that's going to stand him in good stead, you understand?"

"Yes, sir."

"You could use a little more of that yourself, you know."

"I'll try," said Desmond, and though I couldn't see him, given I was eavesdropping per my dearest habit at the time, it was easy to envision him standing directly before Faw with his hands in his pockets and eyes averted downward.

"Don't try, do."

"Yes, sir."

"That's my guy."

Stuart Hollander, the Pannett and Neden of Pannett & Neden who were producers, Beth and Howard Silliman, the del Russes who were the Geiger accountants—as best Djuna, with my help, could make out from Faw's handwritten notes about the dinner, which he scribbled out at her behest—all were showing up within the hour, and here were two dozen woodcocks skewered on their own beaks, heads skinned, trussed like intricate kites with baking string, standing in almost military order on the butcher block counter in the kitchen and turning before Djuna's and my eyes from the sallow gray and pink a healthy woodcock ought to show, to the green tinge of the fungus that grew up the stone wall at the easternmost corner of the yard opposite the orchard. Djuna looked out the window at the wall. Her face was blank; the game was tainted. How was it possible? They'd been shot that very week (it was Saturday) in the Yucatan or in Guadalajara or maybe it was just Louisiana—wherever Faw and Berg had been on their way back up from the Gulf Stream trip, what did it matter now, now that they were removed from the container? It was nice, Djuna noted, that the guide had taken it upon himself to pluck the birds before he packed them in ice for the flight home. She had seen the pictures of him, a handsome, flat-nosed cowboy of sorts standing next to my father who had his arm draped on Berg's nearest shoulder, each not smiling but rather looking straight into the camera even as they cast their shadows across the fan of game birds laid out on a palm-frond bed at their feet—were there palm trees in Louisiana?

Well, but we were trailing off and away, as sometimes we did, Djuna and I, and especially in moments such as these, where two elements were coming together, forming a trap really—our island world, and the outside world of the people who were coming, whose names were written out on that piece of stationery, a beautiful heavy paper Faw favored for the letterheads of his companies, people all so important to him, we knew, important enough that they could not be sacrificed to putrid woodcocks. Djuna went to Mrs. Beeton's book, her touchstone in running the house. In Mrs. Beeton the woodcock was shown in French as Bécasse, which naturally put me in mind of the question,

"But why?" . . . but instead of saying anything about Bécasse, I said, "Where is Mom? She'd know what to do," not
meaning to slight Djuna, more meaning to redress my
shaky image of Mother.

I don't remember what Djuna said, because the time was
passing, frittering along with no concern for her or Mother
or me or tainted woodcock or the brilliant green watercress
that floated in the sink. She sighed a deep-throated sigh and
it surprised her; that was the same tone she heard herself
make whenever she was losing her cool (like when she
made us turn off the box); then, one by one at first and soon
in an armload she gathered the woodcocks and stuffed them
into the trash compactor that Ernest had installed, and
once they were all in the compactor—they filled it to the
edge of the plastic liner—she pushed the drawer back into
the counter, locked it, and pressed the black, rectangular
button and listened to the birds being crushed together
inside, their tainted skin and beaks and bones gliding into
a single pulp. She pulled the compactor drawer out, lifted
the remains, carried with some difficulty the bundle across
the kitchen, and deposited them outside in the can.

Another low groan as she looked at her hands, which
were wetted with thin blood. Across the floor ran a feath-
ery pink line of the same blood. She would have to go after
that in the morning. There was no time to get out the mop
and pail. She washed her hands then remembered how
sticky blood could be when it dried, and how the flies
would be attracted so she thought better of it and told me
to take a linen hand towel—knowing how wrong it was to
use such a fine piece of fabric, but what else could she do,
there simply wasn't the time to mop—and I dropped the
linen on the tail end of the trail of red. "Women should
endeavor to cultivate that tact and forbearance without
which no man can hope to succeed in his career," the vener-
able Mrs. Beeton observed. And I, who attempted to follow
some avenue toward my father's success by skating the rag
under my hands along that bloody browning-pink line

which crossed the kitchen floor, wonder now what kind of life Mrs. Beeton must have had, what kind of father, what kind of mother. Would she have been able to see a flare man in a tree in England? Would the tact she spoke of have extended to getting down on the linoleum and on all fours wiping up woodcock juice? Her answer, of course, would be that she wouldn't have spilled the blood in the first place.

And Djuna read again from *Household Management*, "Accidents, of course, will happen (though but rarely with proper precautions)"—what a scolding old bitch she was this Mrs. Beeton—". . . fires will not always burn, nor ovens bake as they should . . . the gas supply may be deficient; but if the joint, or whatever it may be, cannot be done to time, do not send it up only partially cooked, but ask for a little grace . . ."

For what? We laughed together, Djuna first, then I, and it seemed so funny to us (even though it wasn't terribly) that I had to run to another room and stamp my feet hard in order to stop. I looked out the window, to see that there were shadows cast by headlights from the side driveway. One of the guests was arriving, the headlights of a car reflected off the trees and trellises near the kitchen's windows. Djuna had dropped Mrs. Beeton to the floor where the veneer of fowl blood—I hadn't been very thorough in my clean-up—had already begun to dry into patterns; oh, indeed, we could already hear the flies pinging against the screen. She went to the wall phone and dialed the number in a kind of haze of defeat mixed with efficiency. Ernest was going to bring over some whitebait. Faw might wonder where his woodcock had gone off to, but the evening would not be lost.

Berg came down into the kitchen, uncomfortable in his tie and blazer, but rather superior for his social apotheosis.

"I see you've got your shirt on with buttons forward, Berg," Djuna noted. "Isn't that against your principles?"

"Sometimes it is, sometimes it isn't."

"Faw had to tie his tie for him," I added, recognizing this as one of the few moments in my life when the tables were turned, and I could tease him without fear of immediate retribution.

Djuna said, "I guess it would be a little hard to wear a tie with the shirt on backwards."

"Faw wanted me to tell you they're here." Then he left.

I eavesdropped dinner, with Desmond at my side. The voices we could not connect with names. I heard Mother speak only to offer more wine, or to call Djuna out from the kitchen; her exclusion from the conversation was of her own choosing, but was not, so far as I could make out from my blind on the landing at the head of the stairs, contested by her guests, whose attentions were directed toward my father.

Where sphinxes hide their riddles in silence, we mortals bury ours in banter. No need to recount the laughter and the jokes. Desmond, bored, tiptoed from our listening perch to my room, and climbed out into his treehouse to do whatever it is he liked to do out there. I overheard, after he left, two remarkable things, though—one, that in honor of their first trip as men together, Faw had decided to make Berg a vice-president of this Gulf Stream Trust thing, "to get his feet wet," and Berg, over Mother's mild protest, got to sample his first sip of champagne, having been toasted by Pannett, or Neden, or one of them. The second matter was much more perplexing, because Berg's premature blossoming as the newest flower in the Geiger festoon I saw for the parental bribe that it was. Faw was buying some good behavior, was what I figured—after all, what good would Berg be to some French woman in some church on an island in the Caribbean?

"What woman, what island are you talking about?" Neden asked. They all seemed drunk except for my father. He may or may not have explained to them what he was referring to, but the matter was so bizarre that I misunderstood along with the others. Whoever this woman was and whatever was her role in the Gulf Stream deal, were matters either so very tangential to what my father's colleagues were doing in their roles as employees of the Sprawl that none of them wanted to commit a faux pas by expressing some opinion that would show them to be ignorant of the inner workings of Geiger, or else it was more complex than heads pleasantly adrift in champagne and wine would want to bother to comprehend. Everyone, it seemed, wanted instead to crowd in with his own bizarrerie.

The hour had gotten late. Dinner had been cleared, Desmond had come in from outside because it had gotten too cold and went off to bed. Mother with Beth Silliman and Mrs. del Russe retired to the kitchen, where Djuna'd built her evening fire. The Sillimans were going to sleep in the guest room downstairs, and the others were staying at the Peconic Lodge over on the island. This was a weekend for these city people, in other words; it was going to be a late night.

Faw and the men—Berg still among them—isolated themselves in the library, and I listened in through a heat register, pressing my cheek to the warmth of the grate, and straining to hear what was being said. They were discussing Gulf Stream in entirely different tones than what I'd discerned at dinner.

"But what are the parameters on setting up a not-for-profit on foreign soil, Chas? I didn't think you could do that," Pannett, I believe it was Pannett, quietly said. The smoke of their cigarettes staled the heat that rose through the register. A decanter clinked against a glass, I could smell cognac. It made my tongue dry, and the back of my throat mildly sore.

"No, you can't," Faw answered.

"Well, how does it work?"

"We operate out of Cape Hatteras, there is a storefront church we have there—actual church, the pastor we've got there is something like a Unitarian I think, so far not much in the way of membership about five families. But the church is nondenominational—"

"You mean its denomination is money, right?" cracked Neden.

And another voice came in, which was del Russe's. "What we're doing here is that 2 or 3 percent of profits of all the Geiger entities will be donated every year to this trust. It is an amount that is not unusual and should not attract any attention if someone is going over the books. Given that all the Geiger companies are incorporated in the state where the individual technology for each of the products is located, where the manufacturing base, or the warehousing base, say, is set up—like say, we make those baseball bats and the bowling pins with the limited edition star signatures out of upstate New York ash, turn them up there, both those companies are New York limiteds, you see—there's no reason for anyone to connect them, the different companies, in any kind of interstate way, you see. It's all generally legal."

"Generally?" again Neden pushed.

"The purpose of the trust is to honor mariners who have given their lives in the interest of trade. And about this I'm very serious"—I wanted to laugh, knowing my father as I did, but no one laughed, and I bit my cheek— "and so as one of the outreach programs, missionary program as it were, we're raising money to salvage derelict vessels from the Gulf Stream gyre and save them for posterity, making a contribution to the history of international trade—because these guys were the pioneers."

Pannett—or Neden, their guttural voices were similar, then did laugh, and said, "Absurd."

"You know what the Gulf Stream gyre is?"

"Can we skip ahead to the point?"

Faw continued, "The Gulf Stream gyre is a circle—"

"This whole thing sounds more like circles than points—"

"—or it's shaped more like the outer edge of an amoeba or a squash or something, but it's a circular path in which the warm water runs through the cold water of the Atlantic. It's about a ten-month loop. You with me? So, historically, ships get hit by high water and storm-waves that are created by when this cold and warm encounter each other, just like storm systems when you get a thunderstorm because of cold air and warm air colliding. And the crew abandons ship, sometimes they're saved, as often not. It's all in the history books. And your ship is abandoned, and as often as not if her frame and skin are of decent wood and she's still basically seaworthy, she'll get pulled into the Gulf current and go round and round—"

"A ghost ship, now, the point being?"

"So, well, we've got this church, set up as a 501 (c) (3) I think is what del Russe and his friends over at Internal Revenue call it, but whatever, it's a nonprofit tax-exempt foundation, and in the charter there is this outreach program so that part of the organization's activities can run something like this. To salvage antique vessels of historical importance from the Gulf Stream gyre, bring them if possible to port, dry dock, and undertake to restore, and then donate to museums to the Christian memory of the international community of pioneers and traders."

"Unutterably ridiculous, all right?"

Someone else said, "For the final time, the point is what?"

"We have an account in North Carolina, we have an account in the French West Indies, like I was saying earlier, the latter takes project outreach program funds from the donations given to the former—goes through our banks in the city—the latter moves monies into another account overseas, you know, like for holding funds for capital as investment against the costs of repair, which would of course have to be contracted out to specialists in the field, of which I have already put one or two on the payroll, a couple of brothers who live in Gustavia, on St. Barthélemy—Bartholomew being a mariner, by the way, and so that's quite an appropriate place I think to carry on this work, since from what I've been able to learn, he was a religious man as well as a man given to discovery. And to the point, these repairs will or will not eventually come to pass, you with me?"

When he asked, no one said a word, and when he went on to say it didn't really matter that they understood, I detected a tone of satisfaction in his voice; it was as if he had led them point by point through something with the hope that they wouldn't get it. He asked del Russe, who had been quiet, a question, which I didn't quite hear, and all of a sudden del Russe seemed to speak the same foreign language. He assured my father and the others that while over the years the trust would no doubt amass a surplus, quite a large surplus, and would therefore have to show activity, they, Geiger, had set up a religious objects company whose factory in Canton had a guaranteed client in the Gulf Stream Trust—the "Make Mary" ornament, for instance, a figurine of Mother Mary with a smiling face, could be produced in hundreds of thousands of units for not much money and sold at inflated prices to the church, which would then "distribute them."

"In other words, bury them in the sand," said Faw.

"Well, that would be one way to distribute them, to be sure. You could also give them away to believers if you had the time and inclination, though that might not be as efficient."

"All right, then," my father finished.

Whether no one spoke then because they all suddenly understood and had nothing to say, or they failed to speak because they wouldn't know what to ask, I couldn't surmise, but a silence ensued. Faw went on, and as he did, the hush downstairs developed further, and what I heard became fragmented, and engulfed, as it were, in the drift of my sleepiness, which was encouraged by the heat pouring upward from the register, and the lateness of the hour, so that what I am able to remember has become a palimpsest. I record it, because in retrospect, all of what has now come to pass was mentioned—if only in some kind of embryonic way—that night, and it has been the link in my memory that led me to St. Barts, so many years later, quite a different island than it must have been back then during the night of the Shelter Island dinner. What linked, what added up to something that made a one and one makes two kind of sense? In some way, all of it; in some way, none. That church mirage of Faw's and the peculiar films that Pannett and Neden went on to discuss, however, I can now see as smoke and fire.

One of the men said, regarding the films, "You have the equipment here to show it?" and the women's voices in the other room rose and fell down in the kitchen, mingling with the voices of their companions in the library.

"—but those birds, they would have been tasty, though I admit it's sort of horrible the way you have to do them, snip their beaks off and stick them up their . . . oh. But they were going rancid or something—" Djuna talking, and I could tell they thought she was quite a pip.

"I think I'd rather not," Faw told the man.

Djuna, again, saying, "Blanch-*ailles*. It's very fast but it's pretty hard to do, too, so Grace should get some of the credit, she's such a dear, so how you do it is you get the flour, clean linen, the wire drying basket, and you start with the lard to melt into hot liquid in the biggest copper frying pan you can find."

"Is that false cypress or viburnum in the yard out front?"

"So, on this plantation where they grow asparagus—"

"And Neden and I were thinking about making this new one, it's called *Oriental Affairs*, in which these Chinese women—"

"Well, they don't even have to be Chinese, they can be Vietnamese, Korean, it doesn't matter you can't tell the difference, tell them the copy."

"Well, you know you start with the advertising materials

and build backwards to the product itself, of course. That's the only way to assure profitability. And so we've been working on the copy, which goes something like this, goes, The pulsing heart of their sensuous, mysterious souls to each and every man with every sinewy shudder . . . lift their geisha skirts and squirm under—"

"Those aren't called skirts, they're kimonos." My father didn't sound pleased with any of this talk; in his voice there was not only discomfort but (was it possible?) fear.

"It's true that a copper pan'll heat faster than steel—"

"—while silver chains and the emperor's handcuffs clink, they drop their silken stockings, these angels of passion trained in the mysterious ways of the East, where a man's satisfaction comes above all, in the tradition of a thousand suns."

"Very poetical." And yes, I could hear Faw's fear through the sarcasm, though I doubt any of the others could.

"The lead female character's name is going to be Jade. You like?"

"—and here it was something the whatevereth?" and they were putting on their coats and saying goodnight and Berg was sent up to bed, I think, "if the real thing is your cup of hemlock, is how the bit will run it's a little rough still but, if you want to see it all and touch it all, if wet and deep and up and down and in and out's your thing, you'll never know how good it is until you see the most steamy seduction scene ever filmed . . ." such laughter, as I myself began to sleep on the floor, and—

Faw had never spanked me before, he did it so gently that although I cried and though it hurt I could tell his heart wasn't in it. My cheeks showed the marks of the heat register the next morning, and I didn't come down because I didn't want to embarrass him. I'd burned my face through my own persistence, but didn't want his guests to think that it was his fault in any way. They must have heard him spank me, must have heard me cry. I was ashamed.

When I woke, Faw was sitting in his reading chair beside my bed. "Grace," he said, "I have something I want to tell you."

What was he going to say? I was sure he was about to tell me that I was going to be sent away somewhere.

"It's difficult to be a parent. You're too young maybe to understand that now, but someday you may understand. What I want you to know is that I'm not happy with what I did last night, and I want you to forgive your old Faw, all right?"

His eyes were dark and tired. Of course I forgave him. I made up my mind that night to doubt everything I had heard; a dream was what I assured myself it was for years, rather than my first insight into what peculiar and possibly grotesque outposts Geiger ranged in search of its ascendancy.

❖

The osprey, an eaglish bird, was disesteemed by fishermen, who took it upon themselves to trap and hunt and poison it wherever it was found on the island. The osprey's skill at fishing was well-known to its human counterparts, who viewed it as a competitive nuisance; and because the ospreys are given to cyclical behavior and return to the same nest every spring, it was quite easy for the fishermen to trap and kill them. It was a slaughter. What traps didn't get them, what buckshot failed to down them, hard pesticides that were insinuated into the food chain did. Once large, the population of course had been all but eradicated on the island. And even though we were too young to know about these particular wars, and who was winning, who losing, at the time, the osprey nest that was perched atop the utility pole, which leaned away from the sea winds down at the farthest edge of our orchard, seemed to us a thing of rarity, a talismanic thing to marvel at.

Marvel we did. That spring, after Desmond (I know I

have thus far avoided speaking of him in detail in my almanac. The only justification I have for this is that it is difficult
for me to address him as a topic, or a character, or with
words. I find him elusive, because he meant so much to me)
and I first spotted the nest, aloft, a vast, stable cloud of
brown sticks in the sky, we kept coming back, to watch and
see if its owner would return after the winter. When she
turned up, we were astounded, so wide was her wingspan
we dropped to our knees in the marsh hoping she wouldn't
catch sight of us. It became one of our preoccupations, to
hide and watch her as she tended to her enormous home,
repairing and adding to it, as she must have done every year
for years, with fresh sticks, strips of bark, vines. Whatever
she happened to find lying around in her landscape, discarded by us wasteful human beings, she saw as potentially
useful in her endeavors. So we watched, in awe, as she
knitted into her nest rope, bits of fishnet, an old shoe, half
the brim of what looked to be someone's straw hat, a rag
doll and toy boat (yes, we saw her import these and fiddle
them both into the weave), and who knows what else to
dress out the house.

I'd seen things dead but never killed before. It rattled me.
She hatched out her brood from pinkish cinnamon, rich-
red-blotched eggs, and with her mate brought plenty of
slippery, death-wiggling fish back to feed her babies, whom
we could hear high up on the pole. She was a crafty and
able killer.

When her young broke out of their shells we listened to
them as they carried on like banshees, maybe two or three
in the brood, screeching with ravenous voices when she
soared in with their food, a pike, or a small bluefish ridicu-
lously struggling in the osprey mother's talons at the end
of her blue-gray legs.

What struck me most about being witness to the way she
glided in, crooking her wings to land, and then went to
work pecking the soon-stilled fish to pieces to feed it to her
hatchlings, was not that the fish's dying was horrible, or

anything like that. I didn't (wouldn't still) philosophize about how nature giveth and taketh away and how all things eventually die so that other life can rise up, strong, to keep the stream of existence going along or any of that stuff. No, what bothered me was how ridiculous the fish looked. It displayed no dignity, it showed no knowledge of its situation, it flipped and flopped and flapped and squirmed and its tail quivered in panic. It showed no evidence of being aware that it had not the slightest chance of escape, and this was a sorry sight to witness. I prayed, with the innocent valor of youth, addressing whatever godless guardian angel looked over me, Please never let me act as pathetic as that fish. And yet at the same time I empathized with the poor beast, or tried to, and believed I was able to understand its terror. What made me feel sad was that I knew that I would behave the same way under the circumstances. I'd felt this empathy for the victim once before, at the circus at Madison Square Garden, when we saw a clown who swallowed some Mexican jumping beans and writhed in the sawdust, center-ring, until some other clowns with faces painted in expansive orange frowns and black eyes came to take him away. How he flailed his arms and whimpered! Everyone, myself included, howled with laughter at that clown, when we should have been revolted or at least left cold by such a stupid joke. Promises to oneself about courage are luxuries, I've since learned, and are often abandoned under the pressure of real terror. Still, then, my empathetic sadness must have passed because I began to giggle or cough softly at the fish, with the same nervous whimpery sounds with which I might have greeted the dead bird in the mudroom had I been the one who found it.

Desmond turned on me. "What are you dumb or something? How would you like it if some big bird went cutting your eyes out?"

"I'm not dumb," I must have answered, whispering in the cover of the purple-budding bushes.

Desmond looked at me, with eyes I'd never seen before, and said, "Sometimes I think you're crazy, Grace, you know, sometimes I just don't get you."

"I'm not dumb, and I'm not crazy."

"If you're not crazy, how come Faw made us come all the way out here?"

"But you said you liked it out here."

Desmond shrugged; he was picking apart a cattail head and putting its white filament feathers into the air, which gusted and puffed. He said, "I know there's no such thing as any lights in any tree, all right?"

Desmond never talked to me like that, and I remember my eyes getting hot, like I was going to cry. "But there is."

"Right, and they talk, too."

"They talk sort of, yes."

"Well, how come I can't hear them?"

"They don't talk to you is all."

"Berg says you're wacko. He says you think you're that witch on that show and that you can make things disappear, but that you're just dumb and you can't."

"What does he know, he doesn't know anything."

"He says he heard Mom tell Faw you're a nut."

"That's a lie," I said, and stood up; I nearly threatened to make him disappear, to freeze him like Samantha can freeze whomever she pleases, but I knew I didn't want to prove Berg right (or myself unable).

Desmond grabbed me by the arm and pulled me back down. "Don't let that bird know we're here."

I then must have started to cry, because he told me, "Listen, Grace. I didn't mean it, I don't think you're crazy, I believe you okay? I just don't get it's all, here I go up in trees all the time and I never seen no flare man."

"Flare man doesn't know you is all, he knows me, he leaves you alone."

"Okay, okay. Stop crying, Grace."

I bit the inside of my cheek, and dug my fingernails into

the palms of my hands, and was quiet, then asked, "You believe me?"

He looked out toward the water, which was partly obscured by the long dune of sand.

"You think he'll find me out here, the flare man I mean?"

Desmond looked up at the osprey nest; the chicks were quiet now. "Fire don't cross water, okay. Now you can stop your crying, okay?"

"You believe me, that they're real."

Desmond shrugged. "If they come I'll protect you, how's that?"

Looking back at what he said I've wondered whether, at some depth in his child's mind, he didn't foresee that afternoon—in those moments of his awe at the osprey and disgust at how the fish was killed—as the osprey launched herself off again back toward the bay to hunt once more before the light failed, that he and Berg didn't belong up in trees, where they loved to climb, the both of them, because boys and people weren't supposed to be up high in the air like that any more than fish were. But I know this idea of mine, this abstraction, is what Faw has always called "privileged thinking," privileged in the sense that such thinking was only done by people who had nothing better to do with their time and themselves.

"I'm freezing," I said, and what happened errs into a misshapen curiosity in my memory. I was teary; I was sorry to have seen the bird murder the asinine fish, was sad to hear my brother call me crazy, was upset to have been the cause of so much disruption to my parents and Desmond, and even Berg. The fog was moving into the darkening evening, and my brother took his glove off (for an instant I flinched, thinking he was about to slap me for not completely having stopped crying) and brushed as gently as he could the tears off my cheek. I must have smiled at him, and he kissed me, on the lips, which I didn't like very much for him to do, but with all that had been said, I knew better than to resist. He made mistakes, he touched me all over. I didn't know what he was doing, I didn't know what I was doing, either. My dress was being muddied, which concerned me. So small, so bare, such flesh with its un-grown and falsely promising slash, white and sad as the pike's gills, is where Desmond tried like a tainted soldier to empower himself, impale me, be the king of the marsh. I knew what I looked like because I had looked there before; at Desmond I didn't look. I couldn't. Nothing was consum-mated, of course, nothing could possibly have happened given how young we were still; but we did hold each other, and it's not impossible that my memory isn't being sabo-taged by sentiment, here now by this hostile teller inside me, isn't fabricating my belief that he was weeping, too, although I have to admit to myself he might have been laughing—my theme for the story: they seem so similar at times. If he was sad, or laughing-sad, it was because he truly did think I was a nut (what kind, as they can be so beauti-ful—just think of the walnut's lush ridges) or else why? He was safe from the osprey. He'd surely forgotten about death. If I could go back and make him cry I might now want him to have cried for different reasons. I'd have him cry because he couldn't be older, be my man not my brother, be some man I never knew. Inside those tears would be a comical joy.

He said, "Grace, don't tell."

I stood up, and examined the mud on my clothes.

"Promise?"

I said I wouldn't tell, and until now I haven't.

❖

"Never complain, never explain," was our father's fondest aphorism. I never told to anyone else, nor have I ever ad-mitted that afternoon to myself in the full richness of its injury or comedy. Maybe no one was injured. The scars I may have are scars I can live with. Maybe it was funny, in the way things that seemed so traumatic can sometimes seem funny once they're safely confined to the past. If Berg hadn't revealed to me, years later, that he had seen us in the marsh, there never would have been any need to explain, or feel vindictive. Vindication is never satisfying, at least to my way of thinking, though everyone around me seems to thrive on it as an addict on her drug. He hinted—as deftly as he was able (Berg in my opinion cannot count deftness as a trait)—that he felt he had come on us in the act of doing something that only he, as the eldest of us children, should even have known about. Yet there was in his voice enough self-doubt to betray to me that he didn't know as much as he wanted me to believe. I had the presence of mind to seize on that doubt. I suppose I lied. No, I did lie. However, we were protected, Desmond and I, by my denying Berg the confirmation he so desperately seemed to want. And that was my objective.

"Grace, you want to look at some of the stuff?" Berg would ask, and to be sure I would, because the films interested me as much as they interested him, but then I'd say, "No," and he would go on, just like the flare man might have gone on, as if I'd just said "Sure," and he'd take me by the hand, and we would go into the library and Berg would tell Desmond to draw the curtain and tilt a chair up under the knob of the door, and then ask, "You ready?"

And I would be ready. And on would come the films, which we watched, Berg running the projector, one of the three of us posted as a lookout (we were able to engage in this activity only when both Mother and Djuna were away from the house), the other two absorbed by the black and white bodies without their clothes, without even bathing suits, as they stuck their tongues out and put them in each other's mouth and in other places, and acted—"acted" is the word, and we were not convinced of the sincerity of all their panting and closed eyes and shivering and so forth—

as if they were having fun. To me they were like horror movies, I watched them with the same combination of enchantment and revulsion.

"This is what you and Desmond were doing but you didn't know how," Berg asserted once, when our brother was not there.

Why wouldn't he just let me watch and see, without having to comment on everything? Here he was, doing his best to be independent, not associated with the family, and most especially with our parents, and yet what was this but an attempt to assign meanings?

"I saw you," and off he would go trying to trip me up into talking about it.

Still, the unhappiness I felt at having had to dissemble, and deny to him everything about our awkward, initiatory, unresolved moment down in the marsh, only turned me away from Berg. Later, when we were in our early twenties, and Djuna threw a small party for me and my one brief husband (more later), Berg—his own tongue freed up by some family champagne (I must link Berg and champagne for some reason, in part because people seem to like Berg and like champagne, while I have all my life had an uneasy relationship with both)—turned to my Warne, and slurred some claim about, "If you want to have a really good go at it, get her out into the mud, she excels in mud, good primal wet gooey vernal mud." It was, in a way that I probably will never be able fully to explain, a moment of Brush behavior in the extreme. Canted teeth and the ability to use them to bite at the most effective moment—yes, this was something of a Brush trait.

Does one try to defend oneself in a situation like that? I think not. At least, I chose not to; but it did set a seed of anger in me toward my brother. Bad seeds always set easier than good, and they're more easily planted, as all of us know. I felt I had tried so hard to be his friend, and he had never been anything more than mercurial and undependable toward me in return.

The question Berg might have asked that would have been more interesting to me, on that occasion of the champagne and his pernicious comments at the reception, would have had to do with what happened between me and Desmond *after* the encounter. He would never admit it, but on reflection, I feel confident Berg spent plenty of time spying on us. He might say, now, in his self-appointed priesthood as cinematographic artist, that he was only playing the role fate had handed him, as one chosen to record the intoxications of childhood, the warping and interweaving of personality, of sexuality, and so much more drivel. Who knows what he might have hoped to gain, even if he'd got to witness what it was he had hoped to see. Had our island lives proceeded in the way we all naturally had expected—had we grown up together, mother, two brothers, daughter, and sometime father—then I suppose it is possible that Desmond and I, being kids, being profoundly alone, being drawn over time into the secret world that can be created in solitude, might have provided Berg with the dirty secret he so hoped to have, to save, to do with as he might please. Who knows what he would have been capable of saying at my reception had Desmond and I actually provided him with fodder for some flash of catharsis? Who knows what he might then have brought out at just the appropriate moment as barter in some postadolescent blackmail?

Desmond and I visited the osprey nest dozens of times before winter came forcing its inhabitants to migrate, and we became each other's best friend. We knew no one along the beach road. We were outsiders in school. As my confidant, not only did he learn to believe what I told him about the things I sometimes saw, but his curiosity about it all somehow alleviated my combined hope and fear that the flare man would eventually catch up with me.

"Let him catch up," I wrote in my diary, in terms that seem to address Berg as much as the flare man. "He can't do me any harm, because Desmond won't let him." I then wrote the facing panel for my diptych, "Things to do on the beach in the summer. Bury my feet in the sand. Bury Mother's feet in the sand. Bury my whole laughing brother in the sand. Wade. Watch the sand clouds in the water that the waves make. Pee in the ocean, the fish don't care because the ocean is so big. Watch the brown pelican dive for fish. Make a stick turn into a boat. Make a lake in the sand. Get sun poisoning. Hate aloe, hate your redness, hate the itch in the middle of your back where you can't get at it and your brother won't scratch it for you. Cry. Be hungry. Be at the hot dog stand and not have the change to buy a hot dog but eat the vendor's relish and drink his ketchup when he's not looking. Be thirsty. Want an ice cream sandwich, or lime popsicle. Beg for these, and get them. Be bored but not want to go home. Be scolded. Sulk, and scrunch mussel shells under the heel of your bare foot. Watch the sailboats come around on their moorings. Watch the windsurfer woman fall over into the blue water and get back up again and pull her orange sail out of the water and try again, then fall again. Watch the seagulls drop conch shells onto the stones on the beach to break their shells. Look at people's fat. Daydream. Worry and worry if those clouds mean rain."

❖

What was really going on all along, with us and around us, and we never saw it happening, we children, though I had once seen how it could begin to happen, was that Mother had made another life for herself, right there adjacent to the one she led with us, but one that was growing and growing and began to want not to share her with us, but have her all to itself. Maybe I can forgive myself for not having said or done something about it, because, for one, I was so young, and being young was caught up with the newness of Scrub Farm, the newness of Djuna Cobbetts and Ernest and his boxes of tools, and the newness of the ocean at my feet.

I had experienced a period of nearly a year, come spring 1965, my eighth birthday, of relative health. The megrims threatened—you can feel them, barometric in their distant pressure—but often never materialized. And this, not just to me, but to all of us, was the object of quiet celebration. Faw came on his weekends, and on the holidays. Djuna Cobbetts would produce baked ham and Desmond and I would stick so many whole cloves in it that one could no longer see the meat. Berg, as I say, generally went his own way, whenever he wasn't watching television or showing us the films that he continued to borrow from a file box, marked with Pannett and Neden's initials, which was hidden in our father's closet. Berg was thirteen then, and developed early on his own sense of what mattered, how he might behave toward whatever ends he had in mind—ends that I believe changed daily.

It could be argued that one occurrence was what precipitated the other. And no doubt Desmond's fall from the treehouse to the paving stones of the porch off the kitchen, did bring every other strain the family experienced to a new level of intensity. What unhappiness my mother Erin had harbored about her being abandoned, as she felt it, was not in fact occasioned by the accidental death of my brother, her younger son; the days that followed Desmond's fall were pregnant with revolt, though.

Who was to say that had they not moved to Shelter Island, to Scrub Farm with its rotting porch and ancient cistern, Desmond wouldn't have been exposed to the temptation to climb trees and gamble like most boys do that their limbs will hold them? Aren't there as many if not more perils in the city as the country? The time for such speculation was past, they knew. Charles could with equal confidence have argued that the boys had not been reined in enough by their mother. He could only do so much from the city, he might have contended—and look at Berg, with his smoking, his runaway pals, his language, look at what an undisciplined child he turned into over the course of that first full summer. If he, Charles, hadn't taken matters into his own fatherly hands by getting the boy involved with Geiger, where might he have ended up?

When the accident happened it was August, it was a Sunday, which to my mind has always been an unholy day—the day that Faw went back to the city, the last day of the week, the day that my brother fell. It was the second year at Scrub Farm, and so muggy that when evening finally descended after the long hot day it seemed like a double night that shrouded the orchard and whispering grass. The air wheezed and chortled; the opaque beach was an ashen torpor. Desmond had gone outside into the treehouse, wearing nothing in the hot night. Berg would have appreciated the performance, and I would always suspect that it was Berg who taught him all these tricks that led to the accident. He sat out in the night air, looking at the stars, and smoked secret cigarettes stolen months and months before from the workmen maybe, maybe from Ernest, and giggled, waited to window-peek on me but when my bedroom light came on and it wasn't I, nor Faw or Mother, but this man he'd only met once or twice and whom he didn't like, the one with the strange name, Gabriel Segredo, he tried to duck down but slipped between limbs, and made no sound as he fell. The men came and had taken Desmond away long before morning. Mother was waiting by the bed, and told me what had happened to Desmond. Faw was nowhere to be found—his telephone rang and rang in the city, and she didn't know where he was.

You can understand how it was possible for me to take on the burden of blame for the breakdown of our family? Sure, it's a cliché, sure we all of us are always looking for things to blame on ourselves, when we're not preoccupied with pinning the blame on others. But why else would they ever have come to that place if not on my behalf, if not because Trudeau and Faw believed this was the only way to get me on the road to health? I know it is never right to blame yourself for things that are out of your hands, but I had never been able to kick this thought that what happened between them—Faw and Mother—was also because of me, but by the time I came to know all that transpired during this period in our lives it was far too late to rectify matters. Even if I could have begun to understand how Mother might resent our new life enough to set her doing the things she began to do, I would have been helpless to change it. She has never been able to understand how I didn't, and don't, resent Faw's desire to be off, alone, away from us for most of the time, doing whatever it was he himself had to do in order to make his Sprawl. I don't resent the fact that she couldn't reach him about Desmond's death until late Monday. What he was doing back then when the family was moved out to Scrub Farm must have been overpoweringly engrossing. I have come to see, from the perspective of an adult, how buying and selling things out in the real world, moving money around, moving people around, and on and on, how the range of all he was doing might have torn him away from us. He was always kind and good to me, anyway, and I always tried to be kind and good back, for above all I knew that I wanted to be a good girl, probably in my adolescent meditations believing that in this way the megrims might come to a stop.

As for my brothers, they had been so enthralled with building their treehouse in the cherry, into which they could climb from my bedroom window, neither—yes, Desmond included—seemed to care about either Father's absence, or Mother's agitation. Berg and I developed a mild rivalry for Desmond's time, as it happened, given that Berg wanted to build, and I merely wanted to walk, to visit the nest, to go down to the sea. When Desmond favored me, Berg simply ignored us both and went about tending to his own affairs, fixing his bicycle, disappearing out into the woods along the beach for hours at a stretch. Whenever I did have one of my megrims, Desmond, unlike Berg, was always there to sit by, and do whatever Djuna Cobbetts, or

Mother, told him to. He didn't mind standing out along the road in the gusty autumn rain on the beach road to take the bus to school, either. Whereas Berg as often as not ditched us the moment Djuna turned under her wind-pummeled umbrella to make back for the house.

"Big baby," Berg would chide his brother when he refused to cut school, and I knew better than to say anything in his defense.

Desmond would study the water that pooled and bristled around his shoes grown shiny and heavy in the road-shoulder mud. Neither Berg nor I would have any idea what he was thinking, whenever he withdrew into himself in those moments. He was distracted; we all three of us were. Our silly little children's worlds were disintegrating under our very feet, and we must have known it, each of us in his own different way. I wonder, now, whether because I possessed some kind of separate, parallel reality—or at least *had* possessed such a thing—it made it easier for me to adjust to what was bound to happen. Berg, I must admit, in a real way, suffered some hard blows, as a boy. Though, again (round and round I go) nothing like what Desmond was fated to know.

I wonder what any of them—Desmond, Berg, my parents, even Trudeau and Djuna—would have thought if I had come out and in so many words told them that I missed my light people? There were so many nights when I went to bed, and the window was open, and far, far away I could hear the clanging of the buoy-marker bell and the distant scratching of the waves on the surface of the sand, and I began to wish that the flare man could come, maybe on his best behavior, maybe having agreed not to flash hostile at me, and enjoy such peace. Wouldn't that have made him, them all, warm—hot—with joy? As often as they had "misbehaved" (I can't remember whether this was Erin or Djuna) and terrified me, I would find myself caught up tight in my own arms in the bed and rocking myself and wondering how they were faring back in the old ailanthus.

Wondering whether they had some new friend to over-whelm with their wild powers. And now I had Desmond to miss, as well.

❖

The church with the old lady at the window, up there on the side of the hill, lighting her votary candle and shielding its flame against the breezes by cupping it in the palm of her hand until it took well into the wick—she was part of a recurrent dream of mine after the dinner. I could see her, all alone, in her rustic adobe church, and she looked out to the sea to keep a keen eye out for the lost sailors. She was a mild figure in my imagination, and had nothing of the authority of the flare man, or my brother. Unlike them, she didn't seem quite so real. I knew that she was a dream. How peculiar it is that of the three of them, the light people, Desmond, and this vigilant candle-bearer, only she, this last, would prove to have had an actual power. Before I sat down to put this all together I secretly went to find her. Maybe she knew something. The water below changed from the grays of the East Coast to the heavier blues and turquoises that set off the sea south of Cuba. I knew that she would be there. I had no doubt of that. But what else it is that would be there I wasn't sure. All the threads that seemed to have no purpose, that seemed to lead off into nowhere, I knew might lead to her door. (I don't mean to be elliptical, don't want to be mysterious, and don't care whether I am being intriguing—threads are what they are.) And I thought, It may not be a church, she may not even keep to her schedule of burning those memorial candles every night, but I won't mind—that part doesn't matter, in the end. What matters to me is that the overactive imagina-tion that was my burden and my release as a child is not operative now. I refuse to be like the little boy who cried wolf one time too many. This is why all these strands must come together, wild and in disarray as they might seem on the surface. That was, I thought, the only hope I have of sheltering my father the same way he once had sheltered me. When I got there, I still didn't know how much harder it would be to do what I had wanted to do. The Sprawl by then was too wide for any single wish to umbrella it.

❖

"Ghosts are men and the houses they inhabit are women."

I wrote that in my journal, which I worked on more and more after Desmond died. It was a way of talking with him, though it was, I knew, only I who did the talking. But since when I wrote it out, everything was silent, I felt I could hear him, or could better imagine what he would sound like if he responded. No one knew about the journal; I found the book, an old calendar book, in the attic. It bore the signature of another owner, one of the Merriams, but was otherwise full of many blank pages. I ignored the dates, as the calendar was for a year long past, and began to concentrate on my own history. In summer 1964, Scrub Farm was a ghostless place. But now that had changed. "I'll be a house if you'll haunt me," I wrote. I think I meant it.

The first time Desmond became an integral part of the megrim sequence, the scent of apricot saturated the room. She—this Grace that was I—reached, pushing against the air in the room with her palms out and her white fingers extended like twigs on a smooth-bark birch, to block it. Faw, who sat by the bed, reading to her, to me, about a man who was turned into a mule, didn't notice that the room had taken on this odor, and had even changed color. Shahrazad looked on, from a corner; her eyes were upside down.

Grace knew the scent could not be blocked. It diffused across the walls and the bedspread, wafting and waving like a lascivious ribbon until it formed itself into a figure and lay its apricot head beside her head on the pillow. It caressed her hands and hair and it flowed over her childish jewelry—the plastic ruby ring, the friendship bracelet Desmond had given her—which she never, ever took off, not even when she took her bath and went to sleep. It moved tardy and heavy as it began to take full possession of the bedroom. As this sense of thickening occurred, the apricot scent became more like a liquid muscle of wind, like juice, but was not sticky so much as chalky, and—as it rose through her throat and settled on the back of her tongue— what came to her then was the thought of all those apricots, and she would be sitting in a tree of apricots, say, and she saw that she was an apricot too, with the other apricots, meaty and browning and rotting. As soon as she saw herself as unclaimed fruit she fought back toward what she knew to be Grace, to be her, and she swallowed hard and rolled onto her side to stare into the fire that Faw had made in the fireplace.

She stared because she wasn't too sure she wanted to be an apricot tonight, since usually being an apricot meant that it was going to hurt. So she worked on making up fire-animals that flickered off the logs. A bark ember in the fireplace popped against the screen there, then fell to the hearth where it paled from peach to white, and shrank until it was no longer an independent glowing bulb but a fragment of char. It reminded her first of the gills of a fish, the osprey's pike's gills, the gills on the salmon that Faw had caught on the river in Maine and brought back with him packed in ice. Now the ember became a shrew's tooth, like the one her uncle Vernon had given her with instructions not to make more than three wishes on it, lest it turn back into a real shrew that would come and get her. For safety's sake she had never bothered to make any wishes on the tooth, and doubted its miraculous powers, anyhow, since Uncle Vernon was a practical joker, as Faw always said, and because it looked more like just a person's tooth, stained yellow and chipped. Then she saw the ember turn into a monkey's face and, last, black as a poppy seed. Faw in the chair by the bed hadn't witnessed any of these occurrences that had reshaped the room in which he was sitting.

Smelling nothing, ignoring the monkey-face fire, he went on reading aloud to Grace, even as she closed her eyes, and left the dying fire behind, and decided that since she wasn't sleepy enough yet, she would take the apricots away with her into another story, a very different one, all her own.

"That's all for tonight," was what her father said. It always startled her when he spoke again in his regular tone of voice, and not in the storytelling tone.

"No, more, please read more," she pleaded, from a pocket in the megrim.

"You're sleeping through the whole story."

"No, I want more."

He read another half-page from the "Tale of Ali bin Bakkar and of Shams al-Nahar." Shahrazad's voice rose back into that of her father, or so it was she perceived it, and she closed her eyes once more, and heard ". . . I know that I am about to be lost past recourse, and the cause of my destruction is naught but love and longing and excess of desire and distraction," and as Ali bin Bakkar beseeched Allah to deliver him from his perilous predicament, Grace swooned, or thought she did (her father heard her merely snore, which made him smile a little as he closed the volume of *The Arabian Nights* and placed it on her bedside table).

He ran his palm over her forehead, and watched her lids flutter and race over the fluctuations of her moving, dreaming eyes. He whispered goodnight to his daughter and turned her lamp off. Finding himself distracted in the room, he stood listening to her breathe, and used the rhythm of her lungs as a frame in which he might bring himself back from the voice of the story to the preoccupations of his own incautious dealings. A pale, unconcentrated light split through the branches of the tree out her window, entered, and coaxed patterns out of the wallpaper; eunuchs, the caliph, Ali and Abu al-Hasan, graven gold and sherbet. The clock struck down the hall. He left the room.

And then it was once upon a time, and the wasps came,

as unable to recognize her for the girl she was as to resist that apricot perfume which emanated from her skin. With the shimmery needles that dangled from their abdomens they pricked her along her neck and temples, causing her to feel sick to her human stomach. It hurt to wince. She tried to stay calm and quiet and pure of mind. There was an instant of tumbling down a set of marble stairs that weren't the stairs in Scrub Farm. These cold stairs had been polished, for the feel of the veined stone treads as they rippled under her and kneaded the backs of her thighs, one step after the other, was like razors.

On looking closer it became clear the stairs were not marble, but were fashioned of brilliantly sparkling wasps. As they stung her she got bruised, and then she began to wonder whether the wasps were not wasps, were not stairs, but were fragments of light carried in the arms of a summery wind. Wind like those sandy mistrals or williwaws or siroccos she read about in school, wind like Shahrazad's desert wind, astringent wind that bore these dead wasps and chips of electricity shaped like wings in its wake.

What followed was the vertigo. Where the wasp-wind was hard to see, whirling and piercing in the apricot tree, the vertigo was, as an agent of changed perception, impossible to see. It was not that Grace was dizzy. Grace was central, was in the middle of it all, and she wasn't moving. The room was what was in a twirl. Grace's head, cradled in her pillow, lay still, while the walls, the fireplace, the bureau, the ceiling, grew dense until in a lavish silent explosion they broke off into a kind of marine plant life that was (as with everything) composed of light.

The other apricots fell from the tree and the wasps carried on williwaw calmed down a bit, and more nonchalantly began to take advantage of her as they burrowed up her nostrils, and snuggled, comfortable and menacing, into the depths of her ears. The vertigo, however, clipped her stem just like that, snip, just like a pair of good, sharp garden shears, and down she plummeted through the lay-

ers and levels of suckers, earning her nausea as she fell. At
this point vomit restored dampness to her flying world and
she, as girl-apricot, was wet once more, and full.

There was, down in her half-conscious, exhausted,
thrumming self the hope of what she knew would next
come toward her just as the ground comes rushing to the
apricot that has dropped through branches of the tree to
earth. The scent, the solitude, the wasps, the wind, the
vertigo, were steps taken—descending—toward the aura.

What an adult word, she thought. "Aura."

And if she were to look in the bureau mirror, having
given up the game of the apricot tree, and the tales and
notions of wasps and wind (which got her through the
pains of it), she knew that what she would witness was just
what she'd witnessed before. She got up quietly and looked.
And she saw it, just as she thought she would—saw herself,
saw her hair as a pink-blue halo of icicles and she had no
face, no face in her head, and above all she understood as
she had before that she had no *idea* that she ever had a face.
Neither face as something forgotten, nor face as something
possible.

It was horrible, it was beautiful. Her visual analysis of
her room and of her body was being impaired even while
her sensorium—there was a word she liked that she had
learned from Dr. Trudeau, she liked it because it seemed
majestic—was otherwise clear, and the megrim was on her
and there was no going forward and no going back. Her
hair was made of a kind of ice that would not melt because
it wasn't even freezing, or anything. It was so pretty she
wanted to comb it, the hair light, the rays, and she smiled
a lipless smile knowing that it was all hers and she saw it,
was the only person who could see it, with eyes that must
have been hidden deep in the void at the halo center.

When her father had shut the door, stealthy as a country
owl out her bedroom window the dead boy climbed a little
higher in the tree and looked in on her. That tree was his
tree, the tree where he had lived ever since he had fallen

out of the house they'd made up there in the branches with planks of lumber filched from the building site down the road.

Grace didn't weep when Desmond died, for one reason: she didn't believe it was true—not that Mother would lie to her; it was just Mother didn't know the truth. None of them did. Death might have taken Desmond away from all of them, but not from her. His flight from the limb to the pavement had occurred without a scream, without the merest capitulation to fear. He was so brave, was Desmond. It was as if he went down to his destiny with mute exuberance, and when she meditated on what it must have felt like being at the center of such a deed, giving the body over to its quick journey from the reluctant branch through close night air to reach the earth, she found she could invent it up to the moment of impact.

All Grace could imagine was that impact meant coming into a sort of new freedom wherein the gist of what was human in him, his flesh and personality, was simply torn and shuffled, like a silhouette under scissors. In time she came to understand that death did not care for all her little metaphors, her little hopes and sorrows. It had no intention of giving him or anyone else back to life just like that, for free. Death was selfish as a miser, and strong as a bull. It broke Desmond, and it broke him, it seemed, for a reason. She might never know what that reason was, but for her to be able to visit him after that she, too, would have to break, or at least rend. It was a necessary exchange, and she was willing to do her part in making it take place.

The branches of the tree seemed to miss him, though not as much as she did, and when they scratched across the skin of the glass of her window under the force of the wind—the breath of Arabia cooled by the sea—she looked to see if he was out there again, tiptoeing over bark and rustling leaves. Sometimes he was, sometimes he wasn't. Sometimes she asked him to come, but he came in when he felt like it. She soon understood that her desire to commune with Des-

mond seldom coincided with his materialization. The one
thing she did feel certain of was this: he depended in some
enigmatic and profound way on the tree. Without the
slightest fleck of proof she was steadfast in her conviction
that without the tree Desmond would be disenchanted. He
would be cut off from her forever. She wept with gratitude
that she'd been able to talk her father out of having the tree
sawed down.

The limbs groaned and gave tonight and here he was up
in the tree again, naked except for his origami hat made of
newspaper, ship-shaped, and she wondered how he lived in
that wild cherry tree without freezing or starving—he
never once ate the food she laid out in its branches for him,
the warm chicken giblets in the tinfoil tray, the lamb chop
she took from the kitchen—she knew that the cherries were
inedible. Desmond had bird's balance in his body now, but
he wasn't hungry. When she told him to eat, he stared at
her and screwed his face into the most quizzical look. He
didn't understand anymore what eating was. Tails flashing
like plumes, the squirrels who bounded over from other
trees were first to get to the pieces of bread she put out
using long sticks lashed together. What the squirrels didn't
want the starlings and jays carried away in their beaks.

Desmond watched her through the rippled old glass.
You could see through him, but he wasn't a ghost. He was
like an image superimposed in a film upon another image—
that was how he looked; solid and palpable and real, but,
well, a little translucent. For her part, she assumed that out
there in the snow-tipped branches of his tree he felt sympathetic pains toward her suffering, but she wondered sometimes how could a person in his position—he must have
powers, surely, living where he lived—sit by like an idle
sovereign, while her face disappeared in those coffee-glitter
lights, leaving a doughnut in the mirror, and nothing more,
no eyes, no lips, no face.

Somehow, though she never told him in so many words
of her feelings, he had changed. His attentions were not

tendered in a way she might have wanted. She knew that tonight he would come to her, having been distant, unapproachable, and would burn clean through the glass, burn clear into her forehead, in a way the lights in the old ailanthus had never done.

Desmond bided his time until his sister—her skin flushed with megrim, her hair damp, her head dully pounding—was drowsy. Djuna locked, as always, the double-sash window, and while Grace could hardly stand she crept from the bureau mirror to the window, eyes closed against the icicle lights, and turned the latch. She wanted him to realize that even though she didn't know if he would come in or not, she was waiting. She looked at him across the night glass and thought she saw him nod. Sensing that if she didn't stand at the window and invite him he was more likely to join her, she went back to bed, and curled into a chrysalis of expectancy. He had developed an indefinable, contrary personality, had Desmond, and she knew that this was all she could do.

She waited for what seemed a very long time. A fluttery and scant breeze—where from?—cooled her forehead. And then he drifted, was the word, drifted rather than leaped or even flew from the branch where he lived, to the sill of the window.

The window drew up quietly, or seemed to. Had the breeze come from there? The light people had never been able to do that. As he came closer, she wondered how it must be for one who is used to living in a tree, the leafy-in-summer, barren-in-winter cherry tree, to be inside her room. She had read about the flying fish, and other beasts whose needs and habits took them from one world into another (what were we to make of the earthbound caterpillar destined to flutter away into the air with its painted wings?) —and what was Desmond's sense of coming from there to here? She would have asked him, but she knew that he wouldn't understand the question.

Grace opened her eyes and studied him as he knelt beside

her, saw the details of his face, fine hair between his narrow
eyebrows, the fanning wrinkles at the corners of his eyes,
wrinkles that were more common in a man much older
than he must have been. His boldness was unexpected.
After brushing aside the comforter and sheets, he carried
her from her bed and placed her on the old prayer rug by
the dying fire, then raised her hips off the floor, pulled her
pajama bottoms down to her ankles, rolled her over. At first
she trembled pleasantly to the feel of the wool against her
belly. When he ran the stiff bristles of the coal broom over
her buttocks Grace's megrim crimped just like it was made
of foil or curtain cloth and sprang right out of the side of
her head, and she felt liberated all of a sudden from its dry,
idiotic pain. She dared not move. The andirons stood like
sentinels over her, smiling and knowing, and the poker and
shovel and log forks she could see were instruments any of
which might find their way into his hands. Inasmuch as
they might, she knew that they ought to, in a way, ought
to because she felt it was she who must atone for what
happened; and since everything in life is first the discovery
of balance versus imbalance, second the understanding of
how absolution may come to pass, third the will to sacrifice—she knew he would never do anything to her that
would be unmerciful. He had found balance she knew just
by the way he was able to walk the branches of the tree like
some seasoned acrobat. He had found understanding, she
could just tell, by the way he'd carried her, and touched
her, and by how he had seemed somehow to become a man,
unlike the boy under the osprey nest who knew nothing.
She was willing to sacrifice whatever he might want her to
sacrifice, and knew that he wouldn't want something that
she wouldn't happily be able to give him. He would never
punish her, as such. This was a thought not made of words
or intelligence, rather like a sensation that she kept before
her as the boy spanked her with the coal brush, rather
methodically, while at the same time caressing her cheek
with his free hand. She kissed his hand and her pillow (how

had she been moved back into her bed?) not caring which was which but just rejoicing in being able to touch him again and be touched by him. As she kissed, her experience became concentrated at the base of her spine. It was warm.

She tried to stiffen, to show him that she was confused. He must have known. There was a smell of mayonnaise, yes that was exactly what the air had come to smell like then, which she attempted to wipe off her mouth onto the sheets. It was as if she'd fallen into a cactus plant like the ones they had found on the dunes, yellow and barbed to protect themselves from animals that were thirsty and would like to eat their green flesh, and Desmond began to work his mouth along her lower spine and her thighs, which were spread apart as far as he could make them give. He was kissing her through what seemed like impossible curves, and she bit her knuckle so as not to scream out, which she both wanted and didn't want to do. To steady herself, she hooked one knee over the side of the bed. Was this what was supposed to happen? she thought, and made the thought travel through her back down into her pelvis, and spread through her buttocks, all over her flesh, through her naked pubis, and again, as the thought traveled the thought itself knew there was no fact of Grace but for the dense, magnetic scent of apricot and Desmond and mayonnaise, all of it mingling into something delicious, into which he sank his tongue, his mouth, his face and, ultimately, his whole head, which she understood to be . . . well it had to be impossible, for he would have had to open her up between her legs in a way that they just wouldn't be able to be opened, to fit his precious head there, but it seemed so simple and not the result of such violence that he was moving in and out of her slowly, deliberately, and when she thought what it meant, thought of her brother's head, the delicate brain tissue (she had seen brains once, in a restaurant, and watched Faw spoon it, it was like burnt tapioca, into his mouth, unable to eat her own food as she was so overwhelmed by what he was dining on, what it once had been) cradled within his bone-bowl, his cranium, and thought of his soft ears, the silken hair that now was running damp with her, and wet with the oil of forgiveness, it became concrete and imaginable, and therefore familiar, and she gave herself over to it as not just a possibility but what was happening to her, the magnificent wisdom of what she had needed to have happen to her, and sensed new clear distinctions such as the grit of his tongue passing over her, again, and having her, again, and her control was gone, she was moaning and heaving and she didn't care whether Djuna or Berg or Faw or Mother or all of them came rushing into the room to find her with Desmond there on her bed, crazy with the pleasure of being bold, and just as the scream rose into her throat he stopped and rested his soaked face in the small of her back.

Between her legs she ached like fire under bellows and prong. He clutched her tightly, kissed her hair, chewed—even roughly—at her temple and on down her cheek. What happened then would prevent her from ever understanding the nature of Desmond's love for her, because what appeared to happen to her after this delay was that her head in a fever was gently knocked into the mattress, and he hardened over her, binding her hands with his, raging with his mouth over her shoulder and down her neck, until her megrim was abstracted so that she could shove back, with him and at him, and when he felt her moving at him and with him and against him he entered, except that now she was on her back and he was under her, his arms wrapped around her chest, his ankles wrapped around and over her ankles.

Lights like crystals started up on the ceiling. Their sharpness seemed to have nothing in common with the bite of Desmond's hips and thighs. They were measured, she soon realized, against the beat of her own heart. Once she understood this her eyes and throat began to hurt, as did her fingers, her neck, and before long her whole body. She carried on, forward, thrusting by herself. Desmond somehow had maneuvered himself out from underneath her and stood beside her on the bed and burst into light over her face and breasts and belly. The room was full of the apricot scent, and Grace, breathing hard, began to worry again that the smell would escape the room, creep under the door, to give her away here at the height of their freedom, bring the others who loved her into the room from without and bring her to some kind of new shame and with it an absence of freedom.

But it didn't happen. Desmond, again himself, was already out on the ledge, and back into the tree.

The window was ajar. The house was silent. The wind buffeted the branches in the cherry tree, and the waves knocked as ever on the stones. The sheets and blankets on her bed were mussed with their extraordinary perfume—a perfume that reminded her then of her mother's potpourri—and she pulled them, and the perfume they gave off, back over her against the fresh chill in the room. This was how the ravishments began.

PART II

COECLES INLET AND OTHER DESTINATIONS

The answer to the question of what Gabriel Segredo was doing in my room will never rest easy with me. He was looking for a scarf for her to wrap around her head, a brash, brilliant skein of silk to frame her treacherous face—this was the object of a search that ended with Desmond being frightened from his perch to his death. I'm glad I didn't know this detail until later—when my mother decided to get it off her chest in one of her letters to me—or else I would have gone after the both of them with a kitchen knife, I swear it.

He was looking for the scarf because she, my poor unwitting mother, asked him to look for it, and already he was so trapped by his conviction that he wanted to have her for himself that he would do whatever she wanted. How these desires revolve in such ironies. Segredo's needs and his wants slowly rotated around his belief that this Erin Brush, while married, and while a mother, was not an impossible target; and yet, despite his pluck, he was never, in my eyes, a strong person—emotionally—not then, at least. Strength as often as not can work against you, and so in Segredo's case I believe it was in part his emotional weaknesses that drew my mother into his orbit as much as anything. With him, she could have her own way, for once, or so she thought, and in that capacity he was dutiful, whether he meant to be or not.

If she had shown the courage to pack her belongings and leave her family on her own, I can't help but think my brother Desmond might be alive today. The same thought has bothered her over the years, I know because she's confessed as much to me. We've each seen our way clear to forgiving her—indeed, Desmond's responsibility in his own demise has not escaped us—but forgiveness never

quite washes anger out of all the dark corners where anger
clings. It may not be fair to feel anger toward her after
having truly forgiven her, but I don't see by what standards
I'm supposed to be fair at all times. Fairness is part of my
nature, it is deep in my skin and bones; it's not in my blood,
though. Blood judges for itself.

I knew he was in the house that day because I noticed,
from the library window, his car parked down the road,
and from a second window saw him walk—a large, heavy
(strong, not fat) man dressed in loose, drab clothes, a red
and black kerchief tied around his neck—across the field
toward our house. There was an air about him, maybe it
was the deliberate way his hard shoes came down to meet
the dirt as he moved toward the house, maybe it was the
way he kept his eye averted and his bark-brown hair toppled down over his forehead, that informed me not to run
out and say hello. He seemed grim, determined, powerful.
I heard him stamp the dust off his boots on the mat on the
porch, and stayed where I was. Their voices, rather more
quiet than they should have been if nothing was afoot, I
strained to hear; soon enough their intentions became
clear. He brought a few suitcases up from the cellar, and
he commented, I heard him, on the mildew that had begun
to destroy them. "Set them out in the sun for a while and
let them bake it out," is what he told her they would have
to do with the luggage sometime. He was trying so hard to
make it sound as if nothing of any special importance was
going on, so soft and purposely even was his voice, and so
ostensibly simple were his concerns. The suitcases, the
damp basement, the mildew. It was all so easy, in fact, that
despite my pounding heart I failed to notice when it was
they had gone upstairs, to the master bedroom—I forget
what I was watching on the box, but for all my natural
inclination to know everything I wasn't supposed to know,
see things that were supposed to be hidden from my sight,
I continued to stay where I was, agitated, but not inclined
to move upstairs after them. Djuna was over in Orient, her

day off. Faw was, as I've said, in New York. Berg was down
at the shore shooting his air gun into the crests of waves,
like the Irish king Cuchulain that Mother said was one of
her distant relatives, using pellets instead of a sword to slay
his phantom sea monsters. It was all so well planned, plot-
ted, timed, in other words, Segredo's arrival, the discreet
placement of the car in which they would leave, the way
in which they carried on inside the house, I can still
scarcely believe it. Time has its way of piling experience on
experience, crowding data and whim and reaction and
error and triumph together, one upon the other, so that
whatever a person experiences in a life will someday, like
the person himself, be buried under by his own myriad
gestures (this is, by the way, why suicide out of shame
never makes sense)—but, sometimes, to this day, I have
wondered how she could look back to that August evening,
and stand herself.

You see, just as Desmond is the hitch that prevents me
from being able to care much about what was behind her
desire to get out of her arrangement with Faw and the rest
of us—I have no quarrel, objectively, with her desire to
make a different life for herself—Desmond was the hitch in
her own considerations. He was supposed to be off with
Berg by the sea, or in with me watching television. He
could generally be counted on to be with either of his
siblings. But this once he'd gone out on his own, climbed
into the cherry tree. Of course, when he fell, Erin and
Segredo's plan collapsed. It occurs to me, did someone
break the law? Did Desmond have a clear moment, before
he slipped off his branch, in which his eyes met those of this
man who was about to betray him? If I knew more about
the Bible, would I find it ironic that the last person Desmond would ever see in his life shared the name of an
angel? Or would I merely find it disgusting? The television
was projecting its beehive of grays and blacks and rollick-
ing with its canned laughter—once I knew what was happening in the house, in a general sense, I'd turned up the

volume. A helplessness spread through me like megrim apricot. I wonder, since none of us heard him fall, how long my poor brother was out there all alone before my mother's screams carried across the yard? I wonder how she managed to put me to bed that night, knowing what she knew, knowing that by waiting until morning to tell me she would save her Gabriel from the implication of any guilt. I wonder why it is that canned laughter sounds like the chatter of waves when they come into a rocky beach. The waves made the most sultry and unique sounds that night. They laughed and laughed. I believe to this day they were laughing at my mother. That is what I'd like to continue to believe, because otherwise they were surely laughing at me, who stayed in the library, watching whatever was on the screen, as I pressed my hands tightly to my ears.

❖

Grace wasn't alone in observing the beginnings of Erin's revolt. She saw it all starting to fall to pieces not because she had nothing better to do with her time, but because it seemed to her that more and more Erin had something better to do with hers. The way Erin had left it to Djuna to get Desmond and Grace dressed and fed and out of the house to school on time. The way she told Djuna that if Berg was being tiresome she ought to take it up with his father the next time he was in from the city. The way she said she had to run some errands, and she might be late for dinner. The way when Charles did come on Saturday afternoon to be with the family, some of Erin's stories about what happened during the week didn't align with what Djuna herself had thought happened.

For a while she was content to believe that what she thought had happened maybe hadn't. Djuna didn't for the life of her want to confirm what she'd begun to suspect, but as she well knew, what one wants and what one gets can be different as cats and canaries. This is what she told her uncle Webster—in whom she'd confided her fears, since Webster never bothered to gossip, indeed hardly ever condescended to talk with anyone besides himself. Webster told his niece he thought Mrs. Brush might have the right to feel lonely.

"Why is it married women are always the ones who've got the right to feel lonely?"

To that, Webster had no reply, and went back to his task of cleaning with a penny nail the facets of the fanciful white pavilion carved into the bowl of his meerschaum pipe.

A friend in town clued Djuna in as to what Erin Brush was up to that October, but Djuna felt it only right to say, "Jenny, mind your own business, would you?" And Jenny said something honorable like, "I'm only trying to protect you, Djuna," and Djuna thanked her, and changed the subject to weather, or sea conditions, or old Ann Nicholls and how silly she was to keep up the pretense of going to town in her buggy drawn by draft horses.

But, no, it was no good, this business of Mrs. Brush being away from Scrub Farm so often and for such long stretches of time. The farm had come a long way since they had moved in, but still much remained to be done before the winter set in—the orchard was a mess, half the furniture in the house needed fixing still, or replacing, the carriage house roof leaked though Djuna didn't feel it was her place to complain and rather than tell Mr. Brush she simply set out pans and pots on the second floor of the little stone building whenever the rain swept through—and with Charles away six of seven days a week, and now with Erin out and about as she saw fit during her husband's absence, much fell to Djuna's lot to keep up with.

Sometimes she only wished she didn't like the children so much. She didn't care about the money, nor about the prospect of having to go back to living on Web's charity. Historically, Djuna harbored no great love of children. Kids, she had always averred, were put on earth to destroy

things, heirlooms and valuable things primarily. They
were here to produce unbearable noises and make unrea-
sonable requests, and register complaints that later in their
lives, if they had the misfortune of remembering how they
had acted, they would recognize as callow and selfish. They
were unformed, as a rule, they were manipulative.

Djuna had discussed her fears with Uncle Webster the
day she had him drive her over from Dering Harbor, and
had warned him not to be upset with her if she declined to
take the Brush job because she thought the children were
unmanageable. When they were returning from the Merriam place out at the end of Ram, Webster could hardly
believe his ears.

"The poor girl suffers from they don't know what, has
these horrid bouts . . . persecuted by the pain of it, from
what her mother was saying." Her uncle was glad, if astounded, for he himself had no interest in going back to
work and, at any rate, hadn't he already carried a better
part of the load since Hibby died and he'd offered to let
Djuna come over and live with him? He thought, Hibby
would have a coronary listening to her go on about this
Grace and Desmond, if he hadn't already had a coronary;
he was buried right near where he was born, over in Orient, but they might just as easily have thrown him out into
the harbor for what good he'd bothered to make of his time
on earth, was what Webster believed. Social security only
goes so far, and therefore Djuna's moving out to live with
these Brush people made a lot of sense to him, who would
be partial beneficiary of her labor.

"Besides," he told Djuna, "being around children will
keep you young where hanging out with an old fossil like
me will just wrinkle you faster than a soak in tea."

Djuna was in her late forties, and yet it was true she
looked to Grace like a grandmother, given how silver her
hair was, how heavy were her wrists and ankles, and with
what warm, old, knowing blue-gray eyes she looked at the
girl. All her dresses were old, too, and the prints she

wrapped about her stout middle were invariable in their large floral patterns and fifties colors—once vivid, now rather faint with hundreds of washings. It was a style of dress that Grace would later pick up herself; through her early twenties she fancied secondhand dresses, layers of clothing, vests over open forties blouses over silk tops. For all her girth, Djuna seemed fragile. One sensed that there lingered just beneath the sturdy outward carapace of competence and forthrightness, of stamina and strong opinions, very delicate nerves, which if strained would produce serious melancholy. In this, she believed that she and the Brushes' daughter shared a bond. Djuna knew what was under her own skin, and she sensed she knew what was under Grace's. She hadn't been around Grace for long before she came to think she understood the girl better than anybody else. She didn't suffer physically in the way Grace did, but she did carry around inside her, she felt, similar problems she wasn't about to let anyone see. It didn't, in the end, matter whether she was correct in all her assumptions of morbid kinship with the girl; the very fact that she identified with her, empathized with her, came through in the various ways she behaved toward Grace. And that was, in itself, a healing thing.

Grace's father must have observed this sensitivity of Djuna's toward Grace because he was not only supportive of her, but was attentive to her needs—in some ways more attentive to her than to Erin. He liked Djuna, though there wasn't much for them to talk about, since they held so little in common, and since neither of them could claim to understand the other. They seldom exchanged more than a few words when Charles was on the island, during his sojourns with the family; nonetheless, the bond was deep, at first because of a mutual affection for Grace, and over time grew deeper out of a common, simple respect.

Perhaps because of her own curiosity, or else because she felt protective not just toward Grace but toward Charles as well, within a week or so of talking with Jenny, Djuna took it upon herself to make some casual inquiry. She'd known most of these islanders since she was a child. She understood that there was no way for her to be subtle enough about it that they wouldn't see through her questions, and therefore she chose to be direct. She asked about Erin, and her suspicions were confirmed. There was no reason to take much of an adverse view toward Erin in a moral way, as such, she told herself; Erin wasn't doing something terribly unusual. She didn't, however, approve of Erin's choice in Gabriel Segredo, and considered going to Erin to tell her, warn her maybe about the downside of what she was about out here.

Instead, she determined to remain silent. All her energy would go toward making the house solid against the trouble that was surely going to be coming its way. She wanted to see Scrub Farm survive. And she didn't want to hear Erin Brush tell her in the same words she herself had used with Jenny to "mind your own business, would you?"

❖

Mother's learning how to drive an automobile was the great moment of liberation for her, it gave her not just the means to effect her freedom but in a way provided her with the reason to take her chances. If she hadn't wanted to drive she wouldn't have needed a car, and if she hadn't gone out looking for a car she wouldn't have met Gabriel Segredo—this was the equation I had constructed, at any rate.

Webster was the one to instruct her. He was rewarded with a water glass filled with stout at the end of their several lessons, and would run his commentary on her progress at the kitchen table while all of us—Segredo included—listened. "She done fair on the straights down the beach road there, but you got to work on the brakes, Erin, too heavy on the brake pedal, nearly blowed us both through the windshield."

"I did, I did," Mother admitted, herself drinking cocoa-

brown stout from the bottle, leaning forward from the edge
of her chair in her black jeans, tapping the floor with the
heels of her cowboy boots (red, like the car), which I had
never seen on her before. "It felt wonderful," and she
spread her knees, put her hands on them, and hunched her
shoulders up. What a beatific smile there was on her face.
She was transformed before us. I had to confess to myself
that if this is what my mother looked like when she was
truly happy, it was a happiness that was alien to her, and
to me who was witnessing it.

And we all laughed, perhaps all of us laughing with her,
with the freedom to which she seemed so openly to have
exposed herself, the same freedom that must have suggested to her that it was all right for her to unbutton the
top three buttons of her blouse, and let her hair tumble
down, literally, over her cheek and one eye. She sat next to
Segredo, and he studied her with loving solemnity. I could
sense so easily what was between them, as human beings,
as physical beings. Who was I—though I loved Faw so
much, or at least the idea of Faw, since as an absentee father
he became more and more an abstraction—who was I to
deny her an unfurled blouse, and this open-mouthed smile
and the stout and all this unusual sexuality she was now so
casually, even innocently, expressing to those of us she
adored at the kitchen table?

She caught right on with the driving business, which
surprised all of us. Maybe she surprised herself the most.
Nothing seemed to make her giddier; yes, it was her independence she was gaining, and she was learning what she
wanted to do with it. I noticed that I had never viewed her
as a person before, but that she was, and within a month,
so quickly the transformation occurred, she graduated
from being just my mother to being more beautiful than
any woman I'd ever seen, there in her car with her delicate
neck craning to left and right, Webster beside her directing
as they began driving down the gravel lane toward the
beach road. I might have asked why it was that now both

my parents found their greatest joy in being away from Scrub Farm, and, above all, away from *me*, but it's the kind of question a child has no will, nor way, to put forward. I was, instead, pleased for her, just as I was overly understanding of my father's crazy mercantile picaresque, and I didn't quite have enough experience with life to know that what all this boded for me was—abandonment. Yet what was I, who had no authority anyhow, to say to this blossoming woman who before now had been devoted only to dead petals in cold vases? I kept my mouth shut.

So she brought over her new friend, whom she met, she told us, after she bought it, this red treasure shaped like a horseshoe crab confident with its fresh wash and wax, its chrome and all its curves, angles, and fins. The pretext was the car needed some body work, was rusting as all cars rust on islands, and the guy who sold it to her said Gabriel was good at such things. Already, though, I believe—this remains hazy to me—somehow they had met before. I was convinced she actually wanted Desmond and me to meet him, to show him off to us almost as if he were a confident red roadster too. "I think you'll like him," she said, as if she were the youth and I the adult to whom she might look for judgment. From my perspective now, and knowing what I know, not only about her, but about myself and how the world and love can work, I admire her for her lack of restraint.

Segredo lived across Coecles (pronounced like "the Cockles of my heart") Bay. At the end of the poorest street on the island he worked on cars in his yard in the day, whenever work came his way, and made sculptures the rest of the time. He worked with metal, he told me. He had tried carpentry, and given it up. He'd tried his hand at a number of other things, but he kept coming back to iron and steel and welding torches. The way he said the very word "metal" was reverential.

Leaning against Mother's car, he said, "People take it for granted, but metal is one of man's greatest inventions."

"Metal is not an invention," I said—I could tell that he was talking to me as an adult talks to a child, and I wasn't going to let him get away with it so easily.

"It is, you don't mine metal. You make it. It's a process, and it changed civilization. Before they learned how to slag iron ore, to carburize, quench, temper, handle hot metal, all that, man had to do everything with stones and bones. You know what the word metal comes from?"

I didn't; I gazed up into his eyes, and yes, they were steely, as was his hair, woven with silver prematurely, for he wasn't even forty. Blue jeans, big buckle, black shirt with sleeves rolled away from his wrists, and black boots—of course, I realized, the clothes my mother had begun to wear were influenced by him.

"From the Greek *metallan,* it means, to search, to search for metal, see, like prospecting, mining. Metal will always be better than wood, for instance. Wood rots. And bones, bones rot."

"Stones don't rot."

He wasn't used to being contradicted by children, indeed he wasn't used to being around children at all. Here he had shifted so quickly from speaking down to me to speaking with me as if we were equals that I found myself out of my league. But there was a lot of child in Segredo, and he himself struck up just the right kind of argumentative tone, and paused before countering, "Metal is stronger than rock, though. You think Grissom could have orbited the earth inside a rock?"

"The Flintstones have rock cars."

"—Flintstones," and he smiled at me a conspiratorial smile, to which I answered with a roll of the eyes, which intended to inform him, No, the joke is on you, man. "Glenn," said I, "it was Glenn who orbited."

"What did I say?"

Was he making fun of me? How would I have attempted to handle Grace Brush if I ever met a Grace Brush? "My father was born in the place where they make steel," I continued, and I should have known then that when he didn't ask me more about that, something was wrong— after all, absent though he was, indeed partly because he was so often absent, no one was more interesting to me than my father; "Pittsburgh" put an end to this fragment of dialogue.

A decade out of college, where he had drifted from major to major before settling into the art department, Gabriel Segredo had himself a yard of cars stripped down to pure metal, cars, discarded propane tanks, trucks, even an old school bus that had been in an accident. When he had tried to sell them as automobiles, trucks, tanks, none sold, and so—following the creative tendencies he had nurtured at school—he decided to see what it would be like to torch them into pieces, reconstitute them as sculptures and live on welfare for a while. Though he would accept the occasional mechanic job as necessary, he became more serious about what he was doing; but none of the galleries in the city, where he sometimes went to show his slides on Saturday mornings, "viewing mornings" for many of the dealers, took him on, and he wasn't able to sell anything on his own. His collection of automotive parts and half-finished constructs, which aged quietly among the thistles and weeds in front of his garage, constituted an informal outdoor museum of rusting debris and works in progress.

Mother drove me and Desmond over to the sculpture yard once. He apologized for not having anything to offer us children and told us that the combination of being a bachelor and an artist whose work doesn't sell keeps his cupboards empty. We did have white bread spread with peanut butter and sliced pickle, cut by Segredo into lovely triangles and squares and "sigmoids." He was deft with the paring knife. I admired him for the little flourish, yet his house on this dead end street off Coecles Inlet was a drear and disorderly place, and was nothing compared to the riotous, garish jumble of raw materials—as he called them—that filled the landscape behind the bungalow. His neighbors didn't seem to mind that whatever boundaries there were along that low bluff which gave onto a treed slope, a narrow beach, and the inlet with its fleet of moored boats beyond seemed to be breached on either side. Tall iron rods reached up and well over toward the east, so that a swing set with molded ropes that was there, its children evidently long since having outgrown it, seemed not so much encroached upon by Segredo's labors, but rather incorporated into them. Desmond and I walked around, picking up pieces of this and that, and climbed up into one sculpture, outfitted with rungs, or so we presumed the series of parallel ribs were that went up its side. We clanged a hammer we found against different lengths of catapulting steel, and made music. Then Desmond had wanted to go back up to the bungalow. I suppose I must have known that Mother and Segredo were in his house doing what Desmond and I had tried and failed to do in the osprey marsh. I kept looking up the hill at the windows and wondering why the curtains had not been drawn. Was I making it all up? It gave me pause, since the alternative was so strange. Is it possible she was so involved with him by this point that the chances of being caught in flagrante delicto by her youngest children didn't frighten her enough for her to bother to hide herself behind some dirty calico? Again, her boldness was extraordinary.

❖

The ravishments for some months in the aftermath of Desmond's death continued. They abated, on the hotter nights of late summer and early fall, when Desmond came out of the tree least. The flare man—I missed watching him do some of his electric tricks—had behaved the same way. I was convinced at the time that the heat made Desmond lethargic. Also, the only time to prune a tree, you know, is in the winter, or late fall, or early spring. If you prune during the warmer seasons the wound will bleed its resin-

ous syrup. It will draw insects, and disease. It will turn a
yellow, the same yellow you see in the blossoms on the
spring forsythia, that most yellow and slovenly of bushes,
when they get heavy on their branches and fall into the
muddy water that stands in puddles at their base. No, Desmond would not risk, it seemed, cutting into me if he
thought there was a chance I would bleed.

So was Desmond a light person now? No, not really. I
have never figured out exactly what he was. Was he just
some reverberant part of my imagination, maybe of a premature sexuality, maybe of an accelerated need to be
loved—a superbly detailed projection of a prepubescent
mind that was left alone too often and for periods of time
too long for its own good? Desmond never did anything
that smacked of the light people's carnival theatrics. But he
did show an ability to come through the glass. If I lifted the
casement window, he came in. If I didn't, he came through
anyway. In other words, even if Desmond had been some
kind of child's projection I, as the child, had no control over
my own skill at persecuting myself.

When you lose someone early in life, I've begun to believe, no matter how dear they had been toward you and
to you, the precise picture of who and how they were
changes. It evolves, it devolves. There is no avoiding it. I
knew, even then, within weeks after Desmond was discovered on the stone patio, that try as I might to keep him true
in my memory, I would never succeed.

I wanted to remember everything, and began to record
whatever I could in the almanac book, and the more I
sequestered myself from going on living in order that I
might make a perfect picture of what I had already known
and been, the more I watched Desmond change under my
very fingertips. I could say or write that Desmond's skin
always smelled of sweetgrass to me, but what would that
finally mean? Would it mean he became associated in my
mind with apricot, and megrims? That this is accurate and
does connect two important elements of my juvenescence

is valuable, at least to me. But anyone might just as easily remark, "Grace, I cannot feel his realness," to which I could only reply, "Neither can I." Which is to say, as much as I had wanted to preserve Desmond, as hard as I'd tried to buoy and nurture and sustain the only Desmond I thought I would ever know, I just couldn't do it. I failed. He kept growing, there was no preventing it. He had stopped living, but he continued to exist, metamorphosing, mutating into whatever my imagination chose to make him.

We all have a desire to be remembered. But how prepared are we to be remembered in such a way that we might not even recognize ourselves? It is dangerous to harbor this passionate wish for our image, our deeds, our thoughts, to fare forward into the brazen new world, tended by others who are assured of molding us into their own preferred image, no matter how genuine and wholesome are their intentions, isn't it?

The night my brother died he became my imagination's toy, like it or not, and I have to face that for what it was and is. I know he couldn't have wanted to do some of what I made him do, made him make me do. There is no man but he becomes a blank slate for those who knew him to mark up with their emotional graffiti once he's left his life behind. We who cherish our privacy as individuals, and our sense of some truth in what it was we did when we lived, can only hope for this: the preservation of our integrity and our personal truth through the death of each and every person who ever knew us, loved or hated us. Awful irony. That those who would mark our lives must join us in that state of perfectly helpless blankness, as tabula rasae unable to mean, or alter, or add. Only when those who loved us join us are we free from the impetuous creativity of memory. Nothing to do about it: we're all grist, we're all mills.

Having thought that, all I could do was apologize to Desmond, and tell him he was too young to understand that ravishment is a two-way street. I did, later that fall,

before the water got too cold, take the almanac down to the
ocean, and swim out with it into the fizzing, salty waves,
and when I was as far away from the shore as I could
possibly be and still have the hope of swimming back to
safety, I let it go into the water. As the waves carried me
back in, and the undertow tickled my toes, I knew I had
done something very pure, and as I cried I thought what
better place is there to shed tears than in the ocean? If only
I were able to shed them backwards, like the flare man had
taught me. I tried, and wound up instead with a mouthful
of seawater—which tasted not unlike the liquid light, but
engendered nothing of its euphoric effect.

I might have spared myself the grand effort of getting rid
of the almanac. As soon as I could find another notebook,
I was back at it, and believe that I got down everything that
I'd so willfully drowned. I suppose purity wasn't something that I was ever able to harbor in my heart for long.

❖

My mother, when she was home with us, and wearing her
other clothes, and being her other self, had become something of a hoarder of bitterness and discontent. That was
something the adults wanted to be, and do, I decided; they
liked to have and hold their bitterness all to themselves, like
a dog his bone, and I felt, Let her have it if she wants it.
So I watched the box. Here trepidation and troubles were
shared by everybody equally. Andy Griffith, and that whis-
tling theme tune, and his deputy thin as a sandpiper's beak
who made all the mistakes so that Aunt Bee would be
worrying all the time, worrying about her pies and
whether they'd cool in time for the big picnic, worrying
about Opie, who was such a moron hick anyway I can't
imagine why anybody would bother worrying about him,
let him go down to the old swimming hole and drown for
all I cared, worrying about Ange, *Aange* is what Barney
called Andy when they were happy and getting along—

well, I watched that show. And I watched others. Gilligan who like me was stranded on an island, only his was made of papier-mâché and plaster of Paris, drank concoctions brewed by that professor who was sneaking around with the sexy woman who had those sequin dresses. He was okay. Sullivan I watched with devotion. All his acrobats from the Alps or Brazil, the bands of the British invasion, Señor Wences that fist with the lipstick mouth painted on, just mystic, just *fab*. I felt I could be friends with the Fugitive, Richard Kimble, the man falsely convicted of murdering his wife, an escapee on the run across the kaleidoscopic terrain of America—what a country ours was! what a place of propriety and obsession! all these people that Kimble met who must have been like the people that Faw in all his travels was meeting—on the run from the awful, long-faced detective who was keen on bringing him in, perhaps send him to the chair, even though he knew, deep down, that Kimble hadn't done it, as everyone on the road who met him knew at once.

Mother was particularly given to quiet hysteria now, and I knew why. On the other hand, Faw was serenely into his burgeoning businesses. I didn't mind being good, since I thought it was just as easy to be good as to be bad, and because I hardly understood what it meant to be bad. Except, I did sense—maybe because Desmond had told me not to talk with any of them about him—that in my secret life with him I was doing something that if they knew about they would think was bad. Even at that, not seeing much of a difference between good and bad, or rather seeing them as distinctions to which grown people paid a lot of attention, people like Andy Griffith and Aunt Bee considered extremely significant, I followed Desmond's advice to keep us a secret less because I didn't want to be bad than because I didn't want to have Desmond taken away from me. And I knew that was what they'd do if they found out about him.

Djuna knew better than anyone besides myself what was

going on in the house, and she took it upon herself to be my friend. I suffered a megrim one night and remembered how she saw me through it alone rather than insinuate my pain into the drama of a crumbling marriage. What Djuna couldn't have known, through that long, exquisitely exhausting ordeal, was that Desmond came inside from his branch and slipped under the quilt, and lay absolutely still down between my legs. She had fallen asleep in the chair by my bed. Shahrazad was someone I could only try to recall, as Djuna refused to read to me. I tried to sleep with my eyes open that night. I know that the Fugitive had to sleep with his open once in a while. It was hard to do, like levitating, or keeping a real friend. Anyone who can do it has my sympathy, and my admiration. I myself never pulled it off.

And then the inevitable stole upon us. It was I who found her note. She wrote it on a piece of Geiger stationery, and left it on Faw's dresser. He was the one whom she intended to have discover it. Her handwriting was more legible than my father's.

"Charles," it read, "you know that I have tried. I went along with the hoax of getting away from the city on account of Grace. I went along with a lot of things that I thought were misdirected. You know in your heart how hard I tried but I can't do it anymore. I'll call."

❖

As a prospective divorcée, Erin had no very compelling case to bring against her husband. Abandonment was a charge that could only, in fact, be laid at her feet. Mental cruelty didn't seem to be viable, nor was it a desirable course to follow because she'd have to go through all the trauma of accusation and then would be expected to back everything up with dates, with facts, with one awful recollection after another. Charles never, to her knowledge, had cheated on her—except in the most metaphoric sense of his having devoted himself utterly, with sexual fervor, to Geiger's companies, which like a harem of mistresses he doted upon, so unabashedly that nothing could be said to have been done behind her back. No, the shopping list of grievances available to one who wants to seek a divorce is, she found, remarkably short. How was it possible in a world of so many ways to misbehave, to cause injury to those you supposedly love and have devoted your life to, that the rubrics of failure were so few?

Mental cruelty. Abandonment. Irreconcilable differences. It was so absurd. With all the complexities there were in any human life, with the strange and diverse directions love could take, how could the demolition of the union between a man and a woman be enacted with tools so paltry as these?

Given that Charles declared that he had no interest in seeking a divorce himself, even though his wife had left her family and was now living on another part of the island with this "half-employed hick," as he called Segredo, this "scam artist," she had to make a go of it with irreconcilable differences. She wished the divorce didn't mean so much to her; she was sure that it meant a lot to Segredo, or she thought she was sure. She would go back and forth on the subject any number of times over the next months. Divorce, differences, irreconcilable, cruelty—all these words were frightening and odious to her. But differences and that they had become irreconcilable were all, she was informed by her lawyer, she had, legally, to work with.

"Maybe you're right," Segredo remarked when she returned from that first visit with the lawyer. "Maybe the divorce just isn't worth all the trouble."

"Well, it's not going to be as simple as we thought."

Then he said, "Not that I don't—"

"I know, look, I want to start over again too, be out of all that Geiger swirl."

"Well, what did this guy say about the children?"

"He tried to call Charles about it."

"And?"

"He wouldn't speak to him."

"No surprise."

"He said, Brown did, there's no way I'm going to get to see the kids unless I take Charles to court. He can keep his money, it's all he cares about anyway."

Segredo didn't like hearing that but said nothing. He knew this was the one topic he couldn't discuss. Sacrosanct old bitch, money. If she could bring against Charles something of substance, something that might sway a court enough to at least grant her the divorce, and at least visitation rights, she would surely stand to come into some enormous amount of the stuff, of money—as he discerned, even a fractional token of Geiger was bound to come to more than enough. He'd like that. For some inexplicable reason, given that Charles hadn't particularly *done* anything to merit his animosity, he wanted to shove it to the man; it'd feel good, for once, to get one up on one of the big fish. Also, a little money would go a way toward dampening the gossip. Segredo wondered why he bothered to worry about what people were thinking, and would think in the future, given that he'd already gone this far playing against the rules. But he didn't want people getting the upper hand on him on the gossip front, if he could help it.

He knew his motives. They were pure—he assured his conscience—because he would want her even if she didn't have access to money, and wasn't he at least being honest with himself about how the money kept coming into mind? He wasn't kidding himself. If he chose not to address money in their conversations (endless, endless, and painful) about the divorce-to-be it was because he had his own system of weights and balances to maintain, too. Sometimes he did do his best to hint at it so Erin herself might bring it to the fore. For instance, just then: "I think you're right. I don't think you and I need paper—divorce paper, money paper, any paper—to be happy together. But I do worry about how this being kept away from your kids is going to

wear on you over time, you know." Nauseating, he thought
to himself; on his tongue as different as chalk and cheese the
truth and this insinuation stuff. He held himself still and
looked at her.

Erin smiled faintly, tried to. She glanced in the mirror
over his couch, that mirror which was artistically crackled
with silvery underlays, and saw how dry was her smile.
What was she doing here? What were these boots doing on
her feet? "I know," and embraced him, and felt the warmth
that drew her toward staying here with him, in the midst
of what was possibly an act of anger, and impractical madness.

Segredo pressed on. "You know, I wonder whether
you're making the right decision."

"What do you think?"

"What do I think means, I don't know, means you're not
answering the question yourself."

"I know what I'm doing, I mean I know as much as
anybody can know—"

"I don't want to argue, this is always the thing that irks
me, you know that, this thing about your having been so
nicely set up in the city, so comfortable, all that, and then
when you had to come out here you were tortured—what
does that mean about me? I'm just a person. I'm nothing
special."

That seemed like a sad thing for anyone to say about
himself, and it struck her. "Gabriel, if I didn't love you I
wouldn't be here with you, all right?" What could she say?

He walked away to the table in the kitchen. He was
having a difficult time keeping his branching concerns
(love of her, need for money, fear of his own drift toward
treachery, fear of the commitment he knew lay ahead of
him) calibrated through the course of their discussions, and
thought to have a scotch, knowing she wouldn't like it, but
also understanding that whenever he did, Erin did not
complain about it, and often changed the subject, trying to
sway his interest from the scotch back to her.

"What are you doing?"

"I'm going to have a drink."

"You aren't the one who needs solace."

"Look, your life isn't the only one that's been turned upside down here. You do it your way I'll do it mine."

"That's so selfish."

He brought the glass, stenciled with Pooh Bear's image, up to the lip of the bottle of scotch, and poured himself a few fingers' measure. He sipped, waited. She had gone to the bedroom. He had no notion whether she was packing her things to go home, whether she simply wanted to spend some minutes crying, just as she had so many days in a row before today, or what. He drank from the Pooh glass, into that heat of booze, and it was eager, brazen, bracing, foolish, relieving. It was great. Works so well, and works so fast, the ultimate wonder drug. She hated it when he drank, but fuck her, he thought, and inhaled the scotch again. Fuck all of them. There were possibilities here, if he followed them through to the end of the line, but did he want to make these steps toward a new life for himself? Why not leave things where they were? he thought. He was so mad, but not at her, not even at himself. Who to blame? Usually he didn't mind when she took off on these weepy forays trying to make him feel guilty, but it was getting old—even after, what, two months was it? All these rich mothers, he tried to tell himself, they were the same in the eyes of the Lord a bunch of nonessentials, a bunch of pedestrians bound to walk the wildest side of all, the hottest streets made, down there in flame town. And what was he supposed to do (he really was rather overpissed given the circumstances, wasn't he?—he brought the glass to his mouth again, and observed Pooh Bear's profile in reverse through the concave surface of glass), what was he supposed to say? which led him to call out from the kitchen, "I'd like to know just what it is I'm supposed to say? Like what is it you want me to do about it?"

Nothing. Quiet throughout the narrow cottage. He

glanced out across the folded-over, yellow grass that luxuriated over the rise, and watched the waves imitate the
grass, folding over and over upon themselves down below,
expressing such enthusiasm on their way toward the flat
sand where together they splayed forward like one long,
flat tongue, and withdrew again, folding back into the
water until the next long flat water tongue pressed forward, maybe a bit farther into the beach, maybe not quite
so far as the last—and he chuckled. Even the fucking ocean
was going to stick its tongue out at him today, and not once,
but over and over.

"Well, fuck you, too," he said, and refilled his glass,
which made Pooh Bear go good and scotch-brown.

What should he do? There was Erin, forlorn as all get
out, down at the end of the knoll, past all his amassment of
spare parts and metal objects that he used for his sculptural
assemblages, leaning against a tree in the gnarl stand, no
doubt crying. He could set his scotch on the table and go
out to her. That was surely what he should do. He could
stay here. He could go away for a while, go down to the
city, leave her until she got it through her head what it was
she must decide to do. He knew, he knew this thing
wouldn't work out. How could it? The bed, no matter how
passionate a place it might be at the beginning of the romance, inevitably loses its charm, wasn't that so? And
speaking of things that lose their charm, Jesus—his eye
skirted the edge of the sea bluff and came to rest on his
half-finished sculpture, which was visible to her right,
nearer the house.

Fuck fuck, he thought, appraising it. Fuck if it didn't
look to him like a ponderous, hideous, crude grabble of
wire, rods, beams, springs, all pitting with rust in the ocean
air, a grand pointless ascending heap with a surly, arty title
like Cat Got Your Nine Tail, or Apocalypse Whisk, or
something, and all he wanted to do was to go down there
and fire up the acetylene torch and cut the sculpture into
pieces, cut the whole damn yard of materials into smaller

and smaller steel fragments until the whole landscape was sheathed in iron leaves . . . and, having thought that, he caught himself thinking that that would make quite an interesting work of art in itself, and then he thought, Fuck you, to himself and turned to walk out the front door, in the opposite direction.

The phone rang. It was that lawyer. When it rains. "She's not here right now." The lawyer left a message for her to call him as soon as she got in. He hung up, finished off the scotch, and peered out the window to see Erin. Instead, again, his attention got caught in the sculptures. They looked suddenly so paltry by comparison to her. Why bother with the stuff when you can live a real life? He studied something he had been working on not a few hours before and thought maybe the piece really ought to be burned into bits. The pile of formless iron could be the new piece. It was something to consider. He'd never seen that before in any of the galleries.

There was music coming in through the open door—it wound in an ascending embrace with the scotch, crisscrossing together like maypole ribbons, or snakes coiling their way up the caduceus, up through his spine and he felt suddenly benevolent toward Erin, looked down to where she stood—he had spotted her by then—and was at once fixed again by the thought of staying with her no matter what. The divorce as such meant nothing to him—what did he care whether she was still married or not? The settlement, he had to admit it to himself, the money that would come into his purview through the divorce, that was the thing that would mean something. He could never tell her, of course; he'd look miserable and grabbing. The reason he would want her to get her settlement was not so much that he wanted the money—he was, or could make himself be, content without—but rather because he sensed the day would come when she was going to miss having it. Then there'd be entire circles in hell for him to pay.

"Turn that shit down," he was now out in front of the

cottage, and marching toward the parked car from which the music was coming. Here he was picking up a whiffleball bat, his face going amber, and all he really wanted to do was maybe climb into the back seat of the car—the two girls, total strangers hanging out here for want of a better idea, looked up at him startled—and go wherever they wanted to go, the farther away the better. Behind the smoked glass, in the passenger seat, a finger rose, as the car pulled away in no great hurry. And yes, it was deflating, he knew, because the music wasn't even all that bad, just an ambience of artillery was all it was and that wasn't too distinct from the way he was now beginning to feel down in his gut. He struck his calf a couple of times with the airy plastic club (neighborhood kids were forever leaving toys in his front yard, what a life just drifting from one gratuitous insult to the next) and walked past the house down to the lower yard in back.

"I mean you realize that what you're doing here is crazy, right?" as he approached her tree.

Erin had heard him reach this dreadful part of the argument a couple of times before. It was the part she didn't like, because it simultaneously reinforced her thought to stay with him and made her feel that he could in fact let her go.

"It's not crazy."

"I mean, look at this," sweeping the whiffleball bat around the yard littered with automobile parts, rusted transmission blocks, truck shells, girders, imploded propane tanks scarred with metal flowers where the breach took place, shovel heads, bedsprings, steering columns, and on and on, this iron cemetery.

"So? It's what you do. I don't have any problem with it."

"Well I do. This is just pure squalor here, there's no future here. I'm a mechanic, not a sculptor."

"Gabriel," she was drifting down the narrow, pebbly path toward the beach, Segredo following, "you're an artist."

"I'm no artist, just welding all that junk together."

"Of course you are."

"I think you ought to think seriously, Erin, think very seriously about going home. It's not too late still."

"Yes it is and anyway I'm not going. If you want me out of here, that's one thing—"

"That isn't what I want, why don't you slow down?"

Having reached the sand, she stopped. The pale fog reclined across a breadth of beach where the water hissed, and as the sun hadn't burned through the cloud cover all day there were no bathers along the stretch. "This is where I want to be. You are the person I want to be with. I myself don't care about legal tidiness in the matter, don't care what the State of New York considers me to be, all right?—"

Again that coalescence of money-wishing stirred, as a rod stirring water in a wishing well might stir the deposit of coins on its floor. "Fine," and stared out over her shoulder, which was pressed against him, toward the fishing trawler out on the horizon, where the ocean was suffused with a color somewhere between pewter gray and butter yellow. The metal seemed alive, once more.

❖

Night. Sparks poured down into the black yard and illuminated eerily the ring of trees that reached up toward the moon at that corner of the welding pit. Segredo stood on a heavy scaffold, about fifteen feet above the ground, and winced against all the profusion of fire he was creating. He liked working at night—the later the better, since fewer neighbors complained, having already gone to bed, thus missing the flashing rain of sparks and the annoying rumble of the generator motor. So there was that. That was one reason. Also, he preferred welding the pieces of his huge, bric-a-brac sculptures together after dark because doing so introduced a randomness into the process. This he consid-

ered aesthetically interesting. You selected your piece of
armature by vesper light, you pulled it over to the work in
progress, used the pulleys and chains to hoist it up into
place, lit the torch and had at it—and in the morning you
would find out what you'd assembled. It was cooler working with the hot metal at night, too, as well as being ten
times more dangerous than working in daylight. All these
elements—difficulty, risk, lack of control—at least gave him
an out: if the sculpture was a grand failure, he could blame
it on his process, and its random nature. If what he
managed to construct seemed successful as a work of art,
then the credit could be reserved entirely for himself. It
was much like throwing I Ching: you read your hexagrams
and trigrams, and if the sticks in their wisdom judge you
positively, then all is well with your throw, and all is right
with the world—if not, and you are a practical person, you
are always free to doubt the reading, question the sticks,
and proceed as if your fate was not something, after all, to
be patrolled by chance.

It was into Segredo's cluttered welding yard that Berg
and I crept, on an escapade. He asked me if I'd like to be
his assistant on an adventure; flattered, I agreed. I don't
think that Berg had a clear concept of what we were to
accomplish, but we were committed to doing *something*.
After all, we had gone to such trouble to sneak out of Scrub
Farm and bicycle over the causeways, and around the head
of the inlet to Segredo's neighborhood. The moon poured
over the land and water. We hadn't encountered a single
car on the road. It was late, and the island had, as they say,
pulled up its sidewalks and retired for the night.

This was some time after the fact of Mother's having left
the family had become a reality to Berg and me. Berg must
have been sixteen, then, and I eleven. Whereas we had
failed as fishing partners, had failed that is at our initial
attempt to convert me into a Desmond figure for Berg to
grow up with, we had, by then, forged a symbiotic relationship that relied increasingly on secrets, and inevitably on

lies. What had begun with Berg's showing me the skin movies, and bringing us into that particular secret world, had ended in a fragile and hard-won friendship. To suggest that I had become a tomboy would be simplifying how far I had gone toward incorporating what I knew of Desmond into my own personality. It might not have been enough to satisfy Berg, but it was enough to be alarming to Djuna. I had transformed, past the megrims, past the light people, past the ravishments, into tough stock. It was a calm, quick, sweet, quiet transformation, and I don't think that it registered itself in an outward way. My clothes, as I remember them, were feminine, chosen by Faw, and Djuna, and occasionally, still, by my mother, when she was able to see me, take me into the city for the day, to have lunch and shop for such silly things as culottes and clogs and dirndl skirts. My habits, I believe, remained more or less as they always had been. Unlike the conventional tomboy I didn't suddenly stop bathing, say, or take a pair of shears to my hair. I didn't insist on smoking cigarettes or shooting woodchucks with a stupid little rifle. No, I knew better than to display to others the forms of my recklessness. And yet the most extreme example of this recklessness—my opening myself up to Berg, my hoping that he would accept me, that he would even like me—did contradict my basic secretiveness, and a habitual mistrust of my oldest brother that I had had since as far back as I can remember. This contradiction, this risk I took in letting Berg know me, is something I can account for only by considering it in the context of a disintegrating family.

We stashed the bicycles in a copse at the end of a street next to a monastery. Through the hedges, we could see the holy fathers' retreat. We walked between some houses away from the grounds of the monastery toward Segredo's, hunched over, moving side by side, smiling with anticipation. Berg had brought his camera. This was, if anything, to be at the core of our adventure—to get something on moving film, so that we could look at it later on the projec-

tor; Berg knew that there was a good chance little of the
footage would come out, since he didn't have access to the
kind of infrared film necessary to shoot in the dark, but he
was determined to try, anyway.

The lights in the bungalow were on, but it appeared that
Mother wasn't there. Segredo's torch blew sparks in an
umbrella-shaped shower over the yard. Once we caught
sight of him back there, Berg dropped to his knees and told
me to get the camera out of his pack, which I did, like a
good assistant. The camera produced a humming sound as
Berg began to make his movie.

I knelt beside him for a long time, and followed him
forward. We were like soldiers in one of the many war
movies we'd watched together on television, using indistinct masses of metal to hide ourselves from Segredo, just
as the soldiers hid themselves behind big fake boulders on
Pacific island beaches, as they made their way toward the
gunner's nest, dancing between bullets and fondling the
hand-grenade they intended to lob up into the enemy's
palm-frond blind. But the more absorbed he became with
the splashing sparks ("Some of this stuff'll come out," he
whispered) and Gabriel's front-lit figure and back-lit sculptural monster, the more bold I was in my own intruder's
heart. I wanted to go inside the house.

"I'll be back," I whispered, though I'm not sure he heard
me, since he kept his small gray box up to his eye, clutched
it with both hands, and held his breath while the film
ran—much the same way a marksman holds his breath
when firing, in order not to disturb the accuracy of his aim.

The front door was unlocked, and inside the rooms
smelled of garlic—their dinner—combined with potpourri.
It was a familiar combination, though the potpourri
smelled more of perfume here, and less of dead flora. I left
the door slightly ajar in case I had to run back out fast, and
tiptoed toward the kitchen. What would I do if I encountered her, I wondered; no answer—it seemed that she
wasn't here anyway. The kitchen was a shambles, and this

was not so familiar to me. Encouraged by the silence, and perhaps by the high blood of the escapade itself, I began to rummage around in the cabinets. This indulgence brought me into the possession of a bottle of port wine, half-full, which I saw as a real means to ingratiate myself with my brother. Why not? It was a question that kept answering all my self-rebukes that night, and I had no ready answer to it; I tucked the bottle under my jacket, feeling very much the profligate, and started for the front door. Because of all the lights in the cottage I couldn't see out into the night with the same ease I'd been able to peer in. Another thought came to mind, though. I wanted to see their bed. I wanted to see where they did it. Since I didn't know who my mother was anymore, I'd decided, this maneuver might give me an insight into what she had become.

I knew there was some danger that she would be in the room, but the temptation was irresistible, and so down the short, carpeted hallway I hurried, my hands gone cold against the bottle. The door was shut, and under it there was no light, so I assumed that if she was in the room she might be asleep.

She was both. I saw their bed, nondescript. The light from the hallway poured over my shoulder and angled down over her. Her mouth was open, slack, innocent like a child's with saliva gathered over her tongue and lower lip. She was breathing, my mother, slowly and steadily, and there was in the rhythm of her breath a maturity I'd never seen in her before; for one, she didn't resent Segredo's nocturnal creativity—she slept, and slept with her body to one side of the bed, leaving room for him to come and join her when he was finished. There was a confidence in the way she lay there, her hand draped off the edge of the mattress, which made her a stranger to me, but a stranger I could admire. What was I doing? There was no point in my standing there, I realized, this was her new life that she was living and it hardly involved me. It is difficult to ex- plain, but I sensed that my curiosity was inappropriate, if only because there was little or nothing with which she could reward it. This was an instant of surpassing emptiness, and it gave way to a release. She was no longer responsible for me, and I was not to be responsible for her—"even-Steven," as Berg was fond of saying.

I closed the door, as gently as I could, and walked, almost ran, back through the front of the house, and around the side. Something had gone wrong with our plan, because when I got there, Berg was gone, and Gabriel was nowhere to be seen, either. A light went off in the cottage, and I crouched down. I had left the front door ajar upon leaving, the same way I had when I'd been inside—maybe Berg would want to go in to shoot some film indoors where he'd said he had the best chance of getting something to develop, I didn't know, it was a mistake, and now Segredo would surely notice. I backed away into a row of bulky bushes, making more noise than intended, and found myself in the neighbor's front yard. A dog barked, and then another. It was just like in one of the Fugitive scenarios, though now my empathic heart raced for myself. Where was Berg?

"Berg?" I whispered, raspy-throated. Nothing. I decided to go back to the monastery.

Both our bicycles were where we left them, and I decided that the best thing to do was to sit down and wait for my brother. I was glad that I'd lifted the bottle of port, because at least if Berg accused me of having deserted him, I'd have this to appease him. I could still hear the dogs, though the wind had picked up in the trees, and the moon had passed apogee and begun to drop in behind them. The stars were going strong, fattened and turned pink by the thin, high mist, and out in Coecles the steady clanking of rigging hardware against the metal masts gave a sweet percussive ground to the buoy bell that clanged, deep and voluminous, farther out in the water, northeast toward where Scrub Farm was across the inlet. Berg, I thought, come on—I wanted to get on the bike and go home, I wanted to be asleep, as our mother was, in my bed. It would

have been fun if the flare man could have come to talk, but
he seemed more distant than ever. It occurred to me to taste
the port, because that's what they did when they got cold
in the movies, they had a slug off a bottle, and that cured
them, but when I uncorked it and smelled the wine I knew
that it wasn't for me. The leaves in the trees gently hissed
overhead.

When Berg did show, he was incredibly agitated. "You
won't believe this," he said, full-voiced, and I shushed him
for fear that he would get the dogs going again. "Come on,"
he half-yelped, half-whispered, and I pedaled home in the
darkest night air behind him, the cold wind off the ocean
along the causeway helping me to keep my eyes open. I
didn't understand a bit of what he was yammering about.
Tomorrow, I thought, tomorrow.

As I fell asleep at home, in my bed, I remembered that
I had left the bottle of port in the bushes. Let the monks
drink it. They love that jazzy vinegar.

❖

What made me change toward Desmond I can't say, exactly. Sometimes, if Djuna would let me, or if she'd gone
to the carriage house for the night and I could get away
with it by keeping the sound low on the box, I slept downstairs in the library, on the couch. Desmond didn't come
there. His branch was on the other side of the house.

What was a rape, if not this unquestioning, mute, overwhelming force that fell upon me at its own whim, its own
chosen moment? The way Desmond more than assumed I
was willing to have him—more than assumed, or perhaps
less than assumed, given he made no display of needing to
know one way or the other about what my wishes might
have been—that was rape, wasn't it? It's like a disease with
the dead, this not inquiring about the living, their desires,
what they need. The living have so often gone to such
lengths to take care of the dead, setting them forth on their

journey into the so-called last night in seven caskets each
of different material, like what those French did for Napo-
leon sticking him inside seven different boxes made of
seven kinds of metal and wood, or bedecking them with
hammered gold jewelry and silk clothing and appointing
their crypts with fancy objects that their souls may delight
in during lulls in their long night (there must be a lot of
lulls, for those who have left life), and even going so far as
to leave wine and food and condiments there with them in
the tomb, lest the poor men come back to life and find
themselves thirsty or hungry. But what courtesies do the
dead show the living?—not that Desmond's visits weren't
necessary for me, but as time moved on, as time does, I
wondered whether he was aware of what he continued to
ask from me, even while in return all I ever wanted was to
be with him again.

Never did I feel shaken from the conviction my brother
loved me. Nevertheless, in my mid-teens, his visits developed into a pattern of slow, musing violence that would
trouble me long past the night he died this sort of second
death. Given my abiding conviction of his love, however,
I never denied him. The very few times when I suspected
I might be making the whole damn thing up were when
he'd get the most crazy, or else cold. I have learned that
when something wondrous or peculiar or impossible that
you've believed to be real comes under a sudden scrutiny
that tells you it may be your own projection you're responding to with such innocent enthusiasm, that's the moment the phenomenon can most take control. I did allow
myself, whenever he appeared at the sill and traveled
through the glass into the bedroom, the choice of being
either happy to have him there with me, or fearful of what
was about to occur. But I didn't have the wherewithal to
deny him, or at least I thought I didn't. I knew it wasn't
right. Every time it happened, no matter whether he was
rough, or was tender, I began to wish a little more that it
would stop.

I wouldn't allow myself to think bad things about Desmond for long, though. What could cruelty possibly mean (if cruelty was the word for Desmond's way of acting toward me) to someone who'd experienced the cruelest truth of all? If he knocked my head against the floor while loving me, who was I to suggest he did it on purpose, who was I to complain—the pains I felt could never match what he'd gone through.

So, yes, as I say, whenever I look back on Desmond and what we did together when we were children, I wonder how I managed to keep the ravishments a secret, a part of my independent thought-world. Desmond never swore me to secrecy about himself (as he had that once down by the osprey nest), or what we did those nights. If I ever did tell, however, that would be the moment he'd have to leave me. It was a prospect that, as I got older, attracted me more and more. I didn't so much mind carrying the weight of our secret around with me, but I did begin to wonder whether someday some man besides Desmond might fall in love with me, and then my brother would be in the way.

"You just stay home like you're supposed to, you look after Faw because look what's gone on with him—you don't want something like that to happen to you do you?" Desmond presented me with a warning one evening. "If you stay here you'll be safe from falling in love with anybody else. You think Erin is happy?"

"No," I answered, though the image I saw while standing near her for those silent moments while she slept belied this.

"No is not the word for it," said he. "She's miserable over there, I've seen her with him and she's miserable. Listen, you want to go swimming?"

"It's too cold!"

That night, the night of the first snow of the coming season, he made love to me in the most gentle way, and after he kissed me good-bye and went back out into his

other world, I found myself questioning whether because
he had been so tender I should trust his words more, or less.

This much I can say, this much I know for sure. Desmond was eleven when he died, in 1965. I turn thirty-three
this spring. I've lived three times as long as he did, and yet
he still feels older, more able, stronger, and in some ways
even wiser than I will ever be. Though you can outlive
everyone in experience or years, whoever was older than
you when you were growing up will always seem older,
and will keep for themselves the prerogatives and powers
you give them for having been older, no matter what.

Even when Desmond had been dead so long that I could
hardly remember what his voice sounded like, or the feel
of his face in my lap—not to mention that extraordinary
moment in which he tried to enter me as a spirit that would
want to be reborn inside a womb that was willing but
unable to shelter him—I thought of him any number of
times during the week. The anniversary of his death never
passed without my private homage. It was the least I could
do. He didn't come anymore, I didn't want him to anymore, so this was my token substitute. Inspired I think by
the image of the woman in the window of the church, I'd
light a candle in the morning, performing a secular Yahr-
zeit, and by the end of the day it would gutter out. I knew
that no one would be overly sympathetic to a grown
woman burning a white candle, by herself, maybe having
a little Irish whiskey and fingering the same half-dozen
photographs of her brother she'd looked at on this day so
many times before, so I kept the ceremony to myself. I had
my own little religion with its personal pantheon; the flare
man, who was like Tiresias or St. John, kind but scary; the
zigzag tongue man was surely a devil; Samantha and Jeannie were White Goddesses. And Desmond? Desmond was
Eros. He still burned somewhere: not in my imagination
but in some other hidden place or places, burned in places
that were dark and quiet. But, in truth, he was gone now,

as was Mother, as was in his own way Berg, who would set off into a decade of utter absence from my life, as would we all, finally, in our own ways.

For me, the greatest proverbs—like, architecture is frozen music, or familiarity begets contempt, or, opposites attract—I have always tried hardest to escape. You only live once. I never had reason to run from that piece of wisdom. But after the night of the first snow, I knew that here was another proverb gone awry. Desmond was gone with it, having proved it wrong. The morning after his last visit I looked out into his tree and could see it had changed. It was physically different in a way I cannot explain.

What I thought I might have learned from Desmond, what I would take and keep for myself out of all this was this: by avoiding the normal paths of love there is an effective way to scale its stranger heights and emerge into a world where mere union may be the least of love's delights. But, of course, any celebrant of the flame knows that even the simplest of rituals are best performed with eyes closed, such as during a prayer, or at least under the blanket of sightless stars. Dark hours are the holy hours. In the dark blindness does become a virtue, and the heart can provide a tempo by which the flesh's music may be played. Like the Sufî poet Ramî, I would sooner consume flame-shaped garlic, though, than any of your manna or celestial meat, or ground walnut mixed with spirits of wine, which Foucault suggests will ease a headache, and which goes to show how little he knew about such matters.

I pulled the curtains shut, went back to bed, and for the first time in my life pretended to have a migraine. Djuna offered to read to me, but I was too old for such things anymore.

❖

Berg showed me the footage. Everything was shrouded in gray. The sparks looked like a white flower. The image jostled because Berg had moved closer and closer to where Segredo had been welding. I was surprised how close he'd dared to get. Indeed, toward the end of that first part of the footage, it appeared that the shower of white was coming down directly on the viewer.

Then, the screen was black for a moment—you could see that there was something Berg had tried to shoot, but in the dark it had been underexposed—and afterward it was gray, and we were peering in a window, someone was moving around in the room, Segredo, and he was naked! I recognized the room, then. It was the same room I had been in, and though the camera was occasionally jiggled, so that the image blurred, I could see her there on the bed, still lying there, but awake. Segredo was talking. Since there was no sound he looked a bit silly, his mouth moving. He was pacing.

He went over to the bed and sat down, and I could see her put her arms around his waist and move her head over so it was in his lap. He was looking down at her, my mother, and even though the film was grainy, and jostling, and dark, I could see that the look on his face was one of contorted mirth. Maybe he was just happy, but to me this all seemed evil.

I didn't want to see any more of the film. I think that Berg called me a big baby. I didn't care, I went outside, and down to the osprey nest. Like most frustrated dreamers, I wished I could fly.

❖

I began to live a back-and-forth life, after Berg was sent away to a private school. It was inevitable that we would eventually get caught, because Berg's boldness seemed to grow by exponential degrees with every fresh adventure. Faw promoted his interest in cameras and projectors, and took him several times a year along on business trips. Canisters of eight-millimeter black and white stock began to pile up on the shelves in his bedroom at Scrub Farm, and indeed his whole room had been converted into a warehouse for tripods, lights, old still cameras he got from who knew where, a burgeoning closet of costumes, drawers of cheap jewelry and other paraphernalia. More than once I'd been coerced to play not just the lead but different minor characters in one of his silents. I'd worn a bear suit that stank of mothballs and urine and chased an old woman—I also played the old woman, with wig and overcoat—and never caught her because, of course, both figures could never be in the same frame at once. I had rowed into the waves like an Inuit princess, I'd run through the orchard as the harvest moon rose, a sheet over my head and my arms powdered white with flour, as part of his great Gothic romance, the most ambitious of all his precocious efforts, and the one about which he had sworn me into solemn confidence because of certain scenes he had in mind for me to play that would involve my doing "grown-up things."

I probably would have been able to do those grown-up things, and with less fear than he might have presumed I would show, had Faw not shown up unexpected one night to find him down in the library, looking at those skin films he was supposed to know nothing about. I've never seen Faw more angry. Even when he had come down the stairs after having read the note Mother left, there wasn't such a stridency about him, nor such a sense of betrayal of trust. I know now why Faw erupted with such unwonted violence, and my knowing why is part of the reason I am obliged to set all this out straight for myself, for all of us really—but then, that day, when Faw shouted, "That's it, I've had enough of you, I've done everything I can do with you," I was crying confused tears.

"We're all going down into the same hole, marines," Berg said, "it's just the matter of when," and then stood there, stoic criminal that he was, and stared hard at me with his mouth cramped shut. Don't admit to anything, was what his eyes were warning me, echoing "Don't complain,

don't explain." And when Faw asked me if I knew anything about what Berg was doing, I lied. This may have
been the only time I lied to him. But just as the truth seems
to be the only way to save all three of us now, a lie seemed
the only way to save us then. Faw didn't want to hear me
tell him I had been as involved with Berg's escapades as
much as I had. Berg didn't want him to know, either.

After my brother departed for the academy up in western Massachusetts, I found myself alone. I lacked whatever
mad energy is required to carry on Berglike adventures on
my own, and his camera equipment, most of which he was
forced to leave behind at Scrub Farm, I didn't know how
to work. He agreed to write me letters from up there, but
after I had sent three or four and never got any back, I gave
up on him, and withdrew into my usual pastimes until Faw
told me, one Sunday soon after, he had decided that it
would be best for me to move back in with him in New
York. The schools were better there, and we could have
more time together that way, he said.

We journeyed this time not in a borrowed and beat-up
truck, but on board a sailboat. This mode of transportation
might have been as eccentric as that pickup had been, and
even less practical—it took us all day, tacking back and
forth in the gusty slate waters of the sound—but watching
him, one hand on the rudder, one controlling the mast,
made me realize once more what a figure of solid centrality
my father was in my life. As invisible, most of the time, as
the wind that plowed into the sail canvas, he was a powerful force, one I couldn't help but respect.

Faw's new place in the city was grander by far than what
we as a family left in 1964. The decade had worked to his
advantage, clearly, in all sorts of ways. We were up higher
than any tree could grow, so the chances that the flare
man—who by now seemed quite a remote phenomenon—
would return were few. (Indeed, that he seemed to me a
phenomenon rather than a being, a man of light, was proof
of how far away I'd grown from my early, almost supernat-

ural experiences. Try as I might, and sometimes I had tried, out at Scrub Farm, to will the flare man back, to conjure any of the light people, I failed. As much as they had terrified me, and as linked as they had been to the megrims, I felt a profound disappointment at my inability to attract them. The Greeks knew of tree-spirits—every tree had its own little resident deity—which were to be feared and worshiped, their boughs were the subject of adoration and beneath them there was orgiastic dancing and ritual sacrifices were made, so I knew that whatever I'd tapped into had some *justification,* however deep or unconscious it might have been. No Minoan, no Samantha or genie, however, I had become a helpless apostate. I closed my eyes, I opened them. Nothing. There was a clear sense, first, of abandonment, just as I had felt abandoned by the family. Second, as I got older, I began to realize that they hadn't forsaken me as such—it was I who had lost my powers, I, who was emerging as an adult, who lacked the child's freedom to create these visions.) I looked down from the twentieth floor, and saw the trees as meaningless brown and reddish blurs in the park and nothing more. An occasional migraine might come over me, like a squall cloud, running over the sea very low, hitting the island with a hot shower, the rain popping in dirt roads and making instant puddles and rivulets everywhere, and then blowing away just as quickly; and it would be oppressive and keep me indoors just like a squall does. The aura, the icicle hair, every portentous, foolhardy, mysterious consequence of the megrim seemed to be lost. And, yes, I was sorry these were lost, given that even in their most extreme manifestations, of which I must admit Desmond as lover might have been the most extreme, they were often the reward for the pain part.

I seemed to do better in school in the city. I don't know why. Heaven knows, by the time I was in high school my island ways had made me just as much an outsider in the city as my city ways, when I was younger, had made me an outcast on Shelter. There's nothing much to say about this

period of my life, except that it was later repeated—in its
odd *absence* of reportable (this is a word?) experience—in
my twenties. Boys I thought peculiar liked me, I think now
looking back, for my own high peculiarities. Glands going,
they figured me for an easy target, but were wrong. I don't
remember any of their names. I don't recall what they
looked like. They are all a bunch of random phantoms
who've gone on, most likely, to lives that wouldn't interest
me. And, harder for me to admit, the girls didn't reach me
either. Maybe I was threatening, maybe plain odd. Among
the most far-afield of outcasts I seemed to make no friends,
not that I tried that hard.

Instead, Faw was my focus. Who was this man? What did
he mean to me, what did he mean to himself and to the rest
of the world, or rather—leaving the world, which hardly
matters, aside—those in the world he touched? The older
I got the more curious I got about the meaning of Mother's
note—the hoax she referred to in it, a hoax she had found
intolerable; what could it have meant? I'd always considered my own fabrications, whatever their genesis, to be the
most creative, the most viable and meaningful audacities I
knew of in my life, but I was wrong. Audacity was my
father's forte. He was a wild force in his field of endeavor,
I began to believe, more wild than religion, more wild than
any sinner who nailed St. Peter upside down on a rood and
spat into his upturned nostrils. Even before I knew
whereof I spoke, the term "hoax" seemed too paltry for
anything my father would do. Hoax was a lowly word,
rhymed with coax, and he never stooped to coax anyone to
do anything. He presented his case, you bought it or you
didn't, and that was that.

The first moment I identified this audacity and understood the sweep of the Sprawl, became interested in its
form and developed a new awe for its erratic energies, was
in the middle of the night, when I was watching an old
movie on the box (a Western, a clutch of men firing flint-
locks on a log cabin, in which only two desperados were

fighting back—the two were killed, the cabin burned
down, end of movie)—and on came a commercial for something called Vintage Library of Art Film Society. Now, the
society, catering to late night aficionados of the so-called
"art" film, about which I will have more to say later, offered, much the way Time-Life offers insomniacs the
chance to collect a series of thin tomes about this subject or
that, high-quality reel-to-reel copies of the finest "art clas-
sics" ever "exposed on film." Was this legal? (Yes and no:
law prohibits advertising porn videos and porn films on
television or radio—but it doesn't stand in the way of somebody putting together a good mailing list of those who've
shown interest in the not-quite-X fare the Society was offering.) It intrigued me, and I even wrote the address and
number down, knowing that I'd never want to become a
member of the Society, but drawn to something about the
way the man who was on the screen presented his case.
Only later did I realize that the man was someone I had
actually met, a long time before. I looked back in the almanac—something I seldom did, because the entries seemed
more and more puerile to me, now that I was seventeen or
eighteen—and, yes, I found what I was looking for. I had
copied from Faw's notes the names of the dinner guests
that one night at Shelter, the night that Berg was invited
to the table, and recognized that the man on the screen had
been Stuart Neden. What was he doing on inexpensive,
early-morning air time? Why wouldn't he have gotten
some peon to do the peddling?

Why shouldn't I ask? I thought; and so I did.

Faw was absolutely disconcerting in his response. "So?"
he said, after I told him that the Sprawl, if Neden was still
a part of the Sprawl, was somehow tied up with an operation called VLAFS.

He was amenable to talking about it, whatever. But the
one-word response stripped me of any questions. What was
I supposed to ask? Was I supposed to change all of a sudden
into some sullied angel, some goodie two shoes? I was sul-

lied, I felt, but no angel—and Faw seemed so comfortable with whatever he had to do with all this, that I couldn't even formulate the next question I would ask, let alone pose it to him. Given what I then asked, I imagine he'd have preferred it if I had engaged him in a discussion about pornography, the sociological pros and cons, the legalities, the negative impact of those real live angels who flapped their polyester wings around the shopping mall cinemas whenever any movie of a "provocative" kind came to ruin their neighborhoods . . . because I did it, I did what I thought I could never do, I asked him, "What hoax was it that Erin was talking about in that note?"

"What note?" he frowned; he was so easy a mark for me, just as I must have been an easy mark for him.

"The note Mother left you."

He smiled at me a smile that said, What were you doing reading that note, that was for me, not you.

"Well, what did she mean, 'hoax.' "

"Your mother, as much as I loved her, as much as I still love her, because you know I still love her—is limited, okay Grace?"

"Yes?" And I waited.

"It was irresponsible of her to have written that to me, and doubly so knowing that you were into everything, worse than a kitten, and that chances were ten to one you'd read that before I did."

"Irresponsible in the sense that there was no hoax?"

"I don't know anything about hoaxes. I can tell you I've never lied to you, or to your brothers, or your mother. It's not how my life works, and I think you know by now, that's not how I want your life to work, either. Hoax. Grace, I don't know. She was bitter. I had my dream and was doing it."

"She had hers too, you know."

"I won't deny that. I still wish her dream had worked out with my own."

"Faw, that's what I want to talk about."

He was sitting with a pile of paper in front of him, and
to me he seemed so fragile at that moment that I followed
my instincts, and stood quiet. I was trying to figure out
how a daughter speaks to her father. Since I didn't know
what precisely it was I was getting at, or hoping to get at,
I couldn't press any further than this. I decided the matter
might best be laid aside. But while nothing revelatory came
of our talk, something very concrete did come of it: Faw
quite abruptly began to address me as an adult. He asked
me what I wanted to eat for dinner. He asked me if I'd like
to come with him to Portugal (I didn't—I preferred to stay
at home, *that* would be my job in the Sprawl, to maintain
the edge on the stationary, to be there, as they say, to be
there for my father). I decided that, albeit his response to my
questions about Neden and my mother's note was obfusca-
tory, clearly fudging, I was going to side with him, no
matter what he was up to, no matter who he was. He was
my father. He had for whatever reasons stuck by me longer
than my beloved flare man, than my dear Desmond fantasy,
than my mother even, and he was my core.

I still feel this way, though the core threatens to melt
down, like that at the blushing center of some insensate
nuclear reactor.

❖

I may as well tell you about my husband, since I was destined to have one. For me marriage was five weeks or so of
bliss, followed by years of ballasting. Even now I don't
dislike my husband—as I say, we've never bothered to divorce, though we've agreed that if sometime one of us
meets someone and would like to get married again, the
other would not stand in the way of a divorce. Various of
his friends have accused him of still being attached to me,
or being lazy about things, and have told him that he ought
to go ahead, given that we have been apart for so long, and
get the matter legally finalized. I don't know—I don't really

care—why it is that he's reluctant to file the papers. He knows I wouldn't fight him. For my part, I find that being married and not living with your husband makes for excellent defense on occasion. I still wear my wedding ring when I go out to parties, or to the movies with friends. It is antisocial as can be, but provides a distance. And while that chestnut about certain men being even more attracted to a woman who has a wedding band on is true, the wedding band can serve nicely in its capacity as a collar with which all comers may be restrained.

The drawn-out process of our separation is more indicative of our relationship than any detailed history of how we met, and fell in love. In brief, though, we met after I dropped out of college. I had gone to New Haven to study Russian. Faw encouraged me, as he believed even then that the next World War was going to be economic rather than atomic, and that a knowledge of Russian would be useful, because Russia was to become our ally—a not unprophetic analysis. But it wasn't in my fate to learn any language but English, and though I switched majors nothing seemed to work for me, and every class felt like an island class—I was the outsider, somehow, and couldn't fathom protocol, couldn't concentrate on lectures, so preoccupied was I with studying what the other students were doing, looking at what sort of pencils they wrote with, what clothes they wore, what quirks and oddities of character defined them. The most I could say for myself is that I became addicted to reading novels, mostly 19th Century, Austen, George Eliot, James; nothing assigned, of course—indeed to escape thinking about assignments.

I had determined to stay on in New Haven (actually East Haven, down near the sound) for a while, I didn't know how long, rather than move back to New York and live with Faw, or back to Shelter Island, where Djuna and Webster held forth—Webster had moved into the main house, to help her with keeping up Scrub Farm, as Faw still had a habit of going out on weekends; it had become more and more the place where he felt he could think most clearly. Often, I took the ferry over from New London to Orient, where Web picked me up, and spent Sunday with them, talking, eating and—when Faw went up to his bedroom to make phone calls—watching television. I loved those Sundays, but after I stopped going to classes altogether, after I made no pretense either to my professors or myself about my interest in continuing toward a degree, it became harder to go to the island and face him, to sit at the pine table in the kitchen and invent subjects that were discussed in classes I'd cut, talk about the Bulldogs and what sort of scores their teams were producing on ludicrous lawns in ludicrous stadiums, and all the rest.

My youthful adoration of Shahrazad, it became apparent those Sundays, was not misplaced. I loved her for the latticework of fictions she was able to invent in order to save her life and the life of her sister, but the more I tried to invent, to lie, the more I appreciated how easy it was to initiate, how difficult to sustain. Faw was no King Shahryar, either—neither so ruthless, nor so easily taken in, he remembered the slightest detail of anything I mentioned, and there was no statute of limitation on his memory. My stories had begun to entangle themselves, much the same way I have seen fishermen who are greedy and not content to be working one line but must have three or five going at once can get tangled while the surf keeps rolling in and the hooked fish begins to run one line over and under another.

I confessed. And was surprised, as ever, by the response. Faw, who professed to hating quitters, presented absolutely no resistance to my dropping out of school. "Fine by me," he said, "what do you think, Djuna?" Djuna was still one to toe the middle course, but allowed that she had never got a degree. "And a fine lot of good that's done you," Webster said, but he was called down with laughter. It didn't seem to matter. "And so what are you doing over there, for godsakes, why don't you come back home?" This was the question I had hoped to avoid, because in fact I didn't know the answer to it, but did know that home was somewhere I wasn't ready to come to yet.

I then told another Shahrazadesque lie. "I've met someone." Djuna placed her fork down noisily in her plate. "Met someone," Faw said. "Yes." "Is it serious?" Djuna asked—it was a straight television line, and I appreciated it, because to that I could make a straight television answer, "I don't know yet."

Whether it was predestined or because I felt myself under the need to fulfill the expectations that were generated by my lie there is no saying, but on a Tuesday—a fall day crackling with dead leaves that tripped down Orange Street toward the red cliffs above the monument park where I had hoped to finish my walk—I met him, he was walking too, the man who was going to be my husband, and we talked, I can't even say exactly why, and sat on a bench, and then later wound up drinking silly concoctions at Archie Moore's bar, and Desmond, and the flare man, and all my childhood and adolescent furies were set free. True, I was a little drunk, but I remember vividly what it was like being with him, the streetlight glow coming down through the bay window in the huge old house where he rented a room. We were in that room for three days. We ate what food he had, but never went out, except for an hour or so in the evenings, to Archie Moore's, which was right around the corner. And the bartender knew what was going on even before we did, he quipped, So when are you going to get married? We got our blood tests on the fourth morning, got our license. After that, of course, what could we do but get married, and so we did.

We drove north for our honeymoon, far up into Canada, because I had got it in my mind I wanted to see the Aurora Borealis. He went along with the scheme, though he told me that the chances we would actually see the auroral lights were slim. I knew we would. We slept in the back of the station wagon we had bought for the excursion, buried

under blankets. The higher the latitude, the more my anticipation grew. We'd been two weeks out from New York
when Warne (spelled self-consciously thus, pronounced
like "warren" of rabbits, an animal we were destined not
to emulate) became impatient with my quixoticism, and we
had our first argument. "Don't you think that we better put
some kind of time limit on this thing?" "Why?" "Because
enough is going to be enough is why, and why is it so
important that we see the aurora anyway?" "I don't know,"
I admitted. "Well, I think we ought to go back. It's ridiculous what we're doing. It's cold up here"—it was, too, that
day, rain in sheets across the rich brown landscape—"and
if something goes wrong with the car—"

I wondered, that night, whether in some implacable and
immature way I was trying to emulate my father, the traveler, the quester, the Don Quixote. My poor husband had
a reasonable point.

To keep the peace I agreed to three more days and
nights, no more. Standing out with him along a desolate
stretch of farm road that was the thinnest line on our map,
hundreds of miles north of the border, and witnessing the
green-yellow pulsing bundles of light, on the second night
of the allotted three, was the high point of the marriage. I
knew we'd see them, the lights, and we did. Discharges
across the length of the sky arced at such great altitudes
before us that none of it seemed real at all. Overhead, and
back behind us to the south, the stars brightened the heav-
ens, and the canopy before us winked and raced with magnetic flames. It was a huge, electrical curtain. The windows
in the back of the wagon fogged with our sleeping breath
that night, and the next morning we turned back.

When Warne took the offer of a job from my father, my
adoration of him—which had been, as I say, so strong for
a short period—took a blow. It wasn't fair of me to think
less of him for having taken Faw up on what was, after all,
not such an unusual arrangement between fathers and
sons-in-law, but I couldn't help myself. There was some-

thing too subordinate in it for *me* (does this sound grossly selfish, grossly unpalliative?); here I was, someone who'd never looked on Faw as a presence, more an absence, and this agreement between the two of them brought him in as benevolent dictator, or so it felt. "He treats me just like anyone else in the company," Warne sighed, not liking the platitude any more than I did.

I proposed several lame alternatives, one of which was to move up to Canada and become farmers. Of course, when Warne countered that I wouldn't know "one end of a pitch-fork from another" I couldn't legitimately disagree. "We can learn," I said, and I could see how frustrated he was with my moody idealism.

He stayed with Geiger, and the breach, having been opened, kept widening until I had to tell him, one morning before he was about to leave our little apartment on the West Side for work, "I don't love you anymore." Perhaps it was the strength of Mother's note to my father when she'd decided to leave him for Segredo, that I drew on—such irony, since part of me would always hate her for that note—because while I hardly knew what I was talking about, I was able to argue with some skill about my decision to leave. "We don't have to be final about anything," was what I said, avoiding, and consciously so, Erin's pattern of finality. He went ahead to work. The subtleties of guilt have never troubled Warne much, and the vigilant work he has done for Geiger over the years probably never rubbed up against whatever ego he's got hidden there somewhere inside his handsome head.

After the marriage broke down I developed a passion for secrecy. What other people didn't know wouldn't hurt them, and by the same token what they didn't know they wouldn't be able to use to hurt me. It was an even exchange, and one controlled by myself, which was the way I was learning to like things, or so I thought.

I packed with every intention of going to Cyprus. Knowing nothing about Cyprus I settled on it as my destination in the same way Faw had chosen Shelter Island. Cyprus drew me to itself by not just an attraction to a sound, or the thought of some shaggy-barked pine; no, there was a logical sequence behind my attraction. Cypress is a tree, and trees are wood. Wood is not metal, and metal is what Gabriel Segredo loved. What Gabriel Segredo loved I was duty-bound to hate. And so Cyprus made irrefutable sense.

There were two problems with my plan, though. For one, unlike Canada, there was strife in Cyprus. And, two, unlike Faw—and later on Berg, too—I had come to realize that there was never going to be solace for me in travel. The road meant only more confusions, more details for me to be unable to absorb and try, and probably fail, to understand. I already felt alienated from myself, from my confused husband, and everyone else around me. Why objectify such loneliness in hotel rooms, listening through their thin walls to conversations in languages I couldn't begin to comprehend? I was in no mood to tear my hair out for no good reason.

Djuna answered when I called. She had aged, which came as a surprise to me, I could hear it in her voice—yes, aged, even though it hadn't been such a long time since last we spoke: maybe it was that I could hear with some greater accuracy. Maybe it was I who had changed.

She was enthusiastic about my "coming home," and disbelieving about the finality with which I spoke of my separation (my comment to Warne notwithstanding). I packed a few things, and left that same morning. It was autumn, dry, and burnt-orange everywhere. The rented car felt consoling around me as the landscape, the warehouses, the overpasses, and industrial mayhem, softly fell behind me, giving way to the flats and farms of the end of the island.

When I pulled into the drive, the first thing I did was to walk down past the orchard to the marsh. The osprey nest was still there, atop its utility pole with its rusted cylindrical power box and salt-eaten lines. It looked more substantial and solid up there on its perch than ever. I realized, at once, why. The ospreys had been coming back every year, mating, raising their brood, and adding to the nest. How could I have doubted that it would still be there? It had become a symbol of stability for me, I knew, as I walked, a plain and shameless smile across my face, back to the house—and I was glad I'd placed my superstitious trust in something as durable as that nest. The next morning, when I got up, I looked out into the cherry tree, and there was nothing there but branches and leaves and sour fruit that the birds were plucking. As much as I liked the sensation of being here, I looked at my suitcase and knew where I had to go. Scrub Farm was close, but wasn't right. Just as I'd been brought to Shelter Island when I was a girl, Shelter was what I should leave to become a woman. I didn't unpack. Djuna was less surprised by all these changed plans than I might have expected. She stood on the porch as I drove away, and I could see her in the rear-view mirror as she walked back inside to telephone my father, as I'd asked her, to tell him to expect me in New York by early afternoon. On the way in I stopped at a roadside vegetable stand after the ferry had docked and bought several stalks of Brussels sprouts, a burlap bag of potatoes, and some squash. I looked forward to seeing my father. I wanted to ask him whether, in all his travels, he had seen the Aurora Borealis.

PART III

AERIE

We looked down seven hundred feet, not even, and it seemed as if we could pluck the Pain de Sucre right out of the ocean. The airplane crabbed left and careered to the right in the fresh breezes, and we saw Les Gros Islets and the port of Gustavia. The deep blues of the water graduated into the turquoises we associated with the West Indies, and we began to wonder why the pilot had the nose of the aircraft pointed sharply down; our chests had tightened, and the heat in the small cabin seemed to have risen, and the bluff, covered in rubber trees, cactus, scrub, succulents, arid paths, and narrow roads, seemed also to have risen. The pilot, a striking black man with a Rolex watch on his wrist and fresh white uniform with natty epaulettes on either shoulder, looked back at us passengers just at the moment we thought it was possible we were not going to clear the ridge, and smiled. Then he turned around and brought the nose of the aircraft up and lit down on the shortest runway in the Caribbean.

This is St. Barthélemy, St. Barth, St. Barts, and as I drove up the steep concrete road toward the summit of Tour-terelle, I could see why it would be an excellent location for something you might not want everyone to have such easy access to.

Cutts hadn't wanted me to make this trip, though of course I hadn't told him exactly where it was I was going. If he'd known that I was down here to find out for myself what I could about this church, and its connection to my father's trust—which more and more I had begun to believe Berg was tied up with in ways too intricate to be innocent—he might have risked even going to Berg, with the idea that the two of them could prevail. I had just met Cutts, and his wife Bea, a few months before; Berg introduced us. Cutts, like everybody I had met, it seemed, worked for Geiger. He was in New York. Like my brother, he was administrative, one of the people that existed toward the center of the spinning axis of the Sprawl.

Through my twenties—I took this trip over three years ago, just before I turned thirty—I associated less and less with anyone who was enmeshed in Geiger; after Warne and I fell apart and he converted into a functionary cog, as I saw it, no doubt putting a disparaging spin on what was likely a simple response (his need of employment) to a sad situation (our separation), I had little use for Geiger people.

Cutts was different, for me. In the wake of the separation I drifted, and continued to drift over the months and years. Where they went, those years, and to what end I had made it through my days I can hardly say. I'm not proud of having nothing to report here about that time. There are those who claim that your twenties should be the best period of your life. I saw movies, I read, I slept with a few men, I helped keep a home going for my wanderer father. Time just passed, is all. And until I was introduced to Cutts nothing stirred me very deeply; there were no flare men out my windows, Desmond seemed like a distant mirage; if my dreams were shot through with any instances of bright sexuality I never recalled them; when I did experience the occasional megrim, it was pure pain, which sent me to a dark and silent room that had no tales of Arabia, nor anything else in it.

What I had told Cutts was half true. "I'm going on a trip," I'd said. He and I had met for a drink, without Bea, and I noticed that evening our friendship was moving toward what seemed to me to be an inevitability. I had never had an affair with a friend, or a married man, and didn't know whether I wanted to or not. I adored Bea, and felt I would have to give up the chance of having a sister in her if I followed my disorderly heart. When Cutts asked why I was going on this trip, I answered with surprising forthrightness, "Because I think it might be good to get away from you for a while."

That he didn't argue told me everything I needed to know. He felt the same way I did about us.

The Moke groaned as I took it back over the narrow pass. I parked it on the side of the road when I saw a graveyard there, since cemeteries and churches are often proximate. The gum trees and cacti were very thick up here, and I sensed that the church might be hidden in the thicket past the graves. The air was dry and sweet. Far off, a hollow bell on a goat's neck clanged. I made my way between the burial mounds, which were formed of sand and small seashells piled over the site. Some of the mounds were decorated lavishly with purple and pink plastic flowers and lined with conch shells. Bees hovered over the graves, lazily, drawn to examine the flowers.

They were disappointed, of course, as was I. After looking around that entire remote part of the island for the rest of the day, I began to conclude that what I'd always suspected was right. I checked into my hotel down by St. Jean, sat on the balcony and watched the pelicans dive for fish. I found myself wishing that Cutts was here with me. The little bit of French I had went just far enough to make me feel even more isolated. I drank from a bottle of scotch a former guest in this room had left behind, and that the maids had somehow missed appropriating for themselves, and wondered how Faw did it, how he managed to feel content inside his own skin while staying on the road all the time. How does a person do it, make the road his home? I decided I would ask around, as best I could, the next day, about the church, but after a sleepless night found myself making arrangements to catch a flight back to St. John, and home. I booked on a flight for the next day. Even with some time to kill I stayed in my room. Saline, Colombier, Gouverneur's beaches, none of them attracted me. I didn't care about the sun. The little lizard that lived in the flowering tree off my porch could have it all to himself.

That night, evening light along the water was bathed in brown-pink, the color of the pelicans I had observed—the same color as the pelicans we had watched as children on Shelter, fascinated by the way they folded themselves into a seemingly helpless heap to make their deadly dive.

Meantime, I had found what I came looking for, which was that there was nothing there to find.

❖

It happened. It had to happen. There was no resisting it. And it wasn't as difficult to do, either spiritually or practically, as I had thought it would be. I existed in unquestioning oblivion for nearly six weeks. Why shouldn't I allow myself to be happy? Other people made it their constant concern, to be happy, to content themselves no matter what the cost to others, so why not I? I found myself able to brunch with Cutts and Bea on Sunday, share the newspaper, waste hours with them at the flea market, and then, come Monday midday, meet him at their apartment and make love with him on the same comforter Bea had bought at the outdoor market the day before. But it wasn't that my heart had hardened, or so it was I assured myself, rather that I had opened myself up to a broader life, one that need not make moral sense in order to strike a balance. If there were unfortunate paradoxes here and there that happened to help keep things interesting, then so be it. After all, I had no strong aspirations to sainthood anyway.

Although I was naturally afraid that Bea might come home to discover us together—that was what inevitably happened in these arrangements, as I had understood from the movies I'd seen in which this kind of thing went on—I reveled in the smell of the sheets, and loved feeling saturated in the combined anxiety of fearing discovery and the absent intimacy of Bea's presence in the room. Sweet Bea, goddamn it all—the scent of my best friend in the pillow-case was profoundly, disturbingly intoxicating, and I would turn my head as far as I could to the side as Bea's man covered me, and breathe in deep in order to draw inside me with this one sense all I could of Bea, while I took inside me the single thing that in this world Bea probably considered all her own, and in this way not only was I able to give myself to Bea's man but I was able to make myself, for just a moment, Bea's home. This was how it felt to me, anyhow. It wasn't that I was purloining, wasn't that I was taking anything from Bea. Rather I was opening myself up to her, you see. Empathizing. I was presenting myself as a gift to Bea, anonymous and secret, quiet and willing. Again, no logician, I can't present a formula that would explain just why what another person would call a simple treachery I saw as an act of humility and love. But that is how it felt to me then, and how it feels even now.

I moved under the warmth, moved down into the mat-tress with my hips, and I supposed that somehow in mak-ing that movement I was able to mark the sheets with myself, and so bring myself into them, become part of their fabric, too. And later, after I left, much later that night I would imagine Bea lying in those same sheets with her man (by then the ambiguity of "her" and whom it denoted would have blossomed like April petals on Scrub Farm's apple trees)—and the thought would be as exquisite as any actual moment spent with either Bea or Cutts. In some ways more exquisite, because I could think of it by myself, extend it and repeat it, do as I pleased with the idea. It wasn't a mean thought, either; wasn't, as I saw it, pleasure from seeing someone else suffer. That was for . . . for whom? I hardly could conjure what kind of emotional gro-tesque (or wacko, as Berg would call it, still using that word as an adult, still thinking that way about me his sister) derived satisfaction from watching another person in pain. Bea wasn't in pain, Bea wasn't suffering in any way. If anyone was suffering it was me, wasn't it?

"I love you," he allowed one day, and his statement struck the most incongruous chord inside me.

"Don't say that."

"Why not?"

"I don't know why not. Just don't."

"But, Grace, I do, it's the truth. I mean I just do."

"The truth? Give me a break," was my response, and we both let it go.

Later on, that evening, back home alone, it came to me why I didn't want him to tell me he loved me. Because by saying he loved me he pushed Bea back further away from the two of us, and I suddenly understood how delicate and improbable was this emotional cat's cradle I found myself entangled in, languorous as a cat myself. He shouldn't say it because for one I already knew he loved me, so they were just dull little words that if anything muted, rubbed, reduced the very experience they attempted to image; and, further, even more important, the words were words that Bea couldn't say to me, and I, in order to be able—somehow responsibly—to have him as my husband, too, had to feel that ineradicable bond between Bea and myself. "I love you" were words made out of blades, and sharp ones at that. They were words that severed, didn't seam, didn't mend, yet didn't lacerate either. They cut clean, and left behind nothing but a sheer imbalance. The formula was: Grace loved Bea, Bea was her husband as much as Cutts. I looked down dizzily at the twin blurs of red, the parallel taillights down the avenue, heightened in the dank drizzle. What a pity to know, without ever having tried of course, that making love with Beatrice would be boring. And what a strange thing to suspect that if Cutts—as he was pressing his body into mine—could cry out, We love you, the spell I was already under would be made unbreakable, that I would be fully possessed by him, by them. Should I have been glad he didn't seem to have a clue how obsessive I would be able to get about *them*?

The next day, the mist-rain was still filtering down

through the streets, creating silver tracery on the windows, and the city was embraced in phosphorescent-gray fog. I whispered, "I hate you," into his mouth as I was kissing him, and tightened my arms around his back. He either didn't understand what I had said, or knew better than to question or contradict the statement, and in his silence unknowingly gained my commitment to him, as I turned myself over, allowed my hands to dangle over the settee's edge, and heard myself moaning, "My husband, my husband," like some perfect slut.

❖

And, with this, the thought that ran through her mind, the thought that made her move better than she had ever moved before, as a woman, as a sexual being, was that she was learning something about who Grace Brush could possibly be.

Who would have guessed?

What she couldn't comprehend, though, was how her involvement with her best friend's spouse (yes, admit it for all the cliché that it was) generated in her not one glimmering of guilt—at least not a glimmering recognizable as guilt—and, indeed, she didn't much try. The point would have been what? It was a moment that begged for practicality, rather, and what did begin to grow was her survivor's sense of the need to shelter their arrangement. Spread the odds, or even nix the downside odds, just as her father would do, if it were a business arrangement. They needed not just a safe refuge, she and Cutts, but a place that would nurture whatever form their lives together could take. It was only a matter of money, and since he couldn't afford it, he said, and couldn't in any very discreet way help her pay the rent on such a thing, given that Bea ran the family finances and wrote their checks, Grace said she would pay the rent. Money could be got, in a host of ways, from the family, and no one needed to be the wiser for it.

The "aerie"—their secret place, named by Grace, of course, and named in honor of the osprey nest—was always filled with sunlight, yellow and brown and gray. And though it faced away from the street, it was always prey to the noise of the city, of neighbors, of trucks, of the deep unnamable hum that spreads through the pavements and up in through the girders and frames of New York buildings, making the glass in every window shiver. It was so different from the island. It took her back to her days of enchantment, her days with the flare man, the light people, her childhood. The light streaming through their window seemed only to encourage whatever flame they were able to generate, and like most city people they'd long since learned how not to listen to the noise. Because circumstances kept them from sleeping there at night, they were never able to test the brightness of their love under the same cover of dark as most lovers—but it didn't seem to matter. Cutts, at least, was content with the arrangement. As for Grace, she had her good days and, after those first weeks of euphoria, her bad days.

The studio was on the top floor of a six-story brownstone, just high enough so that on bleak days the room was flushed in grays and on sunny days scoured by light; yet low enough that it felt protected, hidden within the nest of other buildings, themselves fraught with sufficient private agendas, so that their own—which flashed by each day within these walls—didn't seem so exposed or abnormal. Its cramped bank of windows faced south, out toward Brazil as Grace liked to think, toward frigates and albatrosses, hot beaches and frost flats where other people could sun and freeze, toward the tip of the continent where the wind and water knocked together; they faced away from Thirteenth, the unlucky-number Street, more immediately; and even more immediately, those evocative Village windows stared back, though not too closely, at their own windows, and above the rooftops, from other buildings other windows stared from distances that prevented their being discovered.

A white door with no bell and no nameplate. Just inside, an alcove, and beyond the white plaster archway she had placed a double bed—wrought-iron from the turn of the century, whose head and foot reached up as if to touch the ceiling in clusters of curled strands that Grace thought resembled fiddlehead ferns in the spring, before they had fully opened, and accordingly she'd painted them green. Next to the bed she put an oak side table, and on it a dark wine-glazed Van Briggle lamp molded with dragonflies whose wings spread around its body. In the windowsills some of the starfish collection was laid, and around it she set out a few of her favorite Geiger novelties, including the talking seashell. The closet remained empty, aside from extra linens and a few presents they had given each other, some scarves and unused slippers. This barrenness she'd intended from the beginning to change, since it suggested, to her, a hollowness at the heart of the aerie that was loathsome.

Wasn't it, moreover, false? she might have asked herself—a false emptiness against the fullness of what she and Cutts had worked so hard to get and keep for themselves? By the same token, what else could they have needed, given that they had each other? There was the argument that those who needed to crowd their world with objects and decorations weren't able to be intimate with themselves or anyone else. For any thesis, an antithesis, and what did it matter? To Grace's world that the aerie existed at all meant that she had finally come to a synthesis with someone.

The green bed didn't stand at the center of the aerie although she knew it to be at the center of their arrangement, for she had no difficulty in admitting to herself that sex was not just vital to them, but that she and Cutts were drawn together above all in the cause of their own sexuality, and that the filaments that laced them were made of

flesh over and above any spiritual or intellectual material.
Grace liked to let the sheets go unlaundered for as long as
possible so that the heavy salt-sour smell of them would
persist—it was something she'd always wished she could
have done when they made love at Cutts and Bea's place—
and would be there to greet them along with the whirling-
dervish pigeons that cooed on the concrete sill. Not only
did that scent remind them of why they kept coming back
to the aerie, to that bed, but it played through them a kind
of invocation to begin, each time they entered.

Grace always arrived first. She would put on the kettle
for coffee, knowing that the coffee, too, she made as much
for the smell of it as to sip, because it helped to create an
atmosphere of home, where there was the same licorice red
teakettle, remaking the morning, which was of course by
then a lost thing. She'd already been through this ritual, of
the coffee, the kettle, the not-quite-thereness back with
Charles, but then so much had to be done twice in order
to make the arrangement work. Double life, so this is what
that really meant, she thought, yes because so much has to
be accomplished twice just to create a place or state of mind
where the one thing she did want to make happen actually
could. How did people get themselves into these messes?
And how many mornings did Cutts have to linger in bed
with her, with Bea—his real wife, his acknowledged wife—
to keep his own domestic balances in place? Grace would
never ask. It would upset him, she was sure. He would
refuse to answer, and besides she didn't even want to know,
in the last analysis. Anything in twos meant conspiracy,
meant duplicity, didn't it? The very word double had duplicity as its etymological cousin and given that Grace
didn't care to feel duplicitous she'd learned that it was
better not to press too deeply into areas of Cutts's life. Some
knowledge was best not gained. That is, they were friends,
the three of them; she, him, and her. Grace already knew
the range of not-so-private matters that friends discuss
with one another. Sometimes she'd even had to hear Bea's

girl talk about intimacies between Cutts and herself, how
Bea had noticed that sometime during the last year a really
subtle but you could still feel it, every day, kind of distance
had grown between her and Cutts. It was nothing that
really threatened the marriage, she gave Grace to understand, but since Grace had been married once, well had this
sort of thing happened to Grace? Bea wanted to know,
should she be taking it more, what, not seriously since she
didn't take it seriously, she told herself, or . . . more as a
threat, should she worry? The clock chimed its throaty
mahogany tone when she asked, and it conjured the cuckoo
clock, which always conjured, in turn, the traditional cuck-
old; did Grace wince? She studied the wallpaper in Bea's
kitchen instead. It comprised blotches of dusty-pink blossoms or silly swine-faces, she couldn't tell which. But also,
she tried to consider this, what her friend was asking. She
thought hard, then, before answering, the clock having had
its say, because she knew that she could give Bea an honest
and valuable, if not forthright, response if she could only
concentrate on her own past and on her love for Bea. And
when she said, "I wouldn't worry about it," she felt sure
that there was nothing in her advice that derived from the
deep need in her to protect her own relationship with Bea's
husband. Grace knew she didn't mean to threaten Bea, and
therefore Bea was not in fact threatened by what Grace was
doing. She felt, Grace did, satisfied with her answer.
Whether it was good advice she couldn't know any more
than if she didn't know a thing beyond the surface of her
friendship with Cutts. She was so integrally bound to Cutts
that when she hugged Bea and kissed her good-bye that
time, not the slightest tint of irony or regret or remorse
arose from her own knowledge that these lips and hands of
hers had a few hours before, up in the aerie, spread over the
lips and hands of their mutual husband. If Cutts's lips were
turning cold toward Bea, they would have turned so because of someone besides Grace, wouldn't they? Grace left
Bea behind even sensing that she could somehow enable

Cutts to move closer to Bea physically, and still not relin-
quish him herself. Wasn't there some way all this love
could be deepened, even, for them all? she thought. Some
mornings, when she woke up into the dry linen of her
bedclothes, regretful at their aridity, Grace even allowed
herself to wonder if Bea were made aware of the truth
whether she wouldn't find her way clear to appreciating
the profound goodness in it, in what there was between
Grace and Cutts—she wondered whether even, after the
first shock of betrayal, Bea might not come to accept it,
even welcome it.

On the bed was a crazy quilt (the pattern was Wonder
of the World) and more often than not, for all her lapses
into this sort of peaceable dreaminess about Bea's being
understanding, and welcoming her passionate, lying friend
into her life (for she knew Bea would never understand,
and would either leave Cutts or more likely do everything
in her power to exile Grace), it seemed as if a quilt whose
pattern was called crazy made a lot of sense. All this was
a wonder of the world. For whatever moments she and
Cutts were able to share in the aerie there were as many
moments like the present one, where she stood sipping at
the coffee she'd just made, staring out over the patinaed
roof of the church with its spires rising at the corners of its
dull bulk, daydreaming, thinking that it wouldn't take
much to bring it all to an end. He'd argue. He might even
weep—they both would. It would take weeks, maybe a few
months to answer finally to every question he might raise
in the hope of going on with it, but it could be brought to
an end. Conceivably, though perhaps it was an exalted hope
silly in its lack of practicality, their friendship, hers and
Cutts's, could be salvaged if they moved to end it, and soon.
Bea would never know what had happened and because of
just that—that it had happened, was in the past—it
wouldn't really matter that she didn't know. It would be
over is all, presumably to become a personal, invisible leg-
end, to be pulled out once in a while and fondled, smiled

at, quietly celebrated or scoffed at depending upon the future mood. Grace and Cutts would have had this romance, which like anything else in the world would go dim in time and under the weight of experience. It's common, it happens; let go, let go.

She then felt lazy, as if there were a stream of warm lead pouring down through her veins.

❖

Holidays never failed to quicken if not a worm of jealousy in my gut, some sense of crawling defeat. Like a captured animal, I endured them, from New Year's to Easter, from Independence Day on through to Christmas (always the worst of all holidays, for the false light of celebration it shines into corners occupied by the most resistant, agnostic, even atheist of us all) with Charles—this was expected of me, was a given. And I was dutiful in this regard, in part because I knew that Faw endured them himself, not just because he thought that it wasn't worth fighting them, but because he was caught up in an idea that we, who were for better or worse a family, had best stay somehow in step with the holidays, if only because without them we wouldn't stay in step at all.

Still, there was something tangibly upsetting to me in the thought of Cutts at home, his home, with his own family, his other family, his Graceless family. In the heat of early July, with fireworks bellying rosy and slapping silver-yellow in the night's face out over the water, I knew that Cutts was somewhere on a pier, or in the prodigious trembling streets, or on a roof garden, with Bea, watching the filigrees of color fall and fade, and that he was with his real wife then, while missing me maybe, a moment here or there, when he was reading a menu, trying to decipher Dal Gosht (whose anagram was Ghost Lad) or some biryany at one of the Indian dives that Bea loved so much, she with her stomach of iron, or when there was a delay in the

fireworks display and the sky over the East River went
ash-black and the booming roar ceased until someone
solved the fireworks problem.

On these holidays, whenever I could, I got away from
Faw and his Christmas hearth hung in raiment of holly and
pine boughs, or his table spread with Thanksgiving dinner,
to visit the aerie. Here my jealousy, which I admit to har-
boring, best assumed the form of melancholy. Here I could
accord myself the idiotic extravagance of absolute unhappiness, let it come, let it take over, and slip into the bed with
my clothes on and drink some of Cutts's retsina and curse
him to the Mahler that I would play as loud as the speakers
could handle. Here I would find myself running my hands
over my all-too-familiar ribs, feeling my body like stale
bread in the custodial of the one Catholic church I visited
just for the heck of it once out in the island, grappling my
flesh through the cotton of the sheets and the wool of my
skirt, bringing myself with the orchestra to you know
what. Then I could make Cutts as nonexistent as that last
symphony of Mahler's, the one he always spoke of, the
great one he, Gustav Mahler, was never able to finish.

Mahler would click off, and I, half-dreamy, was reminded of Abû Shakûr of Balkh's attitude toward suffering—To this point doth my learning go, I only know I
nothing know; and just as music and wine annihilated suffering, the thought of dark-eyed Abû's agnostic couplet
here could bring a silly smile to my face, and on his advice
I might sigh, and fall asleep, and forget again how angry I
was with Cutts for choosing to stay with Bea, even though
I had no desire for him to leave Bea, either. When I woke
up and the stars were lying against the glass, reminding me
of the sea stars at Scrub Farm, fat with dust or water, my
headache failed to chasten me while my confusions would
remain as unsorted as ever. Back home I'd walk, my sadness
perishing with my anger, and by the time I went to bed in
my own bed, my other bed, my home bed, doing something
twice yet once again, the holiday—whatever it might have

meant or been—was over, and I was as anxious as ever to see him, this sort-of husband, again. Ah, the fucking tedium unto death!

❖

They met the one morning at Grand Central, and in the great, anonymous stream of faces moving through its passages they kissed, and he had some time so they went down into the Oyster Bar, and locked knees under the small table, and ordered a plate of malpeque and chincoteague and chokomish and kent islands, and never mentioned a thing one to the other about what had happened the day before. Grace had got it in her mind to cut off with him, and Cutts had it in mind to tell her something that he had learned about Charles Brush, just a grapevine sort of bit of information, but something that nevertheless worried him. And they started talking, and Grace moved around and around the possibility of broaching her subject, and she found it was difficult to do. It seemed unusual, because she had experienced not the least hesitation when the time had come to tell Warne that she couldn't go on with him. On the other hand, as Cutts took the oyster shell to his lips to drink the meat and salt water down, he began to question both the validity of the rumor he had heard, and what purpose there might be in bringing it up with Grace. She was, after all, uninvolved with the Geiger Sprawl, at least in any administrative capacity; and what if the rumor he'd heard—which was already deemed by some of his colleagues as pure rubbish, just the kind of smear tactics that he detested—was false, then what? Grace would have to go to her father, tell him about these crazinesses that were circulating about some church somewhere, some mariner's cathedral, and how money was being diverted into its sham coffers in the name of God and country, but was in fact going into the production of—man, had he really thought he'd have the chutzpah to explain this business to her?—

blue boy movies and the like, and that there was a whole fistful of funny stuff going on with the non-profit status of this church (on a fancy island in the Caribbean, too, of all places) and profits from various arms and legs and extremities of Geiger being fed into this Gulf Stream whatever-it-was Trust—and he laughed, laughed aloud, and looked across the small round table at Grace.

"What's so funny?" she said. She looked at Cutts's face, and realized that she didn't want to let him go, in fact, couldn't let go of him, not just yet. Maybe she did love him, she thought. Maybe there were ways to keep on making this thing work.

"Nothing," he said.

❖

The first time Grace brought Li Zhang up the stairs and into the aerie, what was implicit in his mind was more or less just what was in hers. Which was very coincidental, and had something to do with the fact that at the edges of what few words they spoke was the sort of disturbance that can come from a profound expectancy, the kind of expectancy that registers not in thoughts but in the viscera, the flesh of the heart.

It was March, winter was about to surrender to the equinox; it was warmer than it had been in recent weeks. Down in the streets crystal mounds of blackened snow stood forth by the garbage cans and wrought-iron railings, each pile of cold dappled with debris and stained by a film of soot and fumes and filth, looking like ridiculous snow-omens that Grace—later that same night—would come to think she ought to have been able to read. Wherever the sun had sent down its bald light through spaces between the buildings and scraggly ginkgo trees, which rose here and there like exhausted skeletons, the snow had melted, making those clumps of the stuff that remained all the more peculiar. She should have been looking at the bits of rubbish in the mounds, because then she might have gained a little insight into what was going to happen with Li, who'd seemed so nice when they met about an hour before, walking his old mother dachshund, whose chubby back sloped and breast sagged so with age that her coat was almost completely worn away from scraping along on the pavement, her hair replaced by thick liver-colored callus. But Grace just stepped over the grimy snow, talking and walking along with Li and Can Xue (the dachshund was named in honor of the writer Can Xue—i.e., Deng Xiao-hua—whom Li, along with some other disenchanted and idealistic students, met once, having made the pilgrimage to her humble house in Changsha).

At first, Grace and Li Zhang hadn't been walking anywhere in particular. That is, they'd entered into a conversation much in the same way a bather enters the sea, directionless, reading the waves, just going out and out, and Can Xue tugged at her leash, for she was an insistent little beast, Li explained, and then Grace found it impossible to finish the thought, whatever it had been—it seemed drowned in an undertow of words that just swam and swam through and around it now—and she'd picked up Li's discourse and his direction and while, no, she wasn't laughing much at the things they were saying, because Li didn't finally have a very good sense of humor, didn't so much as try to entertain her or make her smile, she was caught up in it all. This man, Li Zhang, seemed to be so engaged, to be so right-there-with-her, and yet it seemed he was simultaneously indefinite about everything.

A siren heard, in the near distance, as a willingly drowning swimmer might hear the cries of her companions back on the beach, awakened her briefly from this word-sleep she felt she was going into, and rather than save her—if that was what the sound, within its metaphor, was supposed to have done—it only made her the more content to keep floating away from it.

When Can Xue paused by one of the ginkgo trees and

shivered as she passed her urine down her blackish legs onto the frozen quarry stones that were arranged around the bole, Grace did say, "Well, see you later."

That was the Grace who wasn't interested in drowning yet, the swimmer Grace who didn't get off on the risk of icy waves and undertows and clasping kelp. She said it of course knowing that it wasn't likely she would ever see him again since she'd never seen him around the neighborhood before, and Li Zhang didn't insist that she stay there and continue talking with him, but instead he continued with whatever it was they'd been talking about.

He was mentioning the stuff about the camphor trees in Formosa and China and how his grandmother took the bark and steamed it over a fire, distilled it—had she ever smelled camphor?—and how his grandmother took it and made soap, and varnish, and perfume from it. Talk about your stream of consciousness, there wasn't even a camphor tree in the city, but that was Li, just flowing along, letting Can Xue's nose dictate the direction, all of which would have led Grace to believe that Li wasn't a willful sort of person, being unconcerned with where his feet carried him; but if that was what she'd thought while they strolled along together, she had been mistaken. For instance, this was not Li's neighborhood at all, Grace discovered, after having expressed surprise that she hadn't seen him and Can Xue before.

No, he lived in Chinatown—"I have the good sense to live where I'm supposed to live, you probably live where you're supposed to live, too," to which she replied, "I live in two places, one with my father, and the other with my lover"—and not taking up the thread, which she sensed he'd thought unnecessary, even gauche, he went on about his dog and how unless she was ailing or tired he took her in a canvas bag onto the subway, rode to a stop chosen at random, and emerged up in the streets where he let her take off down whatever sidewalk she wanted to explore. Li told Grace that at one time or another he and Can Xue had probably been down every block in New York, not that he'd really be able to remember, since just as it was exercise-time for her it was thinking-time for him, and when you are thinking you're not seeing. When Grace glanced over at him, she was struck by how deep the wrinkles around his eyes ran—smile-lines she always called them, though she doubted that Li Zhang had smiled enough in his life to produce them; and then she wondered how old he might be, and realized that he wasn't necessarily younger than she, as she'd first imagined, that indeed he could be much older. She looked at his hand, which held the leash, knowing that hands often tell a person's age better than any other feature, but they were delicate and rather expressionless, and betrayed nothing. The eyes behind his rimless glasses were black, his hair was black and straight and cut tight across his forehead, his clothing was well-tailored and had a homemade look to it—the gray worsted trousers, the gray scarf with purple piping, even the soft green-black leather jacket. And what did he think about when he was walking aimlessly through the cold brick gorges of the city?

She might have asked had she not realized he was now returning her stare (funny how this whole experience seemed as if played out in a fit of exhaustion, how given over to it she felt, just as when in a bad dream you come to understand that you are not going to be able to escape your nightmare-ghoul, and you begin to ease up and accept that the evil your imagination has worked up for you will prevail, at least until you awaken); when she looked into his eyes Grace suddenly lost interest in asking what he thought about while he walked, because she sensed she already knew. Li's quick smile—like an acknowledgment it was—did seem awkward on his lips. That was when she knew she wanted him to come with her up to the aerie.

Now, while neither of them had any particular expectations of what would happen between them alone in the room—a man and a woman who didn't know each other, as such—nor even had the time to formulate specific hopes or desires, or intentions (Li Zhang's behavior in this regard might be seen, in a later light, as harder to explain than Grace's), both experienced an exhilaration.

Both breathed faster, shallower. Both knew clearly what they could do, if they chose, and it is a commonplace that knowing what you can do is the first step toward doing it. The way Can Xue made herself comfortable, turning around in place three times, and then lying down with a warm yawn, only helped them more toward understanding they would probably act on these emerging feelings. People sense what they are going to do, and most especially when they try to convince themselves that they are entering into an episode from which they will emerge not knowing what they might have had in mind (that is, they say, What was I doing, for godsakes?)—though neither asked the other any questions.

Anyway, what sort of question would Li Zhang have asked, before he took the three or four steps he took toward Grace, and ran his palm over her cheek before placing it on her shoulder and drawing her into him? There was nothing to say. There certainly was nothing to ask. He didn't even smile, because when he moved his lips through the shroud of hair and began to kiss her ear, he knew by the way her back curved into him and her fingers clutched into the furrow of his thin neck that there wasn't a need to smile.

She told herself, as she drew the cord that let the blinds down, that it wasn't meant to have been a seduction. After all, the aerie belonged half to Cutts, even if she paid its bills. It just was what it was; it was going to take place, there was nothing to stop it, and no reason for it not to go on. Cutts's absence was of his own choosing. Good choice, given what he'd make of this. It wasn't her choice that Cutts always had to be drinking wine when he was in the aerie—the same wine Li now reluctantly accepted and drank. Grace never told Cutts he had to have wine here. And the scarves of Grace's that Li used to tie her wrists and ankles to the bedposts—Li accomplished all this with such delicacy and determination—had been gifts from Cutts. But she never asked for presents from Cutts. She never much liked the presents he gave her anyway, although they were nice presents (the scarves were silk and colorful). They indicated to Grace more that Cutts felt guilty toward Bea than that he felt generous toward Grace. The scarves were more sacrificial offerings than true gifts. So, all right. Let's make a sacrifice with them.

"You struggle with fate you hurt yourself"—who had said that? It sounded like something Faw would come up with, but though she'd forgotten the source of the statement, Grace had had years of studying that lesson, hadn't she? Of course, any truism was like a trap, a padlock—no matter how unassailable, how finely wrought, how sophisticated, none existed but that it could be escaped or picked. Whether she struggled with fate or not it seemed inevitable that she, or someone, was going to be hurt, so she chose to follow the maxim along its surface, knowing however that she had discovered how to take it to pieces and could easily reduce it, if she wished, to a heap of worthless metaphoric tumblers and cylinders and jaws.

Still, as she lay there, fully clothed and face down on the bed, she wondered how it was possible she felt not the slightest sense of remorse that Cutts's presents were finding such novel use in the dying afternoon.

This would make him furious to say the least. She tried to imagine his fury and how it would feel to see him so angry with her. She closed her eyes and felt nothing, really, except that she liked this sense of being down here in her own darkness, alone and inexplicably strong even while she was being rendered powerless, and as she splayed her arms and legs under the urgings of his hands, her interest in conjuring Cutts waned. What interested her was a stirring, visceral trust she began to feel under Li Zhang's kisses, which were like a cat's, or the graze of emery.

Once Li finished securing her limbs, he asked, "Would you mind if I had a little more wine?" and seeing she couldn't answer, because he had gagged her (the fresh-laundered, bleach-scented men's briefs Li found in the drawer of the nightstand seemed suitable to the task), he poured another glass and drank it off as quickly as he had the first.

"Do you mind if I—" he muttered, politely, as he raised the clacking wooden blinds.

She answered, No, with a deep tongueless "Oh," down in her throat. Let him see me, she thought, under the late winter light that now filled the aerie with its thin glow, Let anybody who wants to see, see.

"Don't worry," he suggested—"dawn wooree be haw-pee," the song passed through her head, and kept going through the next few minutes there was no stopping it until he removed Can Xue's leash from the collar and, climbing on to the bed, gently slipped it under her neck, threading the clip end through the loop of the handle, and drawing it tight. As he was loving her he straddled his knees over her thighs and now and then, quite rhythmically and with ineffable tenderness, yanked her head back a bit with the leash, as he thrust into her more deeply. He had not bothered to do more than push her skirt up and lift her panties aside so that he could have access to what interested him. Or else, given that maybe it didn't so much interest him, where he had to go.

Neither of them made any sound during the fifteen or twenty minutes he spent riding her, his helpless white mare, but as Grace came to orgasm, she pushed the gag out of her mouth with her tongue—reminding them both, at a crucial moment, that her bondage was more gestural than actual—and she began to moan, to which his response was to cease moving.

He laid the leash on her back and sat over her, and said, "What do you think you're doing?" She tried to see his face but he was distorted in her peripheral field, which began to haze up with tears. She arched her hips up, driving her stomach into the sheets, hoping to communicate to him that she wanted to continue, but Li Zhang was not, it became obvious to Grace, going to continue fucking a woman who would come.

The disgust that he exhibited toward her she could feel through the coldness of his fingertips on her back, where he let them rest after emphatically pushing her hips back down onto the bed. Wasn't hatred only for the weak? Li Zhang had already shown himself not to be that; hatred surely was beneath him. So thinking that their lovemaking might still be going on, and that maybe she ought to be more patient than she was being, she took the full dose of his silence and told herself that what he might have been feeling toward her was pity. Yeah, well pity was appropriate, she thought. But then he breathed out hard and she heard resignation in the way he did it. No, she'd screwed up. He continued to rest his hands on her back, and after sitting like dead weight on her thighs for a while, he ceremoniously—anything performed in absolute silence seems ceremonious, doesn't it?—slid the leash through its loop and removed it from around her neck. "Okay," he whispered.

It was over. His flesh, which had dwindled between her legs, he withdrew, snapping his hips back. He dismounted, and dressed.

Grace felt as if she should somehow apologize, should speak now, say something, recreate the word-water they'd floated in before with such pure ease, break up the atmosphere that all their silences had fostered, but she wasn't exactly sure what she'd done to earn this rebuke from Li Zhang. Since she didn't want to bring on any further enmity from him, she lay motionless, breathing as softly as she was able, holding back further tears by concentrating on—of all things—the label on Cutts's underwear through squinted eyes, and she pictured the television commercial where the fat men were all dressed up like grapes and oranges and lemons, and the little old matron who was the head of their peculiar brood stood folding their under-

pants, commenting on how strong the elastic waistbands
were, and how long they would last, and how happy were
all her fruit-boys—those poor failed actors who back in
school might never have imagined that all their struggles
to memorize *A Midsummer Night's Dream* would result in the
pathetic calamity of green grease-paint and selling smiles—
and then she imagined Bea at the store buying these very
products for her husband to wear, daydreaming perhaps
under the fluorescent lights in the department store, lulled
into a half-sleep by the raspy buzz the long bulbs gave off
from above. Then she came back from her own meander-
ing, because the door to the aerie opened. For an instant she
knew it could have been Cutts walking in. Then the door
shut, and she heard Can Xue's nails scuttering on the landing outside.

When Li Zhang left, he left her tied up—which Grace
thought rather strange of him. She got free fairly easily.
Had he gotten suddenly stung with paranoia that she
would want to follow him and therefore thought to get a
jump on her by leaving her there to fight with the scarves?
Or else, well, what had happened? She felt immensely flus-
tered. She looked at herself in the bathroom mirror, just to
see whether her face was there or not, see whether it had
been subjected to one of the auras she'd experienced as a
girl. But it wasn't megrim that had been with her. Similar
hurt, similar high, yet her face was there in the glass, eyes
gazing back at her, composed, sad, wanting to look defiant,
but unable.

❖

Can Xue—the writer, not her namesake—wrote a story
about a young woman who lived with her father, Old
Guan, in a wooden hut that was subject to whatever devas-
tation nature chose to visit upon it. When the wind blew,
the crumbly tiles on the roof were blasted with mulberries

that fell from the tree that grew over it. When it rained, as so often it did, the roots of the rosebushes surrounding the hut rotted, and the rose petals soured to a deathly white. Moreover, the hut flooded, and the young woman found it difficult to sleep, lying in the water as she must beside her father in the small bedroom in the hut. Old Guan was in a state of decline and decay, just as was his house, and whenever he munched on some crackers, which he dearly loved to do, especially as a snack in the night when sleep failed to come and take him into its gentle arms and lift him away from his widower's existence for a few starry hours, his teeth began to hurt, and he became convinced that the field mice ran in and out of his mouth, frolicking like mad through the black crevices they found there.

Old Guan prattled day in and day out about the state of his several teeth, and was moved to think many sentimental thoughts about this cracker and that, idly picking his nose as he curled into a corner of their common bed, while the rain dripped into the room and collected in the oil tarp they had spread over the bed in the hope of staying dry. But, as he did, the young woman mentioned something she had begun to notice lately: an ox, which circled the hut, free as it pleased.

The ox was not, of course, just any ox—not in such a black and blurry landscape as this that the father Guan and his daughter strove to pass their lives in. This ox raised cold sweat on the skin of the girl, as it walked lazily round the hut, its ass (which was the only part of the ox's anatomy Old Guan's daughter ever in fact saw, aside from its horn, which it occasionally drove through the wall, butting and bumping it) giving off a purple glow that pulsed, blindingly, and shimmered blue as a blister in the drizzle. We also learn, toward the end of the story, that the girl's mother, Old Guan's wife, had been a sort of minor thief, and having stolen her husband's sleeping pills (understandably, the insomniac hungers for something besides the same old dry crackers in the middle of his night) she ate them all herself so that she never had to worry about waking up anymore.

After all that, what finally happened was that Guan decided, in the wisdom of his years, to poison those nasty field mice that leaped and scurried through the vast cavities in his teeth, with some arsenic, which he planted in generous quantities on his tongue. Only after he did that did his daughter notice that the ox had fallen into the nearby river, to drown. Still, in its death throes, it managed to send up spectacular plumes of black smoke out of its nostrils, as it raised a hammer to smash the mirror on the wall in which Guan's girl habitually stared at herself.

Grace liked the story. In it, things happened unexpectedly, just as they did in Shahrazad's tales—just as they sometimes did in her own life. In the evening light, the steam escaped from vents and chimneys on the roofs and took on a thick, palpable presence, reminding her of the spumes that the suicide ox gave off as he went for his dip. It was funny—was she supposed to feel happy or sad about that ox drowning? How could it raise a hammer to smash a mirror in the hut at the same time as it had fallen, drowning, into a nearby river? What kind of life was Old Guan's daughter going to have there in the hut now that her crazy father and the obsessed bull were gone?

Deep down she must have loved them both, or else why would she have continued to live like that in the hut? She must have found comfort of sorts in her father's prattle; she must have been flattered by the doting ox that had courted her faithfully until he killed himself after finally understanding that his love for her was a big fat waste of time, because she was only in love with herself.

❖

Unless I called him, I would never know whether Li had left behind the book of Can Xue's stories by mistake or design. I found it on the black and white tile under the sink in the bathroom. When I opened it, there they were, as I might have predicted, his name, and his number. Subtle perhaps, but maybe just pedestrian, this bit of leaving a possession behind in order to create an excuse to get back in touch. Oldest trick in the, well yes, book—and yet, admittedly, a wise one, in that the temptation, the thread, was strong and drew me more quickly than I might have anticipated toward the desire to call.

What would he expect me to say? Tell him that what we had done was something I would never do with him again? Plead with him to give me a chance to try once more to get it right (but, of course, what was right?)—or apologize again for having so willfully spat out the cloth he'd placed in my mouth, and cried like some hapless puppy?

Maybe he really had forgotten the book in his anxiousness to leave. I changed the bed in the aerie, washed, and sat by the window, in a state of sudden, inexplicable contentedness. I thumbed through the book, which was well-worn from Li's readings. Or else from Li's readings and from those of all the other women he'd done this with . . . no, that made no sense, or I didn't want it to make sense, because how could he have retrieved the thing each time? As I was reading the story about the ox, the hut, the girl, the father, and the spectacular purple glow (lights seem constantly to be attracted to such sex-magnetized situations) I knew I'd be willing to try again with Li Zhang if he would give me another chance.

I dialed his number, no answer. The glass of wine, which I wasn't all that fond of drinking, seemed like a good idea, just to give myself a sense of what it must have been like to be Li Zhang with the wine in him. I folded up the scarves and put them away. I considered going out and simply depositing the book in a trash bin as I walked along toward home, but I wasn't ready to face Faw just yet—I was far too skittish and shaken for that. So, I phoned Zhang once more, and this time a woman, in her fifties or sixties, answered.

"Is Li there?"

"Yes. What?"

"Is Li Zhang there, please?"

"Who is calling."

Why not, why not tell her, after everything that had happened, I thought, and anyway Li knew where he could find me if he wanted to, so there was no possibility of anonymity left to me. "Grace Brush," I said.

"Hold on," the woman told me, and I slowed my breath as I studied the purple-blue bruise bracelet that had begun to appear around my right wrist and listened hard into the telephone, and wondered why the skin around my knuckles was marred blue, too. I couldn't remember him touching me there—a sympathy bruise. Was it exciting or not that a man whom I essentially didn't know and who had made these marks on my skin was about to speak to me?

Yes it was, no it wasn't. It was exciting yes because he'd given me the freedom to say to him whatever I liked. I could scream, I could demur, and he couldn't legitimately protest. He relinquished his right to withhold my freedom by having carried out his violence on me only to abandon it so abruptly just because I was—yes—enjoying it. Shame on him for having proposed such a thing and not shown the discipline to carry it out. He had just turned everything we were doing into a bunch of sexual amphigory, a burlesque, was what I began to think.

Exciting no (or was this a yes, too?) because no matter how hard I tried to convince myself otherwise, Li Zhang was, indeed, frightening, and I knew that for all my sudden interest in pushing out and out and away from what I felt to be the confines of my life, what Li'd gotten me to do, and all within a matter of minutes really, was unnerving.

Maybe I was unfit for such irredeemable acts, maybe deep down I was still a jittery little girl who preferred to keep this kind of behavior locked behind veils of fantasy, lodged in the mind where though it wasn't safe it was somehow controllable. Naturally, I hated that idea; no one likes to feel overprotected, to feel weak and unadventurous—we all want to feel as if we're stars, strong, vibrant, irrepressible. And it wasn't the case, anyhow, I reminded myself. It was Li who got a sudden fit of cold feet, Li who ran, impenitent and possibly even scared. I peered around the corner into the bathroom mirror to see if there was a bruise on my neck, assuming a violet line where the leash had embraced me might have begun to appear. The skin was lightly flushed with emotions or wine, but there was no evidence there that I'd been bridled like an untamed and ridiculous pet. It occurred to me that it was Can Xue's leash that had encircled and held me tight, its worn-smooth snaky length responding so personally to me as Li Zhang and I made love. Li had refrained from caressing or embracing me, I noticed. But the leather leash he had set down so kindly on the small of my back had comforted me while he sat there breathing, unmoving and unmovable, to give me just enough time to worry what he might do next.

Did he elect to remove the leash, to dress, and to disappear precisely because he sensed no fear coming from me? It seemed very possible that this might explain what he did. Can Xue, who had waited patiently in one corner of the room, curled up like a mink toque, had scrabbled on her dry old nails across the parquet to reclaim her leash. She could hardly wait to go. Hard call: maybe it's true, they were both just bored by me.

At the other end of the line I could hear hollow sounds now, voices talking, something muffled—again, I couldn't make out what was being said—and, after the voices stopped I was sure I heard footsteps and I cleared my throat and tried to get it straight in my head just what I was going to say to Li when he answered.

I needn't have troubled myself thinking about it, because what I heard next was the dial tone, which I listened to as if it were a meditator's mantra, an *omm,* for a while, think-

ing back to Can Xue's story and then musing what a
drowning ox's bellowings must sound like under the ripply
surface of a river.

❖

Berg, who had always assumed his sister's life was less
eventful than his own, or rather believed that whatever
adventures she struck out upon were confined to her imagination, was in fact leading a life that could be seen as less
engaged than hers. Having given up the characters (mythi-
cal, fantastical, whatever they were) of her childhood—or,
having been abandoned by them might be the more accurate way of putting it, since they drifted into a distance, and
became less accessible to her as time passed, until they
would not come to her no matter how much she might have
wanted them to return—Grace now had moved into a life
of the flesh; her encounter with Li Zhang might or might
not have been more frightening in some of its elements, but
it was more demonstrably "real." The way she knew this
was easy: if, indeed, Li Zhang had got it in his head to try
some of the things Desmond had done, he would probably
have had to kill her to actualize the idea. And though it
hadn't worked out, she didn't regret having given marriage
a whirl, superficial as it was. Though she still lived at
home—which Berg found kind of sad, deplorable even—
she did have secret lives and secret places in which she led
them. But Berg, could he make the same claims?
   He had never married. Massachusetts had been for him
a place of stunning boredom, made tolerable only by the
alcohol he smuggled into his room on campus. He was
considered rather an odd bird by his classmates. While they
were busy growing their hair and flooding their lungs with
hash and lazy pot, he declared himself an ascetic, didn't
believe in smoking, concentrated on drinking clear al-
cohols—gin, vodka, certain blonde tequilas and rums. He
wore his hair cropped tight to his skull, and carried a small

pair of scissors sheathed in a leather pouch with him wherever he went, in order that he might trim it wherever he was. He lost his virginity not in college, but when he returned to the city on visits, to crash around on the Lower East Side; it hardly mattered to him one way or another.

Alphabet City—the precincts between Avenues A and C—was the perfect place for him after he finished school, he felt, and the short hair reinforced his air of asceticism, as did, in its way, the slow drunk calm that most often was evident in his manner and response toward what few responsibilities he agreed to undertake on behalf of his father's businesses, whose sundry accounts he sometimes milked as it suited his particular needs. His father knew more or less what he was up to. He knew that the checks made out to unaccountable payees, or drawn for cash, went toward the support of some small mischief. It could have been anything. It didn't matter to Charles much because Berg had turned out so much better than he had ever had reason to hope; let him do whatever pleases him, so long as it remains under control, was Charles's tack.

Berg moved around. His home seemed naturally to be on the road. This habit of Berg's, which resembled his father's, began more and more to take him out of the city; it seemed logical to do a little troubleshooting for the Sprawl in exchange for fare and wage, which was what Charles offered. Berg appreciated the way Charles handled their dealings. It reminded him a little of *Mission Impossible* in that his father had someone else get in touch about what needed to be done and where, in that Berg always had the option to blow it off if he so chose, and in that there occasionally seemed to be a secretive element—Don't mention this to anyone, was a standard tag line, and in a way, whether he chose to admit it to himself or not, he liked that he was being trusted. The "missions" were usually not just possible, but quite easy. Given the itinerary mattered less to Berg than the need to be itinerant, to be on the roam, this father and son symbiosis worked well.

Grace and Faw were interdependent, too, but in a far more familial way. Grace did daughterly things, she coddled her father. Faw reciprocated. Like some lover off at war, he sent her things, flowers, notes, exotica from his travels, a blanket he found in the Southwest that he thought she might like, a Liberty scarf from London, some lace from France. They went through periods where they talked on the telephone nearly every day, just catching up.

While Berg kept in touch with Erin and Segredo, Grace remained distant. She wished she shared Berg's willingness to forgive, but still held them responsible for Desmond. It wasn't fair. It wasn't fair at all. But that anger was in her. She hoped that one day she would be able to release it, knowing it for the curse it was.

❖

So, was that the beginning and end of Li Zhang?

Possibly it was and if so why wouldn't I see it as an obvious blessing since, after all, I wasn't used to that sort of lovemaking, call it lovemaking, call it anger, or man-killing-woman hatred, even. Still, I wondered why I would come (because I did) like that, and, by Li Zhang's unspoken rules of the game, come too soon, come vocally, come without adhering to whatever thought he might have had of maintaining dignity, keeping to my role of relinquishment. I almost understood, and in understanding where I'd failed found that I was aroused again, was interested—what a sublime invalidation of the will, with all of the world's cranky and stupid mores to which it must answer, this kind of love could, if understood and practiced, mean. The heat from my ankles and wrists was exhilarating, I couldn't deny. Felt hot as a summer sunburn on Rams Island, and Li Zhang's refusal to keep it up after I broke the spell, even that could be viewed as a turn-on in the right context. He would say, You must, and I would say, Maybe I will and maybe I won't. It was a perfect game of sex, was the unexpected answer to questions I remembered asking myself as a child, about Samantha and Jeannie. Their men were such prudes, so lobotomized by their heritage and their work, so smoothed out by their upbringings that they were hardly there—I wondered if, behind their bedroom doors, anything at all ever went on. I couldn't imagine it possible. When I got married, myself, didn't Warne in a way turn out to be just exactly one of those men, an all too easily blown like a leaf Darrin? They were, each of these men, spiritual castrati, and nothing and no one could revivify them, given that they had never been enlivened in the first place. Well, I was different, by god, even though I knew that dominance is not the final key to vitality in a man toward a woman. Desmond's ghost had enlivened me, and now I was visited upon again—but who was Desmond's ghost if not Grace Brush? It was, in fact, not weird or cruel or in any way wrong, but the only thing to do, what I'd done with Li. It was the only way for us to find our balance. I felt sure I'd at least glimpsed what he had been after. Here had been a chance at obedience, a strong womanly willful obedience, a kind of obedience that emerges into a personality of strength beyond anger, and I'd blown it. I would do everything possible to get Li Zhang to give the thing another chance.

I decided to keep Li's Can Xue at the aerie. If it turned out that I couldn't get him back it would serve as a kind of remembrance. If, on the other hand, Li Zhang did sometime decide he wanted to meet me again, I would be able to make him a present of something he already owned. As neatly as I could, I tore out the front endsheet of the book, and hid the leaf of paper, with his address and number, between the mattress and boxspring of the bed. I locked up and went outside, trying my best not to look around at fellow pedestrians as I did, feeling myself to be the worst sort of conventional woman, unworthy of some of my idols, genies and witches, the most normal, stock, traditional, regulated and standard person on earth. Did the cab

driver recognize a schoolgirl's guilt in my eyes, and the
tone of my voice when I gave him the address to go home
to Faw? What did he care. All of a sudden I was shot
through with wistfulness. Wistful in kind was the twilight
sky, which gave off a thoroughly disheartened ox-purple
glow at every horizon and up into the stars.

❖

Cutts had no patience with women who were afraid of
being alone. Men, he told Bea, men had to spend so much
time by themselves, and here it was that women were always the ones who got away with turning the phrase
around, saying that men were the ones who couldn't ever
stand to be alone! While women slept soundly at night, who
was up, alone, pacing around, visiting the refrigerator,
looking at anything the television had to offer, finding
themselves caught up in the most mind-dulling adventures
like the one where the lady whale was swept into the shallow lagoon up in Nova Scotia, and the nice American family out on their sailboat trying to have their vacation was
also swept by the storm into this place where there was a
town full of redneck fishermen who had nothing better to
do than insult the family and shoot their rifles at the
stranded whale. It's men at night who find themselves
caught up in the drama of the lady doctor who lived among
all those rednecks, in a beautifully decorated house, and the
drama of the father of the family, who found himself more
and more involved in trying to save the whale, so involved
that he found himself falling in love with the whale and
swimming with her, looking into her brown and human
eye as he tried to do everything in his power to protect her
(Richard Widmark tried to help him help the whale, but his
ornery sons were far more powerful than he, and pushed
for selling the whale to the captain of the pirate whaler
anchored offshore), but not in the least understanding that
while he was no longer in love with his wife, who com-

plained about the abject conditions of the room in which they were put up until the parts came from the mainland so their sailboat could be repaired and they could go back home to Connecticut or wherever, he shouldn't be wasting his time falling in love with the whale, but should be considering how ecology-minded and desirable the lady doctor was—if he'd seen how lazy and boring was his wife, and how enamored of the local girls the two boys, their children, were, he might have begun to think about making a new life for himself with the doctor, and have even offered his wife the chance to stay on with them all in some sort of capacity, perhaps as a nurse or something. Or maybe they could be mature about it and remain good friends. But this whale stood in the way.

That kind of thing, that was what men, in their aloneness, were destined to suffer, Cutts thought, not without a little humor, of course, but not without some seriousness, either. So when he asked Grace how her weekend had gone, and she shrugged it off, he took it to mean that she'd been lonely and was trying not to make him feel guilty about having passed the holiday surrounded by family.

"Did you miss me?" was a brash bit of hubris but he thought he'd try it out on her anyway.

"You know what we've never done?" she said.

That was quite a deflection, and Cutts thought, best not to press it, and answered, "There's a lot of things we've never done, but if you mean spend a holiday together—"

"I don't care whether we spend a holiday together, I never liked holidays anyhow. Holidays are like killing fields for businessmen predators to pluck a little more money out of pockets that are already emptied."

"Uh, Grace—?"

"But what I was talking about was that we've never done like, I was thinking, there's things in bed, you know, that well, we've never tried."

Cutts was relieved that she wasn't going to complain about how his marriage kept them apart, but was disqui-

eted at the prospect of discussing sex with her. Sex was like
loneliness, agendas non grata, you didn't hold colloquies
about it, it was just something you did, and—"Look, there's
nothing I don't like about what we do, I like everything
about you, I think we have a really great—"

"You know, when we make love we always kind of do
it like, well, look right now. You've got your wine, how
come you always have to have that?"

"Because I need to wind down, Grace, I mean for christ-
sakes it's one-thirty in the afternoon—"

"That's not my fault."

"Oh, here we go."

"No, no, let me go on, I'm not complaining is all I'm
saying about the fact that it's in the day, I like that even,
that doesn't bother me. What I'm saying is look how you're
all comfortable there in bed, your clothes are on the floor
there—"

"Let me get this. You would prefer it to fuck standing
up with all our clothes on."

"That's a thought, but what I'm saying is don't you think
we ought to try different things out, like I mean who's
going to stop us, and we might learn things about each
other."

"Grace. I don't know what you are referring to. You're
going to have to get specific."

"Ah-oh, see? Now you're going to call me Grace, whenever you call me—"

"—Grace, why do you want to be starting something."

"I'm not starting anything, I mean, not in the bad sense."

"Well, what are you doing, then?"

"I'm just trying to talk."

"You're complaining."

"What complaining goddamnit I'm not complaining."

"Well, you're going to, listen to you I know this tone of
voice, I know where you're headed here."

"This has nothing to do with Bea if that's what you
mean."

"Of course it does, everything always comes back to that."

"Would you mind if I got an idea in here, it's hard enough as it is to try to talk about these things, but you've got me way off track. You're probably doing it on purpose because you don't want to listen to what I have to say because it might be something you don't want to hear."

"I'm all ears," he said, his voice trailing down toward its sarcastic flourish.

Who was this person? Grace thought for an instant, then said, "What I was going to say can wait," and while Cutts insisted that she finish her thought, even apologized, she decided to slip into bed with him without saying another word so that if he were going to be inside her he would have to get there through the fortress of all her clothing. At one point while he was kissing her he asked, "Aren't you too warm," and she answered no she wasn't, go on, go ahead, and she wrapped her fingers tightly around the cool iron filigree of the bed and pretended it gripped her back with equal strength, as Li Zhang's penis entered her body again in the guise of Cutts.

After she and Cutts had said good-bye to each other that day, she realized he hadn't noticed either her wrists or her ankles, which had darkened to a cinnamon blue, the tantalizing and arrogant color of a fox's tail, which shoots like a flash of fire into a hedge of equally haughty and same-brown bramble.

And Grace thought, Li . . . listen, what happened?

❖

Even as Bea, who brought her knife down through the faint green strings of celery, and noticed as she did how muscled her wrists had gotten (and thought, how'd that come about?—she'd always had the most delicate, wispiest of wrists) . . . even as she smiled at her vanity over something as silly as the delicacy of wrists and then went on with her

knife . . . even as she tried to persuade herself to think that
she shouldn't let her worries about this stuff take over her
mind, Cutts walked along the street and listened to the first
defiant birds of spring proudly calling out in the still-bare
trees and was himself thinking, from his different vantage,
just the same thought. No one has methods when caught
in such deceit, he reasoned. No one has all the answers
when caught in the midst of a refractory confusion, reasoned Bea. Everything ran in all directions at once, unlike
this celery. Everything was cross-grained and restive and
uncooperative, unlike this celery, which offered itself up
into squat crescents in the most pleasant and unargumenta-
tive manner. Knives do talk a strong language, thought
Bea. No messing around with a good sharp knife. Even
these wrists, as substantial and muscular as they are . . .

❖

There was in the book a dream, which was the dream of the
yellow chrysanthemum, and this story had in it another old
man, an odd old fellow named Old Jiang. Maybe I was tired
when I read it, perhaps I was confused by the story because
I was upset with both Cutts and Li, knowing all the while
that my anger was unavailing, and unfair, but the story
seemed to be even more mysterious than the one I had read
the day before, after Li left. Today, Cutts said good-bye to
me, like he always did, and I stayed on for an hour, as was
my habit, and tidied the bed and fussed about. I hadn't
made the same effort to hide the book as I had to hide its
flyleaf. It wouldn't have mattered, since Cutts hadn't noticed it on the bathroom sill. Was I right to be angry with
him? I hardly knew. I had no more right to be upset with
either of them than the young woman who told the story
of the dream of the yellow chrysanthemum had the need to
be embarrassed when she accidentally shot Old Jiang in the
arm with a steel pellet from an air gun. After all, hadn't she,
the young Chinese girl, been shooting at a helpless little

sparrow who had on its belly not a length of meat worth eating?

In this story the reader was led to believe one thing only to later discover it was another. At first I thought Old Jiang was going to be the girl's father, but later on I found out that he was her husband. By then, it seemed a fine point, hardly worth considering too deeply.

Old Jiang started up with his tricks long before the sun rose, assuming that the young woman would fail to notice his absence, as she seemed to be asleep still. Yet, none of us is ever as asleep as we'd like to be, or, in this instance, as asleep as others would like us to be. So when Jiang climbed up a ladder into the tree outside the house and started chopping away at it with his ax, he might have been sure she didn't hear him, but he was mistaken. Industriously, he wrapped up the severed limbs of the tree in torn sheets and, having swept up the chips of wood scattered at its base in order to conceal any evidence of his activities, he proceeded through the rest of his day happy as a lark in the knowledge that he'd done just as he pleased without anyone's knowing about it.

For her part, joining with him in his merry behavior, she shot him again with her air gun, this time wounding him in the ear. Guns are so hard to aim, aren't they? Try as you may try as you might to focus on your target, when it comes time to pull the trigger you can never be sure where the pellet will make its path. I began to like this story after all.

In a feeble attempt to complain about what had happened, Old Jiang mumbled, "One should have an accurate estimation of oneself," which struck me as a statement born out of the most advanced sort of senility, the sort that gave rise to the same kind of senile thought that Socrates, that old poseur, had worked up—Know thyself, dotty mole . . . like know thy preferred hole, boy, and go go go. This is where, still at the beginning of the story, I didn't know whether it was my being tired, or being upset, but I began

to feel that knowing oneself was a pretty silly accomplish-
ment, since it was hardly possible, was it, given that every
day you could do something that would make you who
might have been knowable before utterly incomprehensi-
ble now. And moreover, I knew I was less and less interested in Grace Brush than I was in Cutts and Bea and Li
and Faw and Berg and just about anybody else other than
myself.

But back to the story. I started to skim it. I learned things
about Jiang, that he had a long neck that he would crane
to see things outside the window from the bed, that he had
the wandering fingers of a lecherous idiot, which he let
crawl over the backs of dancing partners. I made some
coffee. The story was beginning to have on me the same
claustrophobic effect that Can Xue's leash had had, but
what was the promise of satisfaction?

The story came to the fall season. The sky was dark and
the nights seemed longer than the longest days of the summer. In town there was a man who went from door to door,
knocking with a bamboo pole. Old Jiang had an idea about
how he and the young woman ought to respond to this
threat: he proposed that the two of them sit back to back
and try their best to dream of tree toads in the rain.

The young woman was unable to do it, though, to dream
of the toads. She dreamed of black holes in the wall of her
room. She heard seas flashing against pebbly shores outside
and in her dream forgot how to walk, falling into soft mud
and nearly breaking her bones. The story got stranger—so
strange and unreliable that I skipped ahead. In the second
part of the story, the needs and behavior of a woman named
Ru-shu and "Old Thing" (which was what she called him)
were just as unusual as those of the earlier couple. Ru-shu
enjoyed crushing white worms between her fingers. When
she and Old Thing strolled along together, discussing how
they might rearrange their bedroom so that it would be free
of all vulgarity, he noticed that her jacket pocket was bulg-
ing. She told him that it was because she'd gathered roses,

and yet he knew that her pocket was full of the corpses of worms.

At the end of the tale my eye fixed on the line, "Whenever I touch the scissors, I cut out an endless chain of high mountains." Li Zhang had underlined the sentence.

It made me smile to wonder whether Zhang knew the game that Desmond and I had loved to play as children—Scissors, paper, rock. One . . . two, we would count with our fists, and when we both shouted "three!" we would form our hands to make paper (fingers out flat), rock (a fist of stone), or scissors (index and middle fingers snip-snipping). Paper you could wrap around rock, so paper beat rock; rock could smash scissors; scissors could cut paper. It was such a fun game. We played for hours, never tiring of it. And here it was, scissors cutting paper to produce endless ranges of rock. Now which of the three could be declared the victor in *that* round of scissors, paper, rock?

❖

After the encounter with Li, I started to get more and more restless. Seeing Cutts midday for an hour or two, and maybe once during the afternoon on weekends, had seemed in our first few months such a blessing—not that I wouldn't have wanted to see him more often, because I would have been happy, or so I told myself, to be with him all the time, day and night, to live with him and be the wife he now and then told me he felt I was. The steadiness of the relationship had become addicting, despite my inherent disgust toward complacency. I had to admit that the mere fact I was able to be with him at all made me feel grateful at first. But, more and more I'd come to recognize that Li Zhang and Can Xue—the writer—weighed against the balance of what Cutts and I had built in the aerie. Can Xue's houses whose roofs always leaked and whose walls were constantly in danger of being undermined, punched through, began to color the way in which I saw the place. What kind of refuge was it, finally? And, by extension, what kind of osprey was I—a clawless, hopeless, flightless beast?

To complicate matters, I began to notice that not a day went by without my thinking about Li. I couldn't remember what he looked like. I remembered that his eyes were wide-set and that his eyelashes were very long. I remembered thinking his voice was earthy and low, which seemed unusual for a Chinese. I must have been wrong about that detail, I thought. I remembered spitting the gag, and remembered how full he seemed inside me. And I could remember how cold the room felt when he'd laid the warm leash on my back and just sat there, saying nothing, slowly withdrawing. That was all, and it might have been a lot, in fact, but it seemed like nothing. I couldn't remember, for example, what he'd been wearing.

Most of all I found myself dwelling on Li's refusal to speak with me on the telephone. I began to turn it around and around in my head, and wondered what really could have happened that one brief time we were together to so revolt him he never would want to have anything to do with me again. I tried the number, a week later, at first thinking that perhaps it hadn't been Li's home I'd reached the first time. I was willing to doubt what I thought I knew as fact, because it wasn't as if I had spoken with Li himself, or would have even been able to swear without a doubt that his was among those muffled voices I heard in the room that first time I called, before I was cut off. When I tried again, however, there was no question I had reached Li—he never announced his name, but the throaty, cadenced words of the message on the phone machine were from his mouth (though it was so unlike Li Zhang to have put such bland and orthodox instructions on the tape: "Thank you for calling, no one's here right now to take your call, so if you'll leave your name, telephone number, and any brief message").

I left my name and number. Then, some days later, having heard nothing, I left my name and number and the message, "I'd like to see you."

I stayed in the aerie for hours, alone, not wanting to miss his call. All I could do was hope that he wouldn't phone me when Cutts was there. He didn't—he didn't call at all. Some days later, I told his tape, "Li, it's Grace, I don't know why you're not calling me back, I can't get into the details about how I don't think it's such a big deal that I did that little thing I did, I mean how am I supposed to know?—that is, this is ridiculous, I don't even know who's hearing this, but, well . . . okay." And I hung up, and then called right back, adding rather maliciously—malicious in the sense that if he had a wife she would at least take him to task, make him explain who this madwoman was, and if nothing else perhaps that would provoke him into response—"Oh, it's Grace again. What I wanted to let you know was that I have your book here, the Can Xue, and I wanted to get it back to you. I read it. I hope your dog's okay. Let me know where I should send it, the book." And, as an afterthought to the afterthought, I added, in the full knowledge that whatever reserve I had previously had available to me was now utterly lost, "Your earliest attention to this matter will be most appreciated."

I wished I had never said a word—it was a good example substantiating one of Faw's cardinal rules in practicing business: Always sleep on it. If they offer you the world, tell them you'll have to sleep on it, that you'll get back to them; if they offer you shit, tell them you'll sleep on it, and what you do is, rather than sleep on shit, buy a little time to figure out how best to make them eat it themselves. It reminded me of one of Faw's most impressive moments, and how I wished I had been savvy enough to have used the same line (though in my father's case, no doubt some sizable deal was in the balance). He was on the phone, at home. One of the principals on the line said something threatening to him, who knows now what he could have said to evince this gem: "You kick my cat, I'll kill your dog."

And moreover, Li Zhang was no fool. He would see through the operettalike sarcasm of my "your earliest attention" line with ease. No, here was a missed opportunity, and I knew I couldn't call again, that the time for editing my pronouncements was past.

Li Zhang never returned any of my calls, and in the absence of a response I found myself growing more and more in need of being in touch with him. One afternoon in May, two months after our encounter, I got the piece of paper out from its hiding place, intending to try him one last time, to say to the machine that it was an anniversary of sorts, to say that I would leave the book in the foyer of the building so that he could pick it up whenever he felt like it, and without having to bother to see me, of course. But what I did, after running my finger round the rotary, is I began to cry. How ridiculous, and I saw that my tears had fallen onto the paper and caused some of the numbers and letters there to run. "Just ridiculous," I said aloud, and crushed the paper in my fist. I made it to the bathroom and dropped it in the bowl of the toilet, pushed hard on the lever. I had to flush more than once to coax it down into the miles of subterranean pipes where all the waste of the city flowed along, a pitch of twisting mire in which strange albino animals winnowed about and mated and nibbled. Okay, I decided, I'll keep the Can Xue. Enough was enough. If I left it in the foyer, Li would never turn up to retrieve it, someone would take it home with them and put it in their bookcase, or else use it under the leg of a wobbling table.

I read from the flap copy that Can Xue was a woman my own age, in her middle thirties; I found myself wondering what Can Xue's house was like—did she write at night or in the morning? did she sit in a chair or on a mat? what color ink would someone use ideally when writing tales such as these? No, no—given the calm unkindness of Li Zhang's silence, I knew that Can Xue was mine now.

❖

More weeks passed. The sun pulled back up into the expanses of sky overhead. I felt the warmth amassing in the new leaves of the trees and could hear it rising in the birds' songs, and through the course of those weeks in which spring gave itself over to history, I gave up that odd need to feel myself connected to, in possession of, Li Zhang. As the days pushed Li further and further back into the past, I began to realize the obvious: that I wasn't going to be able in the least to hurt Li by taking some sort of emotional possession of Can Xue and her stories. He didn't care. I wasn't proving anything to anyone.

And yet, despite a renewal of my commitment to Cutts, which I newly promised myself I would protect and nurture, I did notice that for no particular reason I'd grown more friendly toward people, mostly strangers, mostly men, than I could remember myself ever having been before. This amicability, this benign fondness for everyone, was (was it possible it all came down to such a frivolous little word like) fun. But, yes, the little world around me became fresh, and its confines seemed to fall away. Who was I to complain about that?

So, there was a shift, and like the broken shards of transparent rock tumbling in the chamber of a kaleidoscope, everything shifted with me. I was positive and expansive, and more loving than ever toward Cutts; I helped Bea with her (late) spring cleaning—a putative adventure for each of us, since neither of us really minded clutter or dust or the faint patina of mildewed air—and we spent an afternoon drinking pots of coffee until we were giddy, careful not to throw away anything that might be useful to someone else, setting out sweaters gone at the elbows on the stoop for

anyone who might want to have them—and not once did
I think any of my bad thoughts about Cutts, and how he
had two women and shouldn't; not once did I allow jealousy toward Bea to crowd in upon me. I came very close
to telling Bea about Li Zhang, and what had happened, but
caught myself before I'd made the mistake. My guard was
down, and it felt good. It was one of those idyllic moments
when I found myself wondering why we couldn't just all
come out and tell each other the truth about what was
going on among us, and take the decision to live somehow
together with one another. I held on to the sensation as
long as I could, without testing my conclusion that it would
never work.

Post-Zhang, I was determined to behave the opposite of
Can Xue's women, who were all so tormented, a condition
into which I imagined Li perhaps would enjoy having
thrown me. I would spit out the gag more than once now,
in a manner of speaking, since he refused to tell me why
I shouldn't. I would make it my business to live with a
bright heart, just as had Mother all those years ago when
we moved out to Scrub Farm—except that where Mother
had failed, I assured myself I would succeed. So I decided
to fix up the aerie—what a shame Bea couldn't be with me,
given what a time we would have!—and hung a painting of
a pretty Rhineland valley autumn scene, with cattle under
trees and curlings of smoke trailing up from cottages in the
village like so many green bracelets into the clouds. I laid
a colorful rag rug on the floor and I brought some of my
favorite clothes from Faw's to give the empty closet some
life, some sense of home. I asked Cutts to help me paint the
place, and the hours we spent doing it were among the best
we ever had together since we'd become lovers.

❖

When Li Zhang called, Cutts answered the phone expect-
ing to hear Grace's voice at the other end. She'd left him

a note on the pegboard—another recent domestic addition to the aerie—saying she had to run an errand, and she'd be back in half an hour.

The windows in the studio were open, letting a fresh fluttery wind feed through. Cutts squinted into the distance. He'd never noticed how much the iron-embroidered fire escapes resembled the filigree in that ornate Iranian jewelry that Grace liked so much. Should he buy her a necklace, or some earrings, to celebrate this renaissance of the aerie? he wondered. He glanced down at his shoes. One of the laces had frayed, and looked as if it might break sometime soon. He was sure there was a shoe repair shop on the corner downstairs; he'd have to remember to stop in after they left.

"May I ask who's calling?"

Li Zhang told him his name.

To which Cutts responded, "She's busy right now. Can I ask what this is regarding?"

"You can ask," Li Zhang said, not mysteriously, just flatly, and Cutts waited for him to go on, but when he didn't began to shift his attention from the shoelace to the tightening he sensed in his throat, so that when he repeated, "What is this regarding?" his voice had made a climb, and betrayed anxiety. Having heard the subtle change, Li said, "May I leave her a message, please."

"All right."

"Just tell her I called, would you please, and that she can call me whenever she gets a chance."

Cutts maneuvered his voice back to timbre. "All right. What's the number?"

"She has the number."

"I'll tell her you called," attempting indifference.

"Thank you," and he hung up.

What struck Cutts first about his own response to this call was how it bothered him that Li Zhang hadn't asked him his name. That Li was so blandly straightforward about giving his own name suggested to Cutts there was nothing much amiss here, nothing to be suspicious of, though naturally he had to wonder how it was possible someone had the aerie number—unlisted—and obviously knew Grace, but whom Grace had never so much as mentioned in passing to him. Six months ago, when things between himself and Grace were rocky, that tickling tightness he'd felt gathering in his voice might have choked him, and would no doubt have sent him flying after Grace in a rage of questions. But now, aside from that brief, physiological tic in his throat, which he'd easily restrained, he didn't have a bit of rage available to fuel jealous questions. In fact, what he concluded, as he heard Grace's footsteps coming up the stairs outside, was not to tell her about the call. Nothing ventured, nothing lost. The only conclusion he could draw was that this guy was some kind of delivery person, or something—conceivably, this Li Zhang was instructed that if Cutts happened to answer the telephone he should not let on what he was calling about. Yes, Cutts had figured it out. Grace had bought him a present, and it was to be a surprise. Now for sure he'd have to go out and buy her those earrings.

Discreetly, Li waited several days before resigning himself to having to make another call. He tried at different times, day and night, but didn't get through until she answered late morning the week after he'd spoken with Cutts.

"What do you want?" she said, even before he had finished saying his name.

"Didn't your friend give you my message?"

"What message—I don't know what you're talking about."

"The man who answered the phone, he said he'd tell you that I called—" (silence followed, and finding himself out on a limb he went on) "—I don't know what his name—but, look I, I was calling in part because I wanted to tell you that Can Xue died, she just fell asleep last week after our walk and didn't wake up again."

Grace found it impossible to read the flatness of Li's vocal tone, and dipping into her hurt over the way he had treated her, she managed, "So what."

A silence expanded through the white noise in the line.

She picked up, "No, I mean, I'm sorry to hear that, she was a nice dog and all, but I don't see what I'm supposed to say about it. What can I say? You and I have an awful lot of problems for two people who've only spent about an hour and a half together. I don't understand why you didn't call back. I don't understand why you left like that. I really don't understand who you think you are just calling me out of the blue and leaving your name with, with this man you don't even know who he is or whether it's going to affect—"

"I'm sorry. I couldn't call—okay?"

She considered hanging up. These telephones, weren't they invented for convenience and privacy in communication, and just look what they did—scuttle privacy and make life hard. Li didn't deserve the consideration she was giving him. "Oh, ah. You couldn't call," she said, sardonic. "Well you seem to be able to now, don't you."

"I had my reasons for what I did."

"I suppose you had your reasons for leaving me in that ridiculous position, too, right?"

"You weren't, look, I had my reasons, I did what I did— it wasn't like you weren't able to get free."

"Look, Li, I didn't mind what you did, okay. You don't have to make any explanations to me for what you did. It's what you didn't do that bothers me."

"It's none of your business why I did or didn't do whatever. I've apologized once. That's it, now stop."

Grace was surprised: leashlike words. Fair enough, she thought. He hadn't asked her to explain who Cutts was, after all. "So why the call, you want your book back?"

"What book, I don't care about any book. I want to see you."

"No, I don't think so, Li."

"I understand if you don't want to but I want you to know I do."

"You understand?—you don't understand anything at all. I'm seeing someone, I can't do what I did with you, you hear me? I shouldn't have done it in the first place."

Li Zhang was quiet. Grace sensed his nonresponse couldn't have been because he was upset that she had someone else; Li's was not a jealous temperament. "I don't get it."

Grace almost said—and it would have been smooth repartee if she had, she knew—Well, Li, I don't get it either; but what she said was, "What's there to get? Look, I've got your phone number and what I think I'll do is I'll think about all this. I'm not saying no, but what I'll do is I'll call you if I feel like it. All right? If you want your book back—"

"Keep it, keep it."

"—I can leave it downstairs or something but we better leave things where they were before you called."

"Fine, Grace," he said, so uninflectedly that there was no chance of deciphering what the words could have had as their emotional core. She began to construct an image of him in the room he was in, tried to decipher what his face must have looked like when he said "Fine," and "Grace," talking to her on the telephone—because he was saying something, and she wasn't listening—maybe now feeling some frustration at her not giving in to what he wanted. It was just then she wondered why was it she was at the same time so willing to believe that what Li Zhang wanted from her were things she wanted to give him, but didn't know how to give him, and yet she was always denying him, too? How did that work? Denying him the chance to go ahead and make love to her just as he pleased, after inviting him up to the aerie to let him have his way, in fact—denying him the chance to see her, after she had called him up and left all those transparently pleading messages on his machine. What did she want? Why would he bother to have anything to do with her? It seemed all so far beyond Shahrazad and Samantha and Jeannie and even beyond Can Xue, that she knew she couldn't rely on things she felt she understood. She'd have to risk exploring new ground, and felt for an instant a sense of extreme spiritual agoraphobia.

A healthy dose of cynicism toward this line of self-inquiry might have been useful, but even when she muttered—maybe even aloud—"Right . . . fine," to reduce Li Zhang to an ant or else anything, it hardly mattered what just so long as it was lowly, just to break him down the more for having ignored her, she found she couldn't summon that up either, and instead was cutting in on him, saying, "All right, when do you want, when are you free?" He said he was free now, and she said, "In an hour," and just as they hung up Cutts's keys rattled at the door, and he came in, all smiles, and handed her a small box tied with a gaudy crimson ribbon.

❖

What was wrong with me that I felt shot through with the most exhilarating combination of guilt, nervousness, and amusement when I put on the earrings he had given me, knowing that there was a strong chance that Li would be taking them off, or filliping them where they dangled loose flashing their little mercurial beaks (the earrings were stainless steel hummingbirds)—how had it happened that after all we had been through together I could so quickly have outgrown Cutts? I could locate in my heart not one bit of ambiguity with regard to this moral lassitude, this ethics-free brilliance I suddenly felt, kissing him good-bye, getting him out of the aerie so that I could be left alone for a few minutes before this other man was to arrive. I didn't feel empty, I felt indifferent. The desire to see Li Zhang must have been building up inside, I told myself, for it to have gone like this, for it to have occurred both so suddenly and with such ease. And just when I thought I had gotten him—like Christians try to get the devil—behind me.

When Li Zhang turned up, however, I was conscious of a shift back toward Cutts-attachment; Zhang seemed very different without his dog with him. He seemed a little like an amputee. And, of course, he wouldn't have the leash with him today, which made me feel—and a ridiculous irony this was—less trusting toward him, less comfortable in his presence.

"That's too bad about Can," I offered.

He frowned when I leaned away from his kiss. "I miss her," he said.

I was grateful for the sound of a baby crying, and a mother yelling, in the distance, as it brought into the aerie a kind of sense of there being other people nearby. A silence began to get awkward, and I broke it saying, "Here's your book."

"Grace?"

"What," and I focused on his mouth. It was dry-brown, somewhat heavier than I remembered. He was wearing, I was pretty sure, the same clothes he wore last time, gray trousers, gray scarf, white shirt, the heavy aubergine boots; like a uniform.

"I'd like to start over," he said, softly emphatic, eschewing the preliminaries—though, of course, we two had yet to bother with preliminaries—even as he proposed them. "Do you think that kind of thing is possible to do?"

"Very artificial."

"That may be, but I'm willing to try."

This sudden direct communicativeness, and its gentle tone, seemed discrepant with the uniform, the lips, and everything I recalled about the way he'd acted before. Why did I find it provocative rather than merely incoherent? "What do you do for a living, Li?" and sat down at the table—pressing on with the thought, All right, give him a chance to reveal himself, small talk, so what's to lose?

"Fold shirts."

Insipid; why was I always asking myself, Who is this guy? why do I feel this way? "No, really—here you are telling me you want to start over again and then you fall back on some stupid racial humor, and that's how we're supposed to get to know each other?"

"What makes you think I want to get to know you?"

That was him, there he was. "I'm not asking you to get to know me, I'm asking you about yourself because I think it might be a good idea to know a few things about *you*."

"There's nothing to know."

"You think I should care that your dog died, care that you want to begin again whatever the hell that means, let you call me when you feel like it but not return my calls, not answer any questions—"

"I answered your question. I fold shirts, sometimes I deliver them when the regular kid is out sick."

"Oh come on—"

"I don't know why you find that so hard to believe. Grace, I think you ought to stop with the questions. What I think is I think you ought to take your dress off."

"We didn't need to take anything off last time."

"Yes, but this time I want you to take it off."

"Why should I?" now seeing how the uniform complemented orders.

"Because that's why you let me come over here."

"I let you come over because I wanted to see why it was you were bothering me, I mean, why you were on my mind—but now I don't think I want to know."

"I was on your mind because you liked what we were doing and probably you didn't do that before with anybody and you wanted to do it again."

"Oh, listen to this. Who fled the instant things started to warm up? Not I, I can tell you."

"I didn't say anything to the contrary. That's a different question. Women's minds always work in tangents."

"Why did you leave like that?"

"I left because you were missing the point."

Grace more or less laughed. "What point?"

"Take off your dress, Grace."

"What?"

"You heard what I said—it's what you want me to say, I can tell. I think you ought to just do it."

"What if I do?"

Li Zhang crossed his arms. He wished he had a cigarette, I could tell. He seemed bored, a fact that perturbed me enough that I got up and walked over toward the bed, saying, "There's no point to it, it's just—what's the point?"

"You had it—'the point'—when we met, when we were walking along that day, and then you had it for a while here, and then you just lost it, you just reverted back to whatever it is you usually are which is what I was hearing on the phone machine and which is why I couldn't call you back, you weren't even the same person, how was I supposed to call you back and talk to you, I didn't even know who you were."

Li Zhang I didn't much like I now began to know, but I thought that for all his cheerless rhetoric he was close to, indeed, identifying something that might be valuable to me, not with regard to any relationship with him—which in any case I now knew for certain I wouldn't want, wouldn't allow—but having to do with myself, or Cutts, or maybe even Desmond, who knew? I tried to deliberate but found myself undoing the catch at the back of my dress. Curiosity.

This time, he didn't bother to tie me up. I didn't require restraint. I lay there, face down, my cheek resting on the back of my hand, and let him fuck me. He didn't kiss me, and he didn't make a sound when he came—having withdrawn—on the sheets. I had internalized and narrowed my concentration so that I didn't much notice him as he cleaned the sheets with a dampened paper towel. I could sense Li hovering over me and knew him just well enough to understand that if I didn't turn over and say something to him—anything, disparaging, affectionate, anything—he would probably now remain silent. It was my theory that behind his need for this impersonal sex, this conceit of making love only in the most distant manner possible, was just another person to whom intimacy was terrifying, literally, beyond words. I would have felt sorry for him if I didn't know better than to bother. What I was beginning to feel then was a remote kind of gratitude hazed a bit by the sense of how deplorable, how squalid and dreary was all this behavior. The gratitude was what I found most interesting. Yes, I was grateful, not for the introduction to this mild sort of sadomasochism he took it upon himself to practice on me—*mild*, to be sure, given that I, in my childish imagination, had conjured far more potent, more violent and abnormal scenes with Desmond's ghost than anything Li could conceive of; no, it was this: I had begun to feel grateful toward Li Zhang because he seemed to have broken my bond with Cutts. There was some part of me, I would be a liar not to admit, a part that I may never understand that liked the feeling of helpless pleasure. It's taken me a long time to admit that to myself. But the sense that I might have achieved an unexpected severance from Cutts through it was overwhelming. Zhang's love was an instance of plain, unalloyed immoral activity making the way for another chance at finding a life in which there might be some fresh ethic. I was reminded of how sometimes out at sea on those huge oil platforms—I had never seen one except on the news on television, burning vividly on the screen—the only way to extinguish a fire raging hot down in the well was to deprive it of oxygen by detonating an explosive that would itself create more fire than there was air to feed it.

This dominator—it made me scowl to know that I should laugh at having been so gullible, or so needy as to be able to allow for someone like Li to undertake such a role—had left a note. "I'll call," it read. He'd taken the book, which was fine by me because the first thing I did when I pushed myself up off the bed and stood up in the aerie, head twinkling with adolescent, if painless, fireflylike lights, was to call the telephone company and give them a disconnect order. I dressed—taking my time, for there was no need to hurry—and left the aerie, knowing I would never come back here again. I didn't bother to make up the bed, it didn't matter. I didn't bother to lock the door because there wasn't a single object inside the place that I would want to have—except for my favorite starfish, a flare-man pink example with only four legs, a rather pathetic little mutilated fellow, which I slipped into my pocket for good luck, and maybe as a cautionary memento. If a burglar removed the entire contents of the aerie it would only save me the trouble of having to hire someone to go in and remove everything down to the street.

By the end of the week, who knew where that charming Dutch idyll would hang. Would it lend its warmth to some other preposterous hearth, or wind up as tinder in a Bowery can fire, where it might keep some ruined soul warm?

To me it was all the same. Let to it happen whatever would happen, was how I viewed it, let it all come down.

PART IV

THE
ALMANAC
BRANCH

We come to the crisis now, or rather it comes to us. It had been, I know, imminent for years, but the first frightening glimpse I had of it was in the eyes of that man who showed up at the door a few weeks ago. I shouldn't have let him in. But he seemed serious, with his serge suit, his rain-blue tie, his immaculate pomaded black hair all bespeaking some deep, sincere purpose, and he said he was from the National Council of Churches, and there was something about him that suggested to me he had come to help us, or at least act kindly toward us. So I invited him in, and he accepted coffee, and asked whether it would be too much trouble to put some cinnamon in it.

Like any observer, I could claim that none of what he wanted to discuss had anything to do with me. Still I wonder how I can have been a presence in the lives of my father and brother and not have had any influential say in the decisions they've made. The three of us are linked—through blood, through shared experiences, through an unholy labyrinth of contractual papers—and yet we have operated as if we were individuals, knowing nevertheless that nothing one of us does can fail to have at least some effect on the other.

Clues there have been, of course; if I had truly wanted to understand how Geiger worked, and asked, with insistence, direct questions of Faw and Berg, I might have come to some of this earlier. Not that either of them would have been able—call that willing—to articulate the pertinent truths about Geiger's phony church.

I can't help but think I'd have been able to protect them from themselves, and from others, if I had known. The little girl running over the dunes in an overlarge bear suit that reeked of urine and mothballs, whose brother chased her with his primitive camera, his recording eye, regretting she was not as wild and strong as he was, and who looked down on her sensitivity as weakness all those years, is the same person who now may have to find the strength to hold our lives together. If this man in the serge suit asked me to come up with a metaphor for where Berg and I stood— tableaux vivants in some museum of late-twentieth-century American hybrids—now, almost two decades later, I'd have no quarrel with letting that image from our childhood stand. Except that now I would follow Berg. And rather than him threatening me I would threaten to bring his sprint to an end. A couple of calls, that would be it, from what I can tell. What he has concocted with these Trust monies deserves to be brought to an end, no doubt. He has learned too well from Faw's dark side, and in his efforts to grow up, and be absolved of having been his father's son, he has ended up baptizing himself in dirty water. He can take his cameras, far more sophisticated than any he ever dreamed of as a child, down to the orchard and over the dunes now where the tide is rising, but what he hopes to find there is gone. I'm not the person he thinks I am, in the same way I wasn't the girl he thought I was. I would challenge the value of any history he might want to try to wrap me, or any of us, up in. His *Almanac* branches from strange roots—and it is not so much that he has been using the money to finance pornography. It's that he's been using the money to make more money. That is what they don't like. And the years he spent dancing in the shadows of Faw, in some ways emulating him, in other ways just manipulating him right back, what use were they, if in his one big attempt at liberation he has only—ironically, and pathetically—brought himself deeper into his father's orbit?

As for my father, on the other hand, I wouldn't have been able to think of a metaphor. He has wandered and proliferated. He has been a continuous flow of ideas. He has long since, I believe, lost track of the mariner's church with its eccentric Unitarian pastor, and its few families who attend its occasional services and are pleased to get a free meal now and then from the refectory in the rear of the building, and drink the wine left over from communion. While I find it hard to believe that he hasn't got some knowledge of the surpluses that this Trust has amassed over the years, until now never critically scrutinized by anyone, the result of luck and del Russe's quiet brinkmanship, I believe he truly doesn't understand what the Almanac branch means.

So, the man sat with his coffee and asked questions. He put them in a way (the guy was clever) that didn't totally disarm me, but did give me no sense that he posed any threat. Had I known, or even suspected his motives, I would have shown him to the door—or else confused him with a bundle of answers that would have sent him off after another scent altogether. But for a quarter of an hour I did respond. It embarrasses me to record, though I must, that there was some vague sense in this procedure, and in his very politeness, that the council was going to bestow some award on the Trust. If only I had asked.

Oh yes, I had a clear childhood memory of the trip Berg and his father took together down to the islands, when the corporation was first being set up, though of course my brother Berg didn't comprehend at the time what its function was to be, or for that matter anything else about it. It was a funny question, reaching so far back in our family history, but it didn't seem incriminating. He crossed his legs, and took his glasses off, and put them on again. Yes, I remembered the dinner party where some of my father's associates—several of those figures who toiled in the more obscure branches of the Sprawl, Pannett and—

"Neden, Patrick Neden?"

Well, yes, Neden sounded right, but they were men whom I had never met before nor since, but whose names occasionally wafted by, whom Faw was never much willing to talk about, and about them I knew nothing. I hadn't even known that Neden's given name was Patrick. Was it?

"If it is the same Neden," he said.

How did you know about that dinner? I asked.

Someone else had told him about it, no big deal, he assured me. He was jotting some of this down. Did I remember anything more about the party? But I wasn't seeing how this tied in to anything that would interest the National Council of Churches, I told him. It felt a little like the first time I tasted champagne, which was just what Berg had told me it would be like, just as he had remembered it when Faw proudly announced that his oldest son was being made a vice-president in the Trust.

"That's Burke?"

Berg, we call him.

"Berg," noting it.

Because his fingers, well he didn't need to know that, and I was wondering what he did need to know, wouldn't it be easiest to ask me in so many words, but I was remembering how that night Berg had quite a case of the swirlees, and a hangover the morning after that grand dinner. Of course I wasn't going to tell this man any of that. It wasn't any of his concern. He asked about the church and if I could tell him anything about its connection to this wonderfully generous donor, the Gulf Stream Trust. I don't know about the church, but as for Cape Hatteras, where it is, it was always my understanding that this was the northernmost location on the Eastern seaboard that the Gulf Stream truly touched. I knew that my father loved coincidences—as in, things coinciding.

"Well, it is a marvelous program," the man smiled, which put me back at ease. I asked if he would leave his card, so that my father could be in touch with him. He left it on the table in the foyer when I was letting him out, but when I went back to look at it, half an hour later, it was gone.

Maybe I wasn't wrong to have trusted him, I thought, but when he left, I felt a weight in my chest and a megrim's heat played around my temples. I pondered, in my own insular and too-sweeping manner, that evil worked best when it was pitted against love. Love just isn't as strong a force as evil. Look at my experience, evil having taken Desmond away, having polluted my few attempts at making love work for me, and who would I be to contradict it? I put the cup in the sink, and stared at the windows of the building across the way, hoping maybe that something might happen in them that would distract me; they were a blank, though. Back in the study, I took up the envelope the visitor had left behind. From the papers he'd left with me for Faw to consider—which I then took out and read (since the envelope was unsealed)—my opinion of evil expanded.

While I am tending to business, there is another matter I want to address. I hadn't understood it until I went back and reread this, my almanac, hoping to discover some common thread of thinking through it all. It is well known that we least understand what is right there in front of us. How strange it is then to look over these other pages, my pages, and come to the realization that my almanac has turned out to be so much a sexual history. I would never have guessed that it would turn out like this. Everything I have said, for what it's worth, is the truth. Even so, I stand before myself and confess that my life has been largely led in solitude. I've been married to a husband not even for a hundred days before retiring back into myself; so weak was my sense of being a wife that I have never been compelled to push for a divorce. Cutts was not impressed enough with my way of leaving him to raise much of a protest—indeed, I think he might have felt relieved to know I *was* still married and thus less threatened his own marriage. Maybe I was becoming too much of a burden on his sense of personal innocence—he let me leave, and doesn't seem to mind that I hardly ever call him and Bea anymore, haven't seen them for over a year. There is not a woman I know—and, I admit, I don't know that many in any deep way, outside Erin, and Bea, and Djuna—who I feel is not as sexually

experienced as I, and yet look. Bea and Erin I am convinced
have never encountered a Li Zhang in their lives. Erin, I
am sure, has never had an affair: the moment she slept with
Segredo was the moment she must have known she was
going to come clean with Faw and leave the family; to her,
this must have been the only honorable equation. Bea, I
happen to believe, has never cheated on her husband, or if
she has it was an uncomplicated, trivial, almost impercepti-
ble flash of curiosity. Neither, to be sure, has Djuna on
hers, even after she passed into widowhood. So where does
this place me? What does it mean I've been, or am? The
thread I discovered is not one I'd have predicted would
trace its way through the center of my life. Even in the face
of what I've disclosed, I consider myself retiring, ingenuous, and, yes, hardly "sexed-up." I have had some lovers
since I walked out of the aerie and back into my Brush life.
None of them in any way involved with the Sprawl, just
casual things, more or less haphazard as that first encounter
with Zhang, infatuation being a state of mind I have now
thoroughly discarded as a trashy waste of time. The travail
of intimacy seems too hard to press on with given how
probable it is that whatever I get myself into will fail. And
how much should I trust a self who reviews her history
with men and, despite all, still senses that Zhang's malice
was the closest pass at perfect release that love has to offer?
Maybe, in the end, it isn't that I am sexually inexperienced,
but rather sexually detached, disengaged, disinherited.

"You don't know a house until you've spent some time
in its basement, you don't know a house till you've lived in
its attic," one of my teachers at school said once. We were
reading Emily Brontë or Mary Shelley, or one of those old
Gothicists, where these two extremities of the house are the
loci of mystery and where the key to understanding those
who have dwelled in the house is hidden. Cellars are dark,
and dug into the earth, where the chthonian spirits venture
through fissures in the loam to blow their noxious air into
the intruder's gaping mouth. Attics, the other extremity,

are where we store things we no longer want to look at or live with on a daily basis—worn-out furniture, dated clothing, broken typewriters, and back in the olden days, insane relatives. Everything between them is where we live and would just as soon keep living.

At Scrub Farm the cellar was merely a place to put things if you secretly wanted them to be destroyed by rust or mildew. Erin told me in one of her letters (it made me think she wanted to come home, that she missed us and simply had lost the way back), told me that she believed Faw stored her suitcases in the cellar because deep down he never wanted her to leave. It is possible; he, like me, has never remarried, is something of a monk from what I can tell. And given that he works so much by intuition I'd not put it past him to have "thought" that far ahead, when we first moved into the house out on Shelter.

So what about the attic? Am I stretching my metaphor out of form to look on the attic as a place of exposure, as an analogue to this film of Berg's that Djuna has called me, all in hysterics, to tell me about? Maybe so, but if I hadn't had those experiences with intimacy and its estimable, if often bloodless, procedures and ends, then I might have a narrower-minded reaction to this film that my brother is in the midst of making. My reaction is not narrow, though. And it has everything to do with attics, with doing things that we think of as dark and damp as cellars can be, but revealed in a lightness and warmth we associate—or, at least I do—with attics. Moreover, attics have windows, often architecturally whimsical affairs shaped like half moons, or triangles, and if I were in an attic I would be able to look down upon his gestures, and watch him putting other people, actors, through the paces he seems to think might explain our own, and I would open that window and cry out "It's all a lie" to the lot of them moving about like Gumby's ant enemies, descended from the widow's walk to the orchard to prey upon its fruit, below.

❖

The rite of passage—call it a rite, call it passage—from producer to writer-director had been simple for Berg, though he knew it might be more difficult for his colleagues to accept. Berg had lost his creative impulse, as we all are susceptible to doing, in his early twenties, and if Faw had intended to sterilize him, redirect him a little, by sending him to that private school, limit him, and hone him in a bit so that he would loop back into the Sprawl, take up with its activities, be his father's son, he succeeded handily. At least for a while. Why leave flighty things unsecured, was a phrase I once heard postmidnight on the box. The baseball player who said it might have said it in other words—the subject was loans, second mortgages to be exact—but I thought it was an appropriate epigraph in general. Faw had secured Berg as you secure a kite to a stake when you run inside to get another ball of string because the wind high up is running so nicely, and the kite is already out as far as the lead you've got on it will go. The only problem is you can come back outside, full of anticipation, excited at the prospect of tying on the extra length of string with the hope of letting your kite up higher and higher, and find that in the short time you were away the wind had died, and the kite fluttered down. Or else, as in the case of Berg, that the wind had picked up, and the string had broken.

This gnarled world of the art film was governed by fewer laws and forces than that of commercial film making. Money here was, as elsewhere, the prime motivator when people or things resisted movement, and was the most effective tranquilizer when they moved either too fast or in the wrong direction. It was, good old money, usually the ultimate purpose, the end in view of making an art film, as well as a commercial one. So, Berg's access to pure, clean money, his willingness to provide the capital that could push matters along, then swing right around again to bring

back home to the sugar shack more nice sugar was only one
of the assets he knew he could bring to the project he had
in mind. The great green leverager was how he'd thought
of himself before. Now he could be something more.
Granted, money was an idea, but there were worlds of
ideas out there that were valuable in and of themselves, and
Berg had reached down into his past and brought one forth,
all viscous and shivering with promise, wanting to breathe,
waiting only for a surgeon with green eyes and a paper-
thin, green blade to cut it loose and let it go off on its own.
Berg—it was as if he'd been hit on the head so clearly the
whole thing had come to him—was going to be mother,
surgeon, blade, and baby all at once. Hell if he wasn't going
to make a masterpiece.

He'd had enough experience as a producer and enough
financial success with the films he had helped to get made—
few of which he had bothered to see, in fact. His taste for
such stuff had been worn out by the time he was in his early
thirties, his aspirations ran to higher ground. When he told
Analise he had a script idea he wanted to develop and shoot
himself, he had reason to believe her response would not
be pessimistic. Analise was like a sibyl to him, and her
advice was cherished; the two of them had been on and off
lovers for years, and now they were in an off-period, which
meant they were collaborators in making money, and nothing else. It took him a couple of weeks to work up the
courage to present her his idea, in part because he predicted
that there would be aspects of the proposal she wouldn't
like, and he was averse to disappointing her.

She did say, "You don't know what you're getting yourself in for," and she might have even said, "You don't have
the slightest idea what you're talking about," and yet he
knew these words were a sure sign of interest, as was the
fact she remained seated across the table from him in the
darkish downstairs hole on Sheridan Square.

Analise removed her incorrigible white-framed sunglasses—which were so retro—as she filled her role of

devil's advocate. This delighted him, and he might even
have made a note of her penchant for doing this whenever
she wanted to emphasize her point (indeed, he *had* written
a few words about it in the pocket notebook he carried with
him just for the purpose of cataloguing interesting tics that
he could use to liven up characterizations he hadn't gotten
around to developing)—and, well—Analise both withheld
and didn't withhold her opinion.

He wondered whether all this might have gone better if
they were in an on-period, but then remembered that she
was even more straight with her opinions when they were
sleeping together than not. She proceeded, "Like, what
kind of story do you have in mind?" which gave him the
opening to tell her what he thought to do.

"It's going to be a film about a family, it'll have the old
crossbones rating but I want it to be so subtly psychological, and the production qualities unique and fresh enough
that it could win a prize at Cannes. So, the family is made
up of a father, mother, and three children—"

She opened her mouth to say something, interject a sarcasm like, Win a prize at Cannes? but allowed, "Yes, so?"
instead.

"One of the three children—the younger boy—he isn't
alive anymore except in these hyper constructs of the girl."

"His sister."

"Right, the sister. So the boy has died in a freak accident,
drowned in a riptide, you see they live on the ocean, and
there's the possibility behind all this that the sister was
responsible, I haven't bothered to work that through yet,
not sure it'll be useful. But anyway you see how these
constructs of the girl, who is very devoted to the family—
devoted for sure to the dead brother because he's so easy for
her to manipulate, being dead and everything, kind of re-
pressed but a bundle of energies, you see how these fantasies of hers make absolutely perfect vehicles for the graphic
stuff? Family disintegrates. Mother runs off with some artist, say, a guy who wouldn't mind tagging in to the hus-

band's wealth in some kind of way that has to do with his knowing something about an operation in the man's business that isn't altogether on the up and up. The husband married to his work. Ignores all this, keeps building and building. And his daughter, Grady I think I'm going to call her, driven to the edge by this combination of a kind of need to make a family for herself, and all this anger at her own family for having burned itself down, what happens with her is that she has all this fantasy life as a child and then runs face first into the real world, gets married, the marriage doesn't work out, and then she goes on through a series of escapades trying to find the Holy Grail in the guise of a lover."

"Pretty complicated. Too complicated."

"Could be, but it could work for us, for instance it could go into sequels, one, two, threes. I want at least to make it so we see her at two different stages of her life—both when she's going through this adolescent trauma of the brother's death and parental split, and then later when she's somewhere in her mid-thirties, is divorced herself, and she's carrying on with her best friend's husband—"

Analise interrupted now. She had waited just long enough to identify what she perceived to be her cue. Berg was important to her and she wanted to let him down as easily as possible while not jeopardizing her relationship with him. She had seen this before, the producers wanting to move into the art itself; everybody wants to be a star, to write, direct, nobody is content to have the real power, the soft-spoken money power behind the scenes. Why would anybody want to write if he didn't have to make a living? It wasn't even that uncommon for the money to want to get out there in front of the camera—and, she always wondered, to what end? What was it in backers' minds that made them want to parade their stories or their bottoms out there with the others, half of whom—the others, that is—would give anything to leave behind the heavy breathing, the creative thinking, all the alcoholic battles with themselves in front of the dailies, and spend their days reading scripts, shouting into the telephone at delinquent accounts, and letting someone else bring them the lime, the mineral water, the Marblehead bowl filled with organic trail mix. "You realize this is going to cost a king's ransom? There's too much plot to it. Plot means sets, means actors who can act, can remember lines, means technicians who can do lighting and props and on and on."

"It'll cost. That's right. I want it to cost. I want it to cause not a ripple but a wave." He shifted in his seat when this came out, the grandiloquence having sounded a bit pompous even to his own ear. But Analise would forgive him his zealousness, he thought.

"No, listen to me. It can't even be attempted within the numbers you're accustomed to spending, you hear me?"

"I don't care what it costs."

"He doesn't care what it costs." What could she say? She must have known that he would not be thrown by a display of self-interest. "How is it you never said that about any of my projects?" —This was, of course, how they had met. She was one of the very few female directors in the industry, and was looked on as something of a pioneer, a phenomenon to be admired, even studied. Her work was hardly pornographic, in fact, which was part of the attraction since Berg had ever been more interested in the profitability of the industry than the sensational aspects of the films themselves—most of what Analise had accomplished was done through innuendo, versus the standard, established modes of behavior on the screen, which she dismissed as antiquated. In Analise's films—as in those made by Candida Royallie, her mentor and Brooklyn idol—women were the focus, their pleasure, their interests, their lives. Her women tended to be enigmatic, and capable of handling themselves in difficult situations. Her men were prudent and backward, as a rule. It was quite a flip.

"Analise." He drew his hand across his eyes, knowing that the person he was addressing was in a position to look on his as the words of an ingenue, "I think this could be a breakthrough for the art film, could help legitimize the form. It's what you've been doing right along, and it's why I've supported you in it."

"You have supported me in it because I have earned out."

"I would have supported your work even if I lost my socks doing it, and you know it."

Much as she adored Berg she had to demur. She studied her fingertips for a moment. "Look, you make the decision to implement an artistic vision—" (give him *that* much if not his rumpled beret and cold-water garret) "—this vision of tracing the sister, Grady you called her, Grady's sexual fantasies from childhood on forward into when she's an adult, and what you're going to wind up doing is pushing the project over into like a different area in terms of distribution. What you're proposing here is going to limit the thing's commercial viability." Try that angle.

"I don't see why."

"Here you cut out your number one ticket buyer, your regular who doesn't want his honest enjoyment all gummed up by psychological complication, who doesn't give one goddamn that some director is going to try to win a Purple Heart for refining the medium, and where will that land you? They don't have debtor's prisons anymore, but you get my drift. Your story line is great but I can see right now how it's going to get in the way. It's too much menu not enough meat." She'd got her sunglasses back on by then, because she could see that Berg was not hearing what he wanted to hear. Indeed, he found himself wondering whether these weren't exactly the words he'd spoken to her once, back when they first met, and she had approached him needing backing with a similarly improbable narrative.

"Properly executed the idea can work, I know it. Can work both as film and as a commercial property."

"Let's say, for the sake of argument, that you're right.

For the record, I think you're nuts to want a theatrical release and not just go for the video market—it's all very uppity. But more important, have you considered the problem of getting that childhood stuff legally in the can, and out to the theater?"

"I don't understand. What problem?"

"Pretty serious legal jeopardy you've got lurking there in hiring some underage actress to play the part of the girl. Remember the Traci Lords deal—"

Berg countered, "I'll get to that when I get to it, and at any rate it's my problem, just like you say."

He was going to proceed, it was clear. Not without reluctance, she asked, "So if all these problems are your problems what do you need me for, darling?"

Berg hesitated, and then confessed, "I want you to be the mature Grady."

Analise laughed, down in her husky smoker's throat. "Mature? What a sensitive euphemism, it's why I love you, but you know I don't do that anymore."

"There isn't anyone I know who'd be more perfect."

"I'm flattered, the answer is no. I made a pact with myself about it and there's no going back. Ten years ago I would have sleepwalked through the whole package, but no way now. I've moved from in front to behind the camera and I'll never go back."

"It's what I want. You think about it."

"The person who should be thinking about it, giving it some calm, rational, mature consideration is you, dear Berg," and when, with those last words, she brought the glasses back down to the tip of her nose, he did try to listen to her advice, knowing as he might that her redoubtable and doubtful opinion of his film arose not from a philistine's hostility toward "human need" and its various forms of expression, nor from a rival's jealousy, but from an honest assessment that what he was getting himself into might produce some grim results for him personally and financially. *Human Need*—after all, that was the title of one of her own films. Great piece, too. There was a line in it that Berg would never forget. It was a joke about suicide. "The wages of death is sin," it went. You had to see it in context. How the Catholics hated that one, all right.

No, she was a true friend, was Analise. Her advice had come too late, however. Try as he might to turn his attention to other things, Berg found that he had conceived an infatuation for the film, which he tentatively had given the title—maybe prompted a bit by the suicide joke that had proved the pivot point in his decision to go ahead—*A Sinner's Almanac.*

The title remained in his mind rather provisional because Berg was uncomfortable with the word sinner, which betrayed, he felt, some interest in a morality system he held in no high regard. But he couldn't think of a worthy replacement. Wrongdoer was stiff. Transgressor seemed foggy and clerical. Malefactor was so clinical, and wordy. Sinner at least had some bite to it, he supposed. It was a good enough working title, and carried some suggestion of the film's episodic nature. Moreover, he explained on the phone to Analise, who finally did agree to act as an advisor, coproducer, on the picture for him but remained resolute in her refusal to act in it, there was an outlandish irony in making the girl Grady a sinner since, as Berg understood the character, all she really wanted to be was a good girl, to be loved by her father and her siblings. The thought was, wouldn't this only heighten the viewer's interest in her moral failures?

Said Analise, "No, anybody who bothers to buy into the idea that they're a sinner wants to be a saint or else they'd know there isn't any useful difference between the one and the other." Berg jotted that into his tiny book, though he doubted the epigram would stand up to logical analysis.

It was determined that the two segments of the film, girl Grady and adult Grady, would be shot in the same location to keep the budget somewhat under control. If the thing ran longer than three hours—Analise coughed at such a notion but assumed she could talk him into editing it down later—they would release it as two films, though Berg wanted in the worst way to make it a little epic. In order to retain as much artistic independence as he could, Berg wanted to make sure he wouldn't have to depend on any outside financing—he had never tapped into the Gulf Stream kitty as deep as he anticipated he'd have to for this, nor had he ever really risked not being able to replace the funds, as he knew he was with *Almanac*—and so he made several production decisions strictly in anticipation of budget problems. At the same time, he tried to turn every practical constraint into an expression of artistic integrity. Even though the savings would be modest, he thought to shoot the childhood scenes in black and white; it had been done before, but it was a nice effect, he assured himself. He took the position—again, in interior monologues, answering critics who didn't exist—that those early days of Grady's life would be made more evocative if they forwent color, would even be more accurate in a way, since in the early sixties color was still being developed, and black and white was the norm. They would shoot the picture with super-sixteen, which meant smaller crew, lighter-weight equipment; it could be blown up to thirty-five millimeter later on at the lab. Analise appreciated the way he was thinking.

Already the vision of how it was going to look began to shimmer and gain on him. Odd angles, funky miking, rough cutting, grainy footage: none of this, Berg decided, would hurt the film's quality. Quite the contrary. When (Analise said "If") it went into theatrical release, they could situate themselves in the market through comparisons to Russ Meyer, perhaps, maybe to Lina Wertmüller or some of the French makers, Varda say, or that Spaniard who had such success with his kinky matador, even the beauty of the chaos that was vogue among new music video directors. The aesthetic freedoms granted by unabashed use of amateurish means was, in certain circles in and outside the industry, the rage and this, he decided, was the posture he would adopt as his own.

All this positive enthusiasm was useful in the face of reality, however. As the *Almanac* script continued to grow through the summer, Berg couldn't resist detailing props, backgrounds, costumes, and stage directions for every scene as he envisioned them, and with every new idea, every foliation the film wanted to make, an awareness grew inside him about how not just the budget but the physical nature of films and making a film would not allow for such a precise rendering of all those details, in practice. The more he developed Grady's life, the more it became important to him to get a complete documentation of how he'd ideally like to have realized his portrait.

Indeed, one night—humidity and August heat seeping through the walls and windows of the hotel room where he lived those months, reclusive, channeling every waking hour into the script—he wondered whether the film ought to be shot at all. He'd just sketched out a scene where the ghostly brother enters the girl's bedroom and seduces her in such a way that it would be physically impossible to stage. This bit of whimsy, based as best he could recollect on what Grace had confessed to him that once (or had she? the vodka that was constantly at hand through these nights and days sometimes bowed reality like an old board; because, no, he knew he'd sneakily read it in her childhood diary)—of course broke the first rule in any practical handbook on how to write or act. So already he'd have to settle for something less than his vision demanded. What could two actors and a director work out as a substitute to the ghost's penetrating his sister with his head? It was depressing, the knowledge that whatever they would finally come up with would in no way match his idea as laid out in the script.

Another matter began to worry him. He had drawn so directly from his own life that he knew if by some miraculous piece of bad luck the film ever came to the attention of Charles or Grace, or even Erin, they would recognize themselves easily, and all the anonymity he'd worked so hard to maintain regarding his other films (he'd been nothing short of criminal, he had to admit, in the way he habitually withdrew monies from this already sensitive account, unauthorized, in order to invest in films that would make up for money he lost in other parts of the Sprawl—what a mess!), those films he was rather less proud of, all anonymity would be forfeited. And that might, no, it *would* mean serious trouble for him. His father would be forced to cut him off completely, if only to protect his own life's project. Faw would never be able to admit to much regarding the Gulf Stream Trust, since it was such a compromising and anomalous piece of work, in any case; but if it came out that his son had been borrowing freely from its Caribbean church account to make profitable not to mention seedy films, there would be no end of nightmares. Gulf Stream was the only place where all the entities that made up Geiger connected. This Berg surmised, because he had yet to see a tax return for any of Geiger's network of corporations that didn't show at least in one year or another a "donation" to the Trust. It was distinctly possible Charles would sue him through some legal mechanism inside the Sprawl. But it would be too late for any of them, by then; if war came to pass (Berg knew Charles would have every right to sue) between himself and his father there was no question who would emerge the victor, though it wouldn't be much of a war worth winning. Very probably all sides would be destroyed, as the government would have a field day. Yet, every time he attempted to invent, to move away from events in their lives as he remembered them, and as he remembered Grace telling them, the script went sour, or flat, or altogether astray, and began to smack of the same falsity he detested in other people's uninspired and hackneyed films.

Thus it happened that the more he meditated about it and the deeper involved he found himself in it, the more

there appeared to be so many reasons to abandon the project before it had gone any further. Still, he knew he had
to go ahead. For him, there seemed now to be no choosing
because—and perhaps for the first time in his life—he felt
sure about the importance of his understanding his own
needs, and fulfilling them. What he needed was to see what
it would *look* like on screen. And after so many years, he
told himself, of deferring his to the needs of others, namely
his father's, he was determined to see this one vision
through.

❖

I was both heartened and ashamed by how promptly
Mother returned Djuna's call. Djuna had left a message
with Segredo, on my behalf, and he told her that he and
Erin would discuss the matter. When Mother called back,
not a full hour later, she said they would welcome me if I
wanted to come visit. In light of her openness, I felt a little
ashamed that I hadn't shown the courage to make that call
myself. My excuse that I didn't want to risk being put in
the position of having to explain why I wanted to see them,
after so many years, seemed indolent, and thoughtless.

But I had reasons, at least, for feeling backward. I wasn't
even sure what I was going to tell them, or rather, how
much I was going to let them in on the Almanac branch.
There was also my desire not to betray any emotion over
the telephone, nor state anything explicit about what I had
begun to suspect. For all I knew, the telephone line at
Scrub Farm was tapped. My knowledge of detective
dramas had taught me to register paranoia about some
things I barely understood; but even if I was being absurdly
cautious, better to err on the "siker's side"—the safer side,
one of mother's phrases, not Irish, Scottish and perennial
with her—than be sorry. Given the jaundiced clouds that
were gathering out on the horizons of the Gulf Stream
Trust, perhaps she had erred on the siker's side in leaving

us for the quiet of Coecles Inlet and its rusted, innocent goliaths. There was good reason for me to begin to feel that things I thought I knew, I didn't know as well as I'd imagined. For one, how wise had I really been, all this time, to have laid the blame for Desmond's death at my mother's feet, and Segredo's? I wasn't so sure of my judgment in this as I used to be.

What I did know was Berg had done one thing I had failed, indeed had not so much as tried, to do: he had maintained a relationship with Mother, and her Gabriel Segredo. If Berg had never done anything else to earn my respect, this would suffice, I now began to think. I remembered back to the times when he and I would be out at Scrub Farm with Faw, and at the end of dinner he would excuse himself, and drive over to pay them a visit. He didn't even have to say where he was going, we knew. Faw made no comment; without exception he never betrayed his silence, never once revised his original decision to neither chastise Mother nor acknowledge her existence. It was a telling act of will, I thought, my father's flawless indifference. It makes me wonder now if this ability to display such prodigious apathy toward his estranged wife came from the same part of his spirit that allowed him to ignore the legal and moral questions that were raised by the Trust and its bogus ghost church down in the shadows of Morne Vitet. Surely, I decided, he knew about all the imputable activities of the Gulf Stream Trust. It was not in his nature not to know things. All I could think was there must be some explanation that I didn't understand. Not wanting to approach Berg, not yet—given how tied up in bending the Almanac branch to his own purposes he was—and knowing that I needn't harbor any hopes of a response from Faw if I brought it up with him, my hope was that Erin might be able to enlighten me. She was there the night of the dinner at Scrub Farm when Faw discussed the Trust with some of his colleagues. There was some chance she had caught sight of its real purpose. Although I knew it wasn't very fair of me to show up, after so long a time limited to sporadic letters—I could add selfishness to my list of faults—there were no alternatives. None, at least, that I could see.

"Grace, you're so thin," were my mother's first words—funny, because that was just what I thought of her. She'd sent photographs of the two of them, once when they had gone to France together on a sort of honeymoon manqué, and I'd noticed that she was radiant and somehow ethereal, with her hair pulled back over her shoulder, her hands in her skirt pockets, looking out over Paris from one of the bridges on the Seine.

Segredo still looked young. He was a finer man in his manners than I'd remembered as a child. The image I had had of that figure crossing the field toward our house, the red and black kerchief around his neck and the black boots denoting the power that I lacked, the fear he must have felt as his eyes were averted from looking up at the house he was about to rob, fear misread by me—that young girl watching him from the window of her sanctuary—as grim determination, all that seemed inappropriate all of a sudden, when I walked into the cottage. He seemed to have grown up emotionally (or else, I had)—it was evident just in the way he placed another log on the fire in the brick hearth in the living room. They were unnervingly at peace with themselves and their environment and, ostensibly, with their fate. Not a single line in my mother's face spoke of any second thoughts about having left Charles Brush.

"Would you like some port, Grace?" and when he said it I didn't get the wry smile at first—of course, I understood the reference later; how had he known about our escapade that night?

I said yes, and he brought in three glasses and an unopened bottle with a Portuguese imprint on the label, and numbers—a date, and barrel lot—written on a piece of tape around its neck, a good bottle, the kind you drink to new beginnings with. This was clearly something he had saved

for the occasion—which made my heart sink at the prospect of bringing up what it was I'd come over to discuss.
They were being forgiving toward me who had more or
less abandoned them, and here I was, come to raise questions immaterial to the life they had built for themselves in
my absence. We talked for a while about Warne, what had
gone awry with my one attempt at marriage, and about
what I was doing with myself, which seemed, in the telling,
fairly paltry and vapid and wasteful. The second glass of
port kept me from excusing myself and running out the
door in shame. When Mother poured it, though, I noticed
that there was a thin band of dirt under her fingernails and
this helped me to refocus, for reasons I am not so proud of,
in that I recognized her poverty, and her own imperfection, in the midst of all this goodness. We all suffered, and
had suffered. I admired her for not being as fastidious as she
once had been, and at the same time felt more on an equal
footing with her.

When I did bring it up, I was clumsy. It might have been
the clumsiness that made what I had to ask more palatable
to her, much the same way the indication of plain old
mortal dirt had made her available to me. If I'd asked with
a steady voice, and smooth stream of words, she might not
have been able to hear my need for help—her daughter's
need of guidance.

"That's still going?" she asked. Not the slightest tone of
indignation, or anger, or judgment in her voice. Did she
understand what I was saying?

Now, the wisdom of letting them in on Faw's single
great failure might have been questionable—my father
would have disinherited me on the spot, had he known—
but I pressed forward, the port in my heart, and the
warmth of the room warming me beyond the cautiousness
I might have honored otherwise. I told them what I knew,
and they were quiet. Mother didn't show the least surprise
at any of my disclosures. Nothing in her eyes displayed

disapproval; she did nothing that suggested the least hostility toward Faw. The phony church, the dedicated account for this program and for that, all the revenues, which must have run into the millions over a span of two decades, that had as yet eluded the scrutiny of an auditor—she didn't betray so much as a sigh of judgment. Was hers a loaded indifference, willful the same way Faw's had always been? I could only wonder, then; now I know. Neither she nor Segredo allowed themselves a bit of rejoicing over the clear trouble my father and brother had gotten themselves into. For a moment I found myself considering the possibility that they had been the recipients of hush money, or some such thing worthy of a made-for-TV movie. (I note this with amused shame.) This would at least explain why they seemed so deficient, or so honorable, in their response. But then Segredo spoke up, and my fantasy was dispelled.

"Grace, I don't want to interrupt you. Your mother and I are so pleased, I think it's pretty obvious, to see you, okay? We both talked about you before you got here, and one of the things we wanted most to let you know was that we don't want to get in your way, but we would like to see you more often. I guess you could have guessed that." Then he rubbed his hands together, and said, "I'm afraid we already have heard most of this stuff you're telling us about your father. We didn't know about Berg. I'm sorry to hear that he's involved, too. If you want us to try to get in touch with him and talk to him, we're certainly willing to give it a shot. But as for the Gulf Stream, there's nothing your mother and I can do about it."

"I think there is," I proposed. That was quite a piece of whimsy, too, because I believed there wasn't in fact anything he could do about it.

He looked at my mother, and I knew he'd asked her with the look whether he should tell me something. New surprise; so they did have a piece of information I was missing after all.

"You want to come out back? It's been a few years since you were there." I still couldn't tell what response my mother had given to that look of his.

We put on our coats, and went out into the sculpture yard. It was quite an imposing sight. The moonlight guided us through the iron menagerie he had continued to build in the yard. It was beyond my capacity to criticize what he had created; it was also beyond me to like it. Here was a fixed world, Daedalian in its resources, and childish in its freedom. A pair of metal wings glimmered over our heads, and I wondered whether moonlight might have burned the wax in Icarus's wings just as effectively as had the sun's rays. Some boys were just destined to fly too high and descend into the hungry sea no matter what precautions they took or refused to take. We carried the bottle of port and our glasses out with us. The camaraderie warmed me to the marrow.

❖

By October, Berg's script was more or less completed. Whatever he didn't have on paper, in black and white, could be improvised right on the set, he told himself, though he need not have worried over such matters given the over-thoroughness with which he'd spelled out scene after scene. Analise had hired a small crew of people she had worked with before, among them a veteran named Meade who was brought in to do the cinematography. Meade had shot over a hundred films—from arcade shorts to feature-length productions—and had the distinction of having worked for legitimates as well as hard core. That he'd footaged some serious art-world movies was the qualification that led Analise to believe that he was their man for the job. Still she was nervous about Berg's idea of working with a young actress. She had even steeled herself against the possibility, even probability, that her colleague might foul his own nest by going to extremes artistically.

When she brought up her concerns again, Berg announced that he thought they ought to shoot in Mexico or
the Caribbean. "The laws down there about this're bound
to be more slack."

"You're wrong," Analise said, as she drew her karakul
coat around her chest against the autumn chill that settled
over the Ramble in Central Park and breeze-broomed
crackly leaves around their ankles.

"Put some cash into the *jefe*'s palms and you're all set."

"Look," Meade gesticulated magisterially with hands
whose skin was spotted as a wood thrush's belly—"you go
down to Mexico or the islands, wherever, and you go with
whatever locals you can find, not one of them is going to
be able to act worth a good goddamn, okay? The English—
even if we find somebody who can speak it—the English is
going to be atrocious. Then, you're going to have some
mother who's going to take your money for her daughter's
services, and the first time you get her under the lights with
the camera rolling and Priapus primed, guess what, all her
brothers show up out of nowhere, rough us up, steal our
equipment, and get your *jefes* on our case—I don't care how
many palms you've greased up beforehand they know the
difference between bread and butter—and then, just like
that, farewell my friends. I've been in on projects where
they've tried it. It doesn't work."

"Besides, shooting outside the country will send the
costs through the stratosphere," asserted Analise, who
looked, to Berg, suddenly quite solemn and beautiful in the
running light. He found his mind straying a bit. Already,
before they had set up the first light on the first set, his
vision was being gnawed away at by the real world. There
was no way the film was going to turn out as he had hoped
it would. All things being equal, the best thing to do would
be to work fast, accept the constraints that the world was
going to impose upon him—laws, costs, prohibiting
mores—and get the picture going at least, get into it. His
fingers were cold. Autumn was early this year, wasn't it?

He wondered whether Meade had ever been a lover of hers, of Analise's. The thought bothered him. It shouldn't have: he had no right. The wind picked up through the half-shed trees. What was wrong with a young girl's fantasies being brought into life on the screen? He hoped this desire he was feeling for Analise would lapse back down. Not a convenient moment for internal commentaries that ran cross purpose. It was the fact she was so confident in all her ideas that made her so attractive to him, wasn't it. It reminded him—very peculiar connection—of Faw.

Meade was going on, playing the old salt; already Berg was feeling aggravated by him. "—Fiasco is what, if you go ahead in that direction. But look, why don't we just shoot right here in New York? Easily done, there's a good talent base to draw off of, you've got the film labs right here, inexpensive, you've got plenty of contacts for loft spaces. Why make matters more difficult than need be?"

"Forget the studio," coming back to focus again. "The outdoor scenes we have to shoot outdoors, and the landscape has to be out in nature. I don't want anything faked up. I need water, I need an island."

"What do you think you're walking on? you've got the most famous island on earth right under your feet."

"This isn't an island."

"Of course it is."

"What I want is whitecaps, real waves, real gulls, real sand, a whole seascape background type of, because the whole vision of the film is really meant to be pure," and he brushed the air in front of him with his outstretched hands, and just as he gestured it was as if the answer had been there before him, imminent and needing only to be polished to be seen. "There's no need to carry on about it," he extemporized, "you don't want to film down South it's fine by me. I know where to do it, and how." It was the second time he had made that claim.

Meade started to say something, but Analise intervened. She wanted to go back inside. Berg smiled at her; he was excited by his solution. The question was this. It wouldn't be hard to go out to the island when his father was on the other side of the world, but how was he going to be able to get Djuna Cobbetts away from the farmhouse on Shelter long enough to be able to bring in his equipment and his cast and crew, to do their work? The answer came to him when he was bidding the two of them farewell, as they emerged from the park through a rustic, bark-pole arbor on Central Park West. He would send her on vacation. Nothing so lavish as a trip to St. Barts—Cape Hatteras would do fine. One of the church people could take her around, show her the sights. Webster had better go, too. What kind of fish were they catching this time of year down there? He would have to find out. As for Grace, Berg figured it wouldn't matter, since she never left the city anymore. For all he knew, she hardly ever left the apartment. Trait she inherited from her mother. So, yes, fine; he would shoot in the privacy of his own home. By doing it this way, there would be the further advantage of not having to put in too much time recreating the scenes that were written to be set there anyway. Verisimilitude to a degree he might not otherwise have hoped for.

❖

"There was this fleck of a company," Segredo said, "this little aberrant mayfly of a thing that your father had set up as a way of protecting some of his profits, sheltering them as they say in the business, and I knew about it because your mother told me. Your father used to interest me, I guess that's how you'd put it."

"Interest you?" Erin nudged him.

"Obsess me. I used to think about him and who he was, how he got to where he was, much more than I ever should have. He seemed to have such a grasp of how you make things happen in life, was how I looked at it, and since that was something I knew that I wasn't able to do, I felt in-

ferior to him, I suppose. Oh, I told myself that making
money wasn't something that artists should be worrying
about. Making art was for artists, making money was for
businessmen. You with me?"

"Sure," I said. I couldn't face looking at him. Here he
hardly knew me, had every right to see me as a traitor to
my mother, having rejected her because of Faw's unwrit-
ten, unspoken, but quite clearly hard-fast rules, and yet
here he was speaking of his own weaknesses with such
candor that they metamorphosed into strengths even as
they were uttered.

"But still I felt inferior, because I knew what your
mother was giving up when she left the farm over there, for
Coecles, and though I didn't have any way to match him
out in the world, in a practical way, it did occur to me—I
don't know how to say it—that I might be able to change
the way his world worked. Might turn it around on him a
bit. Once I realized that, he began to interest me for other
reasons I'm not proud to admit to you. I was angry at him
for so long because of how he treated your mother, and I
wanted to get back at him, you see. Or that was at least my
rationale. So I had something on him. I knew about this
little festering fleck. Back when Berg was angry with him,
Berg would come over and we would sit back here and he
and I would have a drink or two, and without letting on
that I was quietly collecting and assembling, putting the
disparate pieces together—"

"Like welding."

"That sounds right, welding together this weapon that
I could use against him if I ever felt like it. Berg didn't
know that he was incriminating his father, but his tongue
was pretty loose back then. I did a little research on some
of the things he had said, and it became clear very quickly
that this designer church and the Trust that was corpo-
rately attached to it were shady at least. Berg didn't realize—and for all I know still doesn't—that family members

cannot sit on the boards of foundations and churches if they happen to be sole shareholder family members in the very companies whose donations are floating that foundation. It's called a conflict of interest for a reason. You skim some of your profits and bury them in your own foundation where they can work, untaxed, to your own benefit a second time."

"Did Berg tell anybody else about this?" I asked. I was floored by Segredo's confession, not because I hadn't come to more or less all this information on my own, but because it seemed to me that if he knew so much about it, who else knew? The most surprising aspect of all of this was that the loop—a loop just like that of the warm waters of the Gulf Stream, sequestered, and going around full circle at just about the same rate as a church's fiscal year—had not been discovered before now.

"I told him not to. Whether he listened to me, I can't say."

Here was a difficult question for me to ask: had Segredo ever given in to the temptation to tell anyone? I didn't have to ask it, though. He answered on his own.

"Once I knew that your father wasn't as perfect in his genius as I had thought, the obsession subsided. In the beginning it might have made me feel better to know that I could get him whenever it was convenient, just threaten to drop an anonymous letter to the appropriate party, and down he would come. But then, it became clear to me that this wasn't a viable way to go, either. It made me into a lowly blackmailer, or some such thing. One night—this was years ago now, Grace—I was out back here, working on something, and it dawned on me what I would do. It was so unbelievably easy."

The air was fresh off the inlet, and the tide was heaving in over the stones down along the narrow beach.

"Nothing. I would do nothing. He was one of us, for all his running over the face of the earth, making his money

here and there with all his ornaments and toys and crafts
and games, he was just like me. I've never given any of it
much thought since."

❖

In setting up the project, Berg had taken precautions to
protect his father. If the whole thing blew to pieces it
would be demonstrable that Charles knew nothing about
it; it might as well be a suicide rather than a murder—
something along those lines. His sense of filial loyalty, such
as it was, made him feel more confident about what he was
doing. He knew that the more he could get himself to
believe he was undertaking to produce a work of art, that
the sacrifices and risks were his and his alone, the more he
would be able to convince others to believe in him, too. He
wanted to concentrate. He wanted to do something that
was entirely his own. The more he could detach himself
from his father, and the Sprawl, the better. He was getting
too old to fit in that role that Faw had devised for him one
summer so long ago. The hostilities, the jealousies, the
anger he harbored for the better part of his life could be
exorcised, he just knew it, if he were able to make this one
pure move.

In this spirit, when he created the Almanac branch of the
Trust he did what he could to bolster its legitimacy. He
worked up a logo for the production company—

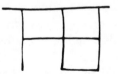

which he liked a lot because not only did it incorporate
the three initial letters TAB into its design, but it had a
cross at its center, which reaffirmed its religious affiliation.

Moreover, the thing looked like the windows in the house out at Scrub Farm, side by side double-sashes with the lintel extending beyond the frames along the top. One of the windows, the left, was open. This was a graphic symbol, to his eye, that there was a way out for his father, should anything go wrong. (Funny how as time wore on, he cared less and less whether the project succeeded or failed, so long as it remained his, the fruit of his own thoughts, own labors.)

Logos, contracts, iconographies. It was just paper protection, but sometimes, he remembered, thinking of that game he used to play with his brother and sister, paper can be stronger than the hardest rock. Whether that was supposed to alleviate some of his feelings of guilt about finessing the till in order to satiate his desire to make *A Sinner's Almanac* he couldn't say for sure. It was far too advanced to turn back, anyway. If the financing of the film were ever scrutinized—following money through labyrinths was often the only way the law could ever catch up with skin traders—Berg could take the fall, could tell the truth about the operation, and possibly prevent anyone from bothering to look past the connection of the branch to the stream, to push a little further to see what kinds of tributaries were feeding the stream itself. He got a friend of Analise's to incorporate the project. Its charter set forth the purpose of the film as a documentation of the many fine accomplishments of the church and its shareholder trust. It stipulated that the large capital equipment purchase Berg had made—all his hardware for the film—and the payments to staff and actors would go toward displaying what wonderful things the Trust was doing with its charitable contributions. "To be shown at fund-raising events," it explained. The Trust had existed now for some two decades without ever having manufactured any real evidence that it was engaged in carrying out salvage and restoration operations, or that its parishioners both in the Hatteras church and down in the ghost-limb outreach church in the islands were benefiting from Trust work. So this would create some fruit for an empty cornucopia. Berg even thought that he, as embodiment of the Almanac branch, could, while funding his serious project, also put a couple of days into filming some nondescript boat yard, maybe find a decrepit wreck somewhere and get the actors to look as if they were going over the skeleton ship with an eye toward putting the old hull and cross braces back together. In other words, actually make something that would protect the Trust while, admittedly yes, exposing the Trust to just a little danger by, well, running these funds out of it, borrowing them interest-free, say several hundred thousand would cover it, surely no more than half a mil. Once *A Sinner's Almanac* was released, the principal would all go straight back into Gulf Stream and no one in the Sprawl would ever know.

These nuances made him feel better, so that he could contemplate what mattered, the film itself.

❖

When the car ferry arrived and I drove down the gangplank, I felt almost at once the sensation of being an outsider. This distance—a kind of disaffirmation of any sense of belonging here—I had experienced before, of course, but never quite so profoundly. I reminded myself that there was no reason that the landing, and the oak and maple trees, and the street that disappeared up toward the island center, should look foreign, reminded myself that I had just visited my mother and Gabriel not two months ago in their cottage, which was three minutes from here, that I had lived, on and off, on Shelter Island for most of my lifetime—but I wasn't able to shake the apprehension.

I drove to the new inn where I had made a reservation. I had registered using Grace as a surname. No one knew me at the place, as it was on the opposite end of the island— somewhere I never ventured, near the public beach. When I settled in my room, I took it out of my bag, and opened

it again, the note I'd received that brought me here. It was
typed out and unsigned. There was no return address on
the envelope. There was nothing about the white paper on
which it was written that would allow me to know the
identity of its author; and this was, of course, intentional:
no Geiger letterhead, no National Council of Churches,
nothing. There wasn't even, in the way the few sentences
were composed, a rhetoric that would give me any insight
into the writer's slant on the situation, or what he or she
hoped to gain from it.

"Your brother is about to make a mistake. You might
want to observe the proceedings. Scrub Farm, middle next
week, it begins. Sorry!"

I hadn't told anyone about this, though I'd been sorely
tempted at least to telephone—of all people—my mother.
She and Segredo had gained my trust when we met, and
had even been in touch on the telephone, just talking, not
even so much catching up, but talking about events, the
world, the government, sweeping impersonal things that
would help us to get our bearings again. But I didn't tell
her about this; I imagined there was some chance she and
Segredo wouldn't want to know. They might think, Grace
is back in our lives and look what she brings, problems,
maybe we were better off before. I didn't want them to
think that way.

The last exclamatory word in the letter does carry a
rhetorical weight, but what kind of weight, and in what
way it leans, I cannot say. Sorry for me, for Berg, sorry for
whom? And does it really mean, sorry, or is there a quiet
snicker behind it, like, "Sorry, but richly deserved"? What
is more, the word "mistake" is particularly *un*loaded—so
light a term it is, within the context of this anonymous
missive, that its rhetorical innocence seems false, and hints
to me that the author of this thing wants me to know that
the mistake is a grave one.

Like a fool, I have come; I didn't see what option there
was. Later, I will go out there. Not in the car, though. My

own anonymity, it occurs to me, might have certain value, but in what regard I couldn't yet say.

❖

Five families used to own the better part of Shelter Island, or at least that was how Berg remembered it, when he was growing up: the Nichollses, the Havens, the Tuthills, the Derings, and the Sylvesters, who had originally owned it all, having had it bestowed upon them by the crown. The island was Republican, as are most islands. In the summers the population would swell to twenty-four hundred souls between the natives, summer people, and the visitors. Islands are like that. A few people do their best to make money during the season, and then are left to survive as best they can through the winter. Berg invented a family that had seen better days. Once an island family, they were now treated as if they were a summer family. Once the toast of the island, once one of the great, glorious, landowning families, the Muellers—as he called them—were quite reduced now. Gone to seed were the terraced gardens, toppled was the fine statuary that once stood here and there, placed by some imported English landscape artist to heighten the effect of this lily pond, or that octagon. The trees on the Mueller estate were overgrown with vines, some of them missing large branches from the storms, some of them dying from diseases or age. The manor—not much of a manor really, just a clapboard farmhouse—was charming, if in a shambles. And the Muellers themselves were charming, if overly devoted to their livestock, the blind goat, the lame mule, the old horse, and the several dogs. The Muellers were caught in their own time-warp, because the stretch of water—narrow though it was—that separated them from the mainland also separated them from the social velocities at which those on the land excelled. Islands are washed by waves, and their clocks tick as irregularly as waves. The sun shows a longer day on an island, coming up as it does right out of the water, and then setting in the water too—no mountains or buildings to keep you in shadow.

So . . .

The camera focuses on a hand. The hand is holding a black fountain pen over a sheet of clean white paper. It is a girl's hand, we suspect, and the pen appears unwieldy, overlarge, awkward in its grasp. There is the suggestion, we suppose, of the black pen being homologous with a black phallus, held so quiveringly in the neophyte's grasp. We note it, the hint, and move on just at the same time the image does, not assigning too much importance to it—the hint—as the hand now puts the nib to paper.

Our earlier thought that the hand was a young girl's is confirmed, and this makes us feel at once satisfied. The words that begin to appear are written in large, rounded forms, and we are sure that the person writing is a child. Although the calligraphy is plain, schoolish, and legible, that the hand is shaking (what is she nervous about? we cannot help but ask ourselves) causes the words to be imperfectly shaped here and there. As the words are revealed, the innocent, fluty voice of the girl hovers over the text with us, and narrates her thoughts as they materialize on the page. No music. The quality of the sound is dry. There was a condenser on the mike in the room where the child-actress read for the sound track. Black and white, a tight shot filling the screen, deep tones of lush gray that almost have in them the quality of old nitrate film stock.

The voice tells us, "I am a sinner, and this is my calendar of days, my confession. This is my almanac," and the theater fades to momentary black.

We can hear the ocean rocking against the shore and the image dissolves into gray waves fanning across sand.

"The ocean is a vast eye," the voice continues, "which has witnessed many things, being an eye that never closes, night nor day."

Then the screen image jump-cuts to a gypsy woman with

one glass eye. "Nasturia was one who knew how to read the lines of a person's palms. My parents brought me, early on in my life, to her, hoping against hope that she could identify the reason for my problems. I had been very ill, and our family had moved to this place on doctor's orders, in the hope of restoring my health. But for all the natural beauty and calm of island life, I was still subject to fits and sinful hallucinations. Desperate about my uncouth nightmares, and my fantasies, which were evident to my parents by the way I moved as I slept, fitfully, moaning and heaving, bathed in the salty water of my own flesh, my parents, frustrated by the failures conventional wisdom and medicine had shown in my case, brought me to Nasturia."

The palmist, in whose own facial wrinkles we are able to read a long, hard life of quackery and falsehoods, smiles a knowing smile. Obscured if not hidden beneath her heavy makeup, we can discern, is a person who possesses both a melancholic understanding of what a bitch life is and a failure to have, herself, warded off its nastiest demon: the demon of growing old ignorant.

She studies the child's hand with admirable concentration. She frowns, as we might expect. Then she looks up to the parents, who stand, worried expressions on their faces, behind their daughter, and darkly mutters, "This bodes evil."

The mother leans forward and tells the palm reader to elaborate.

"How do you feel, honey?" the palmist asks the girl.

Grady answers, most reserved, "Fine."

"You want to go on?"

Grady says, "Yes."

Drawing the hand closer to her dark eye, the palmist reads, "An absent Mount of Jupiter suggests degrading proclivities, the Mount of Venus being rather excessive indicates coquetry and frivolity beyond measure. The Line of the Head reads of a lack of steadiness of mind, I am afraid. None of which is, as you can see, good. However, there is more. Her Line of Life, while being neither normal nor short, is formed of a double J—you see? you see these fishhooks here?"

The father asks, somewhat unimpressed with the palmist's confidence in her craft, about the meaning of the fishhooks.

The palmist smoothly ignores his hostility. "These lines tell of one who shall enjoy success in war."

And she smiles knowingly at the girl, and the girl is seen to smile back at the old hag, her face flooded with innocence.

The parents aren't pleased with the reading.

The palmist stresses, "I can only read what fate has traced there in the flesh, I cannot shape the girl's fate myself," and as she pauses for a moment the camera tightens in on her face, slowly, so that we are close enough to imagine her breath on our cheeks when she says, "One thing I can tell you is this. If she were my daughter I know I'd keep a close watch on her."

The scene was hokey to just the degree Berg wanted it to be hokey, and yet eloquent enough, he believed, so that it achieved precisely the mix of tones he was looking for. Fair enough. It was under way. He'd got his filmic conflict going. The music was to be understated, and that would be a plus, keep it from getting too arty.

When he had first sketched out this opening, he was aware that his audience, now three-four minutes into the action, would be getting restless, maybe begin shifting in their seats, wondering when they were going to be delivered what they'd come looking for, whether it be simple action, or skin trade materials. The palmist could, of course, request to be left alone with the girl, usher the parents to a waiting room, and summon her two twisted sons to the chamber to perform, perhaps, some sort of ritualistic act with the girl to cleanse her of the curse that her palms declared was upon her. The sort of tribal ambience, the narcotized luxuriance of a classic like *Behind the*

Green Door might be effected had he invented a scene like that.

But, Berg reminded himself, classic or not, *Almanac* wasn't to become some piece of pulp porn trash nor a cruddy mail-order tape; it was a family portrait, a Film with a capital "F," and he disciplined himself to stick to the—well, if not facts, as such, at least the testimony his memory wished to preserve on its celluloid canvas.

He knew, further, that he would have to discipline himself to coordinate his need for accuracy in some kind of measure with the market imperatives he knew Analise would have in mind: he wasn't prepared to be irresponsible, given how much money it had by now become evident would have to be siphoned off the Trust to make the thing a reality. So, he gambled the scene that revealed how fate had doomed her was enough of a prelude, and decided not to spend the money and shooting time it would take to further develop and shade the background to Grady's character. He would skip ahead some years and show her as a flowering adolescent, obsessed with her brother.

❖

I felt unhurried as I biked over the first, then the second causeway, maybe because it felt so unusual to be traveling in this childhood mode again, slow and yet covert, and I was enjoying the sea air, and the skittering of the pebbles as the rocks ran fingers through them, foaming and chewing incessantly at the manmade span that led out toward the house.

Enjoying the sea air? I could have laughed if it had been less painful; such a pathetic figure I must have cut in the eyes of those two boys down on the shore, surf casting into the wind, who glanced back to see this woman cycling along toward Ram above them on the road. To them I must have seemed ninety, seemed ancient, with my Soho blacks fluttering into my body, my black ankle boots and black

stockings moving up and down against the pedals of the
bicycle that I'd borrowed from the hotel. In the city, this
was the absolute in feminine garb—at least downtown,
where I had gone so often to meet Cutts at the aerie. But
here, on this rather desolate road, on this island, at this time
of evening, I must have looked like a witch, and a wicked
and ridiculous one to boot. But rather than shout something derisive at me, they ignored me, turning back to the
darkening water and casting again. I could have told them
that fishing here on this side of the causeway was not going
to avail them of any catch, not in this month, at this
hour—Desmond, Berg, and I had tried to fish the bay from
this concrete strait before on many occasions under similar
conditions with no success. But I thought, let them learn
for themselves. That's what I was still doing, wasn't it?
Learning for myself. And besides, they hadn't even
laughed at me. Solipsism, is what it's called, when a person
is so far gone into the sorrows and joys of apperception that
she believes everyone is looking, measuring, admiring, ridi-
culing her. Solipsism is when you think that one of the
primary reasons the sun bothers to rise in the morning is
to show you once more to the world for appraisal. Whatever streak of it I had running through my nerves and
blood and heart I could damned well do without, but it was
in me, like sap in the spring brush, sap out of the wound
of a late-pruned maple branch.
    So. Picture a witch but one without powers, one who
wouldn't know necessarily how to crack a mirror at the
right moment, or wiggle her nose in order to make all the
most inane complications that happen in a life disappear,
and there was Grace, approaching her own house, ditching
her borrowed bicycle in the scrub—plentiful yet out there,
whence the name of the farm originally. The irony (are
these things ironies, or sublime cruelties?) of me coming to
a stop at just about the same place in the road that Segredo
parked his car all those years ago, when he'd come to Erin,
did not escape me—but I did not fight what had by then

become an inevitability, a purpose. To find out just what it was that Berg was doing. And to make up my mind who I was, how I could define myself in the midst of all these other ideas, and movements, all these decisions.

The grounds of Scrub Farm I knew better than my own body. Every tree, every stone, every rise in the grade. I was the most viable insurgent. And—for the solipsist I accused myself of being—the most self-deprecatory. Everyone, I am convinced, has experienced this moment in their lives, when they "snuck up" on someone. Common as grit in a hen's gullet, would be how Web might say it.

The windows cast a yellow onto the holly and junipers, and the tiny berries on the ferethorn burned bright under what had become a convergence of sun afterglow and early moonlight. My old library window, the window that I had stood at so often as a girl, glowed with a butterscotch hue. There were a number of lights on in the house, upstairs and downstairs, though the carriage house was dark. I made my way down toward the far shore where the carriage house looked out toward Coecles head, and peeked in the windows to assure myself no one was inside, then used a key to let myself in the back door. The rooms smelled of (guess what) potpourri, ever so mild. The familiarity of the smell was, in this new context, heartwarming to me, and I could feel my pulse, which had risen as I'd ventured across that open space in the twilight, now return to a regular tempo.

I sat down. I didn't know my way around Djuna's rooms—indeed, even when I was living at Scrub Farm I had only been in the carriage house on a few occasions, once to bring Djuna her medicine, maybe once to help her carry plates of cookies she had made for a surprise party for my father on his fiftieth birthday. Of course, I didn't turn on any lights, but as I sat on the floor in the foyer, my eyes adjusted to the darkness, and soon enough I got my bearings, rose, and walked toward the open staircase—still quite charmingly rickety—and went up to the second story. In Djuna's bedroom the potpourri was positively heady. What was it about these women that would make them want to keep bowls of dead and decaying flowers in their houses? I found her telephone, which was on the bedside table. Without thinking about it I dialed the number for the farmhouse.

Luck was with me, and it surprised me a little that it was, because I hadn't anticipated Berg would allow anyone to answer the telephone besides himself. "Brush residence," she said, the woman who answered; her voice was very direct. That is to say, it was as if she lived there herself, so calm was her tone.

"Is Djuna Cobbetts there?" I asked.

"Hold on a moment, please."

I looked out the window toward the house, which was slightly above me toward that rise which marked the long summit of Rams Island. Evening had come now, and the lights in the windows burned brighter. Light streamed out of my own bedroom window into the cherry tree. These people were incorrigible.

"Mrs. Cobbetts is out of town right now, may I take your name, and I'll have her get back to you."

"When do you expect her back?" I ventured.

"I'm not sure, but if you'll give me your name—" and then I was sure I could hear in the voice the beginnings of anxiety, and I made a small mistake, I suppose, by hanging up. I considered calling back with some line like, We must have been disconnected, but thought instead to leave matters where they stood, and at any rate I had got the information I'd wanted. I lay back on the bed—her mattress was so soft I sank into its downy mass—and made another mistake. Well, not so much a mistake as an unconscious alteration in my plan. I fell asleep. When I woke up, it was still dark outside, and I got up quickly, cursing myself, and saw that the lights in the farmhouse were all off now, except for one. The library window was still aglow.

After smoothing Djuna's bedspread, I went downstairs, out the back door again, locking it, and walked up the brick

path toward the house. Stars blanketed the sky. The air was
damp but not as cold as autumn night air can be. I was wide
awake now. Careful not to make a sound, I walked out
around the house on the orchard side, past their cars and
the garden in front of the house, to get myself in a position
to see what was going on in the library. The light went on
and off, very rapidly, flickering, and gave eerie sprays of
intoxicant whiteness out into the foliage. Berg was projecting onto the wall some footage. He was wholly absorbed
with what he was doing. He looked exhausted, but bur-
nished by the light. I moved in closer and watched in the
silence of the predawn, peering into the window in the
same way that the light people and the flare man and that
ghost boy with the origami hat made out of newspaper had.

What I saw—over Berg's shoulder—was the same old,
sea-roughed rows of trees that Desmond and I had played
in as children, the same orchard I had just skirted on my
way around the house. There was a naked girl and I knew
at once who she was supposed to be.

❖

An orchard. Quiet as Pompeii, or an underwater cathedral.
Shadows running over the grass as heavy as clouds. The
trees lengthening with their fruit. Grady has taken a basket
down to pick apples, or pears, or apricots, whatever remains unharvested. The fruit seems to be fake. Her dress
is diaphanous. Close up on a suggestive, dying flower over
whose pistil a bee has impressed itself. The bee and flower
bob in the breeze, as the camera pulls away, lazily as the
sated old bee, and focuses on Grady, who is now spreading
a blanket beneath one of the trees. She looks around and,
seeing that there is no one in the field, slips first out of her
camisole then her skirt. The delicate beads of sweat that
ring her forehead suggest that an Indian summer's heat has
settled in over the orchard, and makes us feel as light-
headed and sleepy as the girl herself feels. She stretches,

and as she does, the sun and shadow through the leaves dapple her torso. Lying on the blanket we see her narrow buttocks rise and fall as she unaccountably begins to squirm, slowly, distending her limbs, and pushing her fingertips lightly across her muscular, flat stomach down to the hairless mound where her pubis unfurls like some cosmic anemone. Her tongue cowers at the hollow made by her pursed lips.

"Grady?" a voice calls from behind somewhere.

So enraptured with her own movements and the ascendant heat of her game, she hasn't heard him.

A boy, unclothed, his skin luminous, steps out from back in the woods, and walks up to where she lies. "Hi," he says; she squints up into the light at him, but says nothing. A few leaves from the trees have blown onto the blanket, and Grady brushes a leaf out of her hair, which is fanned around her head. "They said I'd find you down here."

She continues to play with a strand of her hair, but says nothing.

"They sent me down to take care of things."

The camera has been moving during his brief dialogue, backing away and around them. The coarse bark of the trees comes into view, blocking them from us, and then again as the camera keeps traveling, we can see them again. He is still talking, she listening, and though the dialogue is obscured by the music of birds, we can tell that something is about to happen between them. The boy seems slouchy, confident as a young cougar. He kneels at her feet, reaches hands out and gently clasps each of her ankles. He lifts her ankles up off the blanket, and her knees fall away from one another. Pushing the backs of her feet toward her raised hips, he has made of her an acquiescent butterfly. We see her face, and know that she has worked herself up into a state of the most dirty desire. Her head rolls to left and to right, and her teeth are gritted in erotic pain. "So that's what you want, eh?" the young man whispers, a satiric smile swarming across his curled lips. "I never say no to anything. If that's what you want, it's what you're going to get, because I hate disappointing anyone," and his tongue now probed the raw, ruffled, floral bloom between her thighs.

"That was how it began," the girl's voice narrated calmly over the image of the young man and the girl now more or less performing a stock pornographic sex act teasingly half-hidden behind the branches of the fruit tree. "Yes. He was my brother. He knew I needed to have him, because it was the only way for me to keep my sanity. He knew I would submit to whatever he wanted, and gladly so. I've always been grateful for those times we had together, and might have stayed with him forever had he not—but I'm getting ahead of myself."

❖

The arrogance of what he was doing had a very different effect on me than I might ever have guessed. Is it possible I was flattered? No, nothing so unambivalent as that. More likely what I felt was respect for Berg's new level of cool delinquency.

Rather than march into my house—yes, *my* house, because it was as much mine as his—and announce to him that this indulgence he was allowing himself was not as closely kept a secret as he assumed, I was suddenly (and strangely) inclined to leave him and his associates alone. Who was I to try and change things now? Let them make their portrait.

If anything, I thought, I ought to go in and warn him about this Council of Churches man, whom I had decided was himself as phony as any storefront church. The eastern sky was by then beginning to turn green and blue, and hum with yellows and pinks, and I knew that I had to make up my mind what to do. It was curious, unaccountable: I felt protective of Berg. I decided to back off, into the field. I retrieved the borrowed bicycle, and rode over the causeways toward the hotel where I had put up. Most of the island was still asleep, and everything seemed pristine and right and calm. Behind me the first lines of dawn light continued to spread over the horizon. To feel as tired as I felt, given that I'd had such a long sleep in the carriage house, was strange, but when I reached my room it was everything I could do to get out of my chilled, damp clothes, and slip into bed.

Maybe I had taken on my brother's exhaustion and needed to sleep for him. Besides, I had nothing better to do than sleep the day away, since I intended to go back again that night, and resume my role as voyeur.

❖

The film is farther along than one might have guessed. At the edge of the orchard we see a figure who has been spying on the boy and girl who made love on the blanket. This is Max. We will know his name very soon. We see the smirk on his face as he looks on, his right hand shading his eyes in such a way that it looks as if he is saluting. Max is not saluting, though. He can see that the lovers are his sister and brother and this doesn't make him happy. He spits. Here is Max, older than his siblings, more wise to the ways of the world, and yet he is still a virgin. The jealous anger he feels at having discovered them here in the orchard is apparent to us when we see the way he grits his teeth, and turns away. His virginity is as yet unrevealed to us, at least in a direct way, but there is something awkward and immature about his gait, in the hands swinging gracelessly at his sides, in the tilt of his head to one side. He is a boy.

On the shore, gathered around a driftwood fire, a group of people is gathered together, drinking from a shared bottle. They are laughing, and singing at their clambake.

Standing sheltered from view at the edge of a woods along the dune is Max, who is shivering a little, because the wind coming in off the shell-shaped waves is cold. It is after sunset, and the moon is a dog's tooth low in the wispy sky beyond where the people linger by the beach fire. Max listens to them, trying to sort out his contradictory thoughts about what he saw earlier, and what he was going to do about his virginity. He didn't feel like going home, knew he wouldn't be able to sit there like a stupid mute at the dinner table, and face his sister and younger brother and his mother, too, knowing what he knew. So he had decided, he guessed, to run away, at least for a while. He would rather be at home, he felt, than out here in the freshening night, but what choice did he have? None whatever.

The fire dances in each of his eyes. If he had had a single ounce of courage, or knowledge about the ways of the flesh—which, he is convinced, are different from the ways of the world—he would have walked over to the two lovers, his siblings, and asserted himself, being the eldest. He would have pulled his brother Dante by the hair, and thrown him to the ground, or else hit his head against the trunk of the tree under which they'd so promiscuously luxuriated. Then, he would have done it to Grady himself, until she came screaming, begging for him to stop, not because she wanted him to stop but because she couldn't take the ecstasy a real man could provoke in her. He didn't know how, though; he didn't know how.

Never could he let Grady and Dante in on his terrible secret, because they would have no respect for him ever again. He was a liar, he knew. A terrible, worthless prevaricator who had never so much as seen a woman with her clothes off, until today of course, when he'd witnessed his own sister from a distance. He'd never touched a woman's skin. He had never kissed anyone except for his mother, and the priest's ring finger once at Mass.

They were so drunk, these partiers on the beach. One of the women was singing by the thick fire, in a slow dirge, mocking herself and the words as she clasped her hands over her breasts:

"Some men go to heaven,
Some go to hell.
Some men buy,
And some men sell."

And Max tried to remember what he had seen, wanted to remember what Grady looked like between her legs, he closed his eyes, and we could see a distorted, parallax view of the orchard, blurry, and we could make out Grady leaning against one of the trees. She wore a sailor's suit, now, with a sailor's white cap tipped to the side of her head, and there was a moustache painted on her face. With her finger waving back and forth like the hand on a metronome she was reprimanding us.

"Some men buy,
Some are bought,
Some men are lovers,
And some are not."

Max told himself that he could have walked right up and grabbed Dante, turned him around and slugged him, wouldn't that have given them both one big surprise.

"Some men row,
Some men bail.
Some men are cops,
And others go to jail."

He walked out, tentatively, toward the festive group. The twilight waves whipped the sand, frost clouds spat out at the earth-fringe, and the heat of the fire wiggled up through darkness past the trees and toward the stars that swirled with the rest of the bonfire sparks thrown up into the air. "Come on over here, boy," one voice cried.

"Some men are crazy,
Some are sane.
Some are strong,
But most are lame."

Max joined the group.

"What's the difference between a refrigerator and a sodomite?" one of the drunks queried. Well, what? "A refrigerator doesn't fart when you take out the meat." That was disgusting. Max tried to smile. The others were laughing so hard. Max shook his head and licked his thumb to ascertain which direction the wind was coming from. Northwest; later tonight it would pour rain. He knew that he had to find himself shelter for the night. He also knew that this haphazardly pitched tent, shelter though it might be, carried quite a cost for what protection it promised to afford. As he is standing there asking himself whether he should stay, or seek cover elsewhere, the camera focuses on an old man who has been sitting closest to the fire, and who looks up in Max's direction with blind eyes, and says—as if he'd been able to read the boy's mind—"Max, listen to me. Don't *should* on yourself."

Max makes his decision to stay. Acceptance into any group is easier than the outsider thinks. Always easier. That there is no secret is the biggest secret of any secret society; that there is nothing special about anything that is deemed to be special. There can't be. If something were special everybody would want it, and what people want they get, because they learn how to take it, and then it isn't special anymore.

Max thinks this. Max knows he is about to learn some solemn, some fundamental lesson. And yet what is there to be learned from this woman who has taken down her panties, grand white bloomers of a bygone era, and put them on her head? And the fat fellow with the checkered pantaloons, sort of circus clown pants, who is barking like a healthy puppy, leaping around on the sand, and licking her naked feet, what pleasure is he seeking, what gaining, and what administering—and what can be learned from such behavior? Max isn't even noticed as he sits next to the blind clairvoyant and warms his hands over the fire, having joined the group, half a dozen men and women of various ages, and they don't even seem to mind when he begins to eat their food, quite a marvelous spread of mussels, clams, olives, pickles, large loaves of bread, and so forth.

One of the women, another circus beast, a moll of sorts with a heavy moustache and hair that roils around a pair of big brutish shoulders, hands him the bottle and nods and gives him the invitation to drink up, by pinching her lips tight, jutting her chin forward and thrusting it up a couple of times. Oh, he drinks, he drinks good and deep does he, does Max. And the fire burns and burns into the clouding, spar-bleak night.

❖

Sleep is a natural antidote to exhaustion. But I wasn't exhausted. I was afraid. Sleep is good medicine against fear, too, much the same way amnesia can protect us from our past.

I couldn't remember ever having slept so much, and still, when I woke up later that afternoon, a cloud of sleepiness lay over me.

I went out into the bright afternoon to get a cup of coffee. No one knew me in town. I didn't recognize anyone, either. That was curious. Here was a small place, the place where I'd grown up, and I was very much a stranger. It made me realize just what an introverted world, a small, half-invented world, we children had grown up in. I could tell you the life histories of so many people on the box, so many characters in books, but of these people out here walking along the streets while the leaves were giving out in the breeze and fluttering along the paling grass, I knew nothing. It was just something I noticed. I didn't feel bad about it. I didn't feel that I'd missed out on anything in particular. Indeed, at the moment it worked out for the best that we didn't know each other. I would have nothing to say to any of them who might have come up and said, "Grace Brush, how nice to see you, how is your father doing, how is your brother getting along, what is life like in the city, I was so sorry to hear about your marriage but someone told me that you hadn't got a divorce does that mean maybe you two are rethinking things?"

The coffee steamed in the cup before me, and I looked out the window. I ordered another cup and drank the second one with sugar, but it seemed only to make me more sleepy.

❖

Home sweet home, reads the valentine card taped on the window. We pull back into a kitchen. The tablecloth recalls the pantaloons of the man on the beach. Here there is no wine flowing. The meal on the table is simple, delicious looking yet rather indifferent in the sense that it doesn't make us feel so much hungry as simply satisfied that it would taste all right if we were forced to sit down and eat it ourselves. There are some sweet potatoes with little melted marshmallows like fish eyes peeking from their slit skins, there is a roast on a platter. The kitchen is tidy. All its appointments and furniture are old-fashioned and homey. There is an octagonal cat-faced clock on the wall, whose hour and second hands are black whiskers, and whose pendulum is a curly tail, and the clock says it is ten-thirty.

No one is eating, because everyone is worried about Max. Grady looks down at her plate in silence, avoiding her brother Dante's occasional stolen glance—boys are such dolts. We can't tell whether she feels ashamed of herself because of her wanton behavior this afternoon in the orchard, or whether her sad mood arises from the disappearance of her older brother. None of the coarseness we saw in her face, none of the lewdness in her lips and rolling eyes, is present now as she sits there, awaiting some word about Max.

"We don't know where he is," the officer tells them. And

yes, while they are all waiting for some word from the search party, he wouldn't say no to having just a small slice off that roast beef. Contemporaneously, he couldn't be faulted for asking himself, where was this woman's husband? Three children, out here alone with them on an island like this, it wasn't hardly proper.

"Excellent," he says, commenting on the meat.

"Thank you," the mother says, her eyes appropriately grave, but with a kind of correspondent shine to match his own, which glow with human hunger. "Why don't you have some more."

Cut to the beach again, where the fire now is burning lower, and a lean-to tent has been erected to keep in abeyance the sea-chill. The party is quieter, and several of the men and women have fallen asleep randomly, it would seem, in one another's arms. The same woman who earlier had passed the bottle to Max is now voicing skepticism about something Max let slip, and we can see that Max is unable to defend what he has claimed to be the truth because he has drunk too much.

She says, "There ain't no such thing as a virgin on this island, on this here earth for that matter. Who you think you're kidding? Virgin!" and she spits—with the same vehemence Max himself had shown earlier, in the orchard—at the crisp sand.

"You think I like being a virgin?"

"You lie. Look here. You come splashing out of your mother's downstairs mouth and she is heaving and grinding like she is riding the biggest stallion in the stable, and she's crying and howling, and it's all just like you were her best lover for then and for ever, and what happens but you start up yelping and howling too, because you must know, like we all must know deep down that, by gum, that was the best time in bed any of us was ever going to have, and everybody's crying and screaming with tears of joy, and there is blood and the oil of afterbirth everywhere, and the rest of it is downhill, man, you sucking your mother's

breast, and you both maybe get a little bit of joy out of
that—she's nurturing and all, and you're getting your milk
and all—but nobody's crying with the birth-ecstasy anymore I can tell you that much."

Max is feeling queasy. Does the woman Meg have to bare
her breast, which is grotesquely long and flat, to illustrate?:
"See this thing here, this has been the cause of plenty of
pleasure to plenty of people I can tell you. But nobody's
given me greater pleasure while nuzzling it than my own
several darlings."

"Why don't you shut up, Meg," says a young woman,
who is off in a corner of the lean-to, lying alone. "Don't
listen to her, Max. Nobody ever got pleasure off that dead
bag."

"Screw you," and she leans into Max and whispers
loudly, "Screw you, get it? It's a joke. It's a joke because
she's never shaken the sheets, get it? So she doesn't even
have any idea what we philosophers are philosophizing
about over here."

"You're so vulgar and stupid you make me sick," offers
the young woman.

Max, feeling full of food, wine, words, has begun to
wonder whether it wouldn't have been better to accept his
shame and go home, rather than to put himself into this
awkward situation. He thinks longingly of his bedroom,
his bed, the duck-down comforter, so warm, his sheets
tucked in tight around him, everything in his room organized and familiar.

"Hey, I got an idea," proposes a rheumy-eyed man.

"That's news," Meg chides.

"No, I do. This here kid thinks he's a virgin, right? And
she over there is a virgin, and well—one plus one—you tell
me."

Meg pulls on her chin. She warms to this idea. "The
moon's up high, the tide's gone out, the seabirds have all
gone abed. I think there's merit here somewhere."

The young woman huddled in the corner darkness says, "Have your fun, but leave me out of it."

Max is poking the fire with the heel of his shoe, and shifts in the sandy bed. Meg moves in close by the boy, and whispers into his ear, "Max, now listen to me, I'm prepared to believe you, that you're a virgin, and all. But now you must prove yourself to me and Bill here and to the virgin there and everyone else, but above all to yourself Max. Are you ready?"

Max is handed a just-uncorked bottle, and invited to drink "five fingers' worth," which he obligingly does. The scuffling that seems to be going on back in the dark recess of the lean-to is kept out of the camera's eye, whose central attention remains fixed on Max's face. A lock of hair dangles over his brow and, encouraged by the wine and the talking heads of several men who resemble those faces depicted by Pieter Brueghel the Elder in his painting *Parable of the Blind* (a reproduction of which the observant cinephile will have noticed taped to the refrigerator door back in the kitchen scene), we are almost able to spot the exact moment when Max undergoes his conversion from an innocent to a wholly debauched monster. The moon, playing one of its commonest roles under Berg's meticulous direction, sheds a glowing light upon the lunatic events that unfold under the fluttering, rickety beach tent. Max half-crawls, is half-dragged, to the young woman, whose clothes have been stripped away by the unbridled troupe of misfits. The scene dissolves to mouse-gray as the camera pulls back to show us how much the lean-to has come to resemble a great, black bird flapping aimlessly on the shore, its wings unable to lift it into the wind, its stick legs helpless to walk, its mad human hatchlings squirming like slugs in dung beneath its smutty shadow.

❖

This scene haunted Berg, and he haunted it right back. While he was trying to edit the passage something he couldn't verbalize pricked his curiosity. It nagged, and he ran it over and over, studying the frames one by one, running it through speeded-up, freeze-framing whenever he sensed he was close to identifying what it was that bothered him. Here he had written the scene. He had directed it, had sent someone by car to the lab in New York so that it could be processed overnight and returned to him midmorning the next day. And now, as he projected it in the moviola, he didn't know what it was he was seeing. That is, he seemed to be witnessing something *through* the images and sounds, and it occurred to him that he might be near an understanding of why it was that making this *Almanac* had been so important to him.

Analise saw he was beginning to be obsessed with the dailies (nights he passed in the library, days when not shooting, in his room since the library was not private enough for his needs). He had managed in two weeks to convert his simple bedroom, with its few pieces of childhood memorabilia on the walls, into a private hell of sorts, with equipment, cables, canisters, clothes, bottles half empty and glasses half full, strewn throughout its interior. Cast and crew were showing signs of edginess, which Analise advised him risked more than just poor performances on the set, more than just losing money in paying out wages to people who were forced to blow off the day in some roadhouse—began to risk losing the whole project before it was so much as half shot.

"I may want to remake this scene," was what Berg explained, knowing how hopelessly perfectionist or dilettantish the statement might have made him look in her eyes. Art film, indeed—the way she left, livid was what it looked like to Berg, though he'd not so much as looked up from the gun-metal-gray moviola box when she'd been there, dressing him down. The spool holder carried this one length of work print back and forth, chirruping a bit, as it could have used some oil, and Berg simply spoke to himself, admitted aloud in the room that there didn't seem to be anything the matter with the scene itself. The scene was crisp, evocative, read on the luminous window of the projection machine as being, visually, even stronger than Berg had written it. He knew he could tinker with the rough cuts, change the order of things around a little, edit together spots with a rather different sense of rhythm. It wasn't a matter of editing, though. What nagged him was the sense—a sense that grew through the hours of that particular night into absolute conviction—that he had lived this thing he was looking at, lived it himself, sometime in his life; whereas, of course, he knew that he hadn't.

As obsessively focussed on the passage as he had gotten, Berg was not lacking in discipline. His colleagues' worry, while surely understandable, need not, he told himself, have gone beyond a concern that this perfectionism would blow the production budget through the roof. But when the youngish actor who was playing Dante up and quit, demanding his pay for the several days of shooting he had been in on, Berg woke up to the problems he was causing. He was the one who was supposed to be solving problems, not creating and fomenting them, and at once he was back to work.

"Where'd he go?" Berg asked Analise.

"He said it was none of my business."

"He signed a release, though, yes?"

"Of course. Before we ran a single frame on him."

"You pay him?"

"I told him if he wanted his money he'd have to talk to you about it."

"Well, he didn't and I don't pay AWOLs."

Analise thought the better of explaining to Berg that an AWOL was precisely what everyone on the film had begun to think he himself had become, including the actor who quit. Instead she asked, "What do you want to do about recasting? You realize we're going to have to shoot that whole sequence again."

"Hell no we're not. This problem is easy."

Every appearance of the Dante character in the film henceforward would be played by a new actor, it didn't matter what he looked like, whether he was stout or tall, black-eyed or hazel. Grady's entire life with Dante was going to be a fantasy. That her figment of a man should change his appearance didn't much matter, as he wasn't a reality anyway. Grady and Max in fact would have no real brother, and Grady would come over the course of the film to understand that.

❖

The seduction was to be followed with a sequence of inter-cuts in which the various members of the party on the beach are being interrogated by the police. This was shot indoors, in the kitchen in fact, with a vast sheet of white cloth hung as a backdrop to the action. We only see the faces of the detainees. They are sitting at the table. All the blinds in the kitchen are down, and the glass windows in the back door are covered with black construction paper. The lighting is stage left intensive, and obvious in its arti-fice.

We're not sure whether these people have been charged with anything or not. We begin to suspect that just as we seem to be sitting in the interrogator's seat; we wonder whether we weren't somehow involved in the surveillance that preceded the arrests the night before. We, the camera, have become some kind of scrutinizing eye. Not only do we assume the role of "voyeur," but we now are participating in the investigation of a crime.

We offer the young woman a cigarette, and she takes it. She looks tired, and not very grateful to us for our little kindness. No matter. We recognize her. She was the one who was the victim of the attack.

"The others," the interrogator says, after lighting the fag for her, "claim they're innocent—every last one of them."

"They're not."

"They say you invited that kid, what's his name, Max, that you invited him to—"

"It's a lie." She's awfully matter-of-fact. Maybe we ought to make a note of it. She could be in shock, or something.

"Can you tell me what you were doing there in the first place?"

"They invited me to a party. It sounded like fun. So I went."

A pause. We see her face now, for the first time, having followed the cigarette up to her lips. We see her face is drawn. She has full lips, a prominent nose, tall forehead, dark quick eyes. She looks like Gina Marie behind the lace curtain in the famous scene from Jean Epstein's *Coeur Fidèle*, or Mona, the tragic wanderer in Agnes Varda's *Vagabond*. Berg would certainly want us to make such comparisons. She also happens to look quite a lot like Grace Brush, though of course she isn't.

"It sounded like fun, and you went."

"I went. Big deal. There's no crime in that is there?"

"A crime may or may not have taken place as a result of your decision to go."

This gets a rise out of her. "Hey, man, the crime was committed against me, all right?"

"The crime was allegedly committed, allegedly against you."

"I don't get it. You're making it sound like I'm the one who did something wrong."

"Nothing of the sort. What would you possibly be guilty of?" The interrogator has said this with such heavy irony that we, along with the young woman herself perhaps, are clearly supposed to begin to doubt the veracity of her accusation, even though we were witness to her violation ourselves.

Fade to this. Max's face against the same indistinct smoky background as the scene before. The interrogator's voice asks him, "What makes you think you could get away with something like what you've done?"

"I haven't—"

"Stow it, my friend, I don't want to hear it. All you people are the same. You think you can get away with anything that comes into your head. But you can't. You don't realize that an island is the worst place on earth to commit a crime. You can't get away."

"I'm not trying to get away. I haven't done anything. I was just doing what the others said I was supposed to do."

The interrogator allows a low, conventional, knowing laugh. "You say you haven't done anything and then the very next thing that comes out of your mouth is a confession."

"That's not a confession."

"Would you mind putting on record what it was the others told you to do, then?"

"Hey, look, I'm not interested in being Nero's fiddle here," argues Max, suddenly rather more mature in his response than we might have expected. "If they want to go out and burn the town down they can do it without musical accompaniment."

Another laugh. "You kids think you know it all, don't you? You spend half your lives glued to the TV, and the other half acting as if you're on it. Well, I've got all the time in the world to wait. I'm on wage, see, so it don't make a bit of difference to me whether you sing now or next year."

Max hesitates before he says, "Yeah, right. I wonder how many cruddy cop shows I've seen where I've heard that same line."

"Don't push me, son."

"And that line, too."

"That does it."

"And that line, too!"

The interrogator's hand, a pulpy pink slab we would not want to claim for our own, now appears on the right side of the screen, as if it were our own, and the cigarette that is in it, the cigarette that has obviously been the source of all the smoke in the dark interrogation room, has been turned around so that it is held between the thumb and forefinger. Max shrinks down in his chair. As always in these kinds of situations, we find ourselves wondering, Why doesn't the kid just get up and flee? In the same way we are often spared the sight of the hapless girl after she has stumbled on the path in her failed flight from the murderer or the monster, here it is left to our imaginations what may or may not happen next to Max.

❖

There was a barrier reef and the cast swam out to it after the day's shoot. There was a lot of horsing around, because everybody was exhausted, and the film was working out. Berg walked out into the waves with them until the water reached his chest and heaved over his shoulders in sizzling foam, but he wouldn't swim the hundred yards out to where it got shallow again. He drifted, standing up buoyant in the sea, spitting out silver water, and watching the others diminish in size as they flailed into the breakers to make the reef. He felt contented; he felt possessive of them all. The sputter and crash of kelp-clogged wash on the sand was punctuated by pure laughter. They were a family, and loved one another . . .

When Berg woke up from this dream, to find himself on the floor of the library with the sun streaming down through the window, he rose to his knees, and felt nauseated at the prospect of facing another day of agonizing over his film. He needn't have bothered to worry about it, however, as he soon would find out.

Upstairs, he took a shower. Cold water on the back of his neck to slow the blood to his brain. After he dried off, and put on his robe, he looked in the mirror. Why had he gotten himself into this mess?

Now that he had used the equipment, he couldn't hope to return it for any amount approaching what he had paid. He had wasted hours of film—thank god he'd decided to use the sixteen-millimeter stock. The lab bills were exorbitant because he had required overnight development, a messenger into the city at the end of the day, messenger back in the morning, in order to stay on a schedule that would get his crew out of Scrub Farm before his father returned. The recasting and rescripting he had thought would have gone easily of course hadn't. He kept having to reject Analise's suggestions (as gently as he could, though because of the pressure he was under he knew that he'd failed at this, too); she simply didn't have the same needs as he—to her the *Almanac* was a work of imagination, to him it was—well, what? Some lousy exorcism? A bit of satirical revenge on his family? As an act of truth, replicating emotional events that he had suffered through, in order to try better to understand himself, and as an act of self-definition, the film was proving to be a radical defeat as well.

He put one bare foot in front of the other, and found himself downstairs. The air of disorganization and discontent seemed to fill the house; he knew he could tell everyone that they could go home, that he had to rethink the thing, and they would go, knowing he had made a fool of himself—but there was the problem of the money. It hadn't been his to lose, not like this. For a fleeting instant the thought of going out to find that beached vessel somewhere to shoot a promotional picture for Gulf Stream seemed a good alternative to confessing grievous failure. He was astute enough, though, to recognize that this, too, would only be a waste of time, that he'd been kidding himself. He had never felt quite so cornered. Even if he produced some short to offer his father as an excuse, the truth of the matter was that Faw wouldn't go for it; why would an operation that depended on the most silent anonymity go out and bother producing a silly promo film? If they were questioned, a hundred hours of film could not serve as sufficient evidence to refute the charges that might be brought against them. He had been doing nothing these last months, indeed these last years, but conciliating himself with pipe dreams.

It was then that it hit him. The house was too quiet. He looked up. A new fear came over him. Where was everyone?

"Analise," he said; and he shouted, "Analise?" Of course. His fears were confirmed. The realization was pressed upon him with the alacrity, the snap of a wasp sting. Everyone had left. He had been abandoned. What a stinking lark. Even the opportunity to make a fool of himself by sending his cast and crew away was denied him.

For a moment he panicked about the equipment, but when he checked the library and mudroom he discovered that nothing was missing. He went for the freezer and the bottle of vodka that was in it. Meade, and the others, he could understand. He had been increasingly difficult—no, he had to admit, he'd become impossible. He hadn't slept longer than three hours a night for the past three weeks, he'd drunk well beyond his fair share of vodka and homemade espresso, he had been open with the cast and crew about the problems he was experiencing holding the thing together. Deplorable, he thought. Never complain, never explain—Andrew Carnegie and his father were right in that. Piteous whining, who needs it, especially when it comes from the mouth of a supposed superior.

Could he splice together what he had into something that might be viable, make back the money so that no one involved with the Trust would find out what had happened? He still had some days left before he had to get everything out of here (What was today, anyway? he wondered as he brought his mouth down to the bottle and lifted back). No, not really.

The vodka got Berg going. He knew he could turn this thing around. He had to depend on himself. He had to depend on what he had done thus far that was useful, to get him through whatever he had done to thwart himself, which meant (for one) to stop reviewing these scenes, stop trying to interpret them, make of them what they were. Give it up, man, like Christ on the rood when he was talking to his father who had put him in the position of becoming ritual carnage in the first place said, It is done. Well, it was done here, too. Some things aren't meant to fly. Could he tell Analise that? Without having to grovel? Of course he couldn't because there he was, already not depending on himself. And anyway, Analise—what was she but a deserter?

This was the same predicament he had found himself in as a seventeen-year-old—exiled then, exiled now. The film was wrong, the whole idea was wrong. Who was he to try to make a portrait of these people he had never understood? Max being Berg, who was Max? Berg, being Berg, could ask, Who is Berg? and know that he would never get it together enough to know. Berg couldn't hope to claim self-comprehension, so why create an image meant to represent an idea of himself that could never, ever be so much as passingly accurate? For instance, Max was no virgin, he knew better. Max might have been a very confused soul, but he understood that those cretins under the tent on the beach represented not shelter, but exposure. So why all the pretense? Why all the playing God—indeed, if there was a God, and Berg was pretty sure there wasn't, he could have it, man. Whatever perks and prerogatives might come with the office surely were overshadowed by these the messiest of questions.

Which brought up another interesting question. When are you exposing yourself and when sheltering? The vodka was not as cold as before, but it still tasted of freedom (tasted of freedom, yes, because alcohol never tasted good, but did smack of release)—and he was able to come to the thought that all these words were tangled up in the most intriguing way, just as he was. You expose film to show things, but you come to an island named Shelter and what right do you have to show what you believe you know? In the skin trade, Berg had learned that those who went in front of the camera were those who seemed—to those who stood behind in the semidark—the ones who were most protected.

When the telephone rang he considered whether or not it was prudent to answer, given the state he was in. It kept ringing. Someone on the other end clearly knew he was here, and intended to let it ring until he picked up. He answered, as much to stop the harsh jangle as anything else. He didn't say hello, just listened.

"Berg? It's me," said Analise.

His heart was beating too fast, and he lifted the bottle again. He knew what she was going to say; he wasn't so confused as to hope that she was about to save him.

"Berg, did you read the contract you and I signed when we started this project?"

He wasn't going to give her the satisfaction.

"I tried to talk you out of doing this, all right, in the first place, you have to remember that now. I never wanted you to let yourself in for it, I knew it could happen, and it did. You wanted to go ahead, nothing I could have—"

"Analise?"

"Yes," she answered, encouraged perhaps by how even was the tone of his voice. She always liked Berg. This debacle was a shame, in fact. Why did he have to be so ambitious and secretive about this film? He was getting in his own way.

"Piss off," said Berg.

And, unprepared for that but not one to be outmaneuvered, she said something to the same effect before putting the receiver down hard into its cradle.

❖

"There are no leaps in nature: everything in it is graduated, shaded. If there were an empty space between any two beings, what reason would there be for proceeding from the one to the other? There is thus no being above and below which there are not other beings that are united to it by some characters and separated from it by others." So Charles Bonnet says in his *Contemplation de la nature,* as quoted by Michel Foucault in his book *The Order of Things,* which I still carry around with me sometimes, though I had loathed him when I read him those years ago in school. I am not French, I am not a philosopher, I am not a scholar, nor was I even a good student; it isn't intended as a pretense on my part to parade this bit of thinking before you, but even though Foucault's recipe for headaches, which I have tried, that business of mixing walnuts and wine, only made me sick—I've always been sort of fond of this quotation of his from Bonnet. Bonnet had this idea about an absolute encyclopedia, in which knowledge, action, language, and everything conceivable would be interwoven. Truths of every kind would be contained in it, and I suppose every sort of falsehood would have to be there too. All words, all acts, things that could never be accomplished. Everything linked, all branches interwoven into a principal beauty. Arbitrariness would stand proudly holding hands with order. Chaos and the sublime would form its grammar. Faith, charity, evil—you wouldn't know your ass from a hole in the ground, as it were, and yet in a way you would, since there would be a steady progress in which all systems would be both partial and universal. A divine mishmash, and all at once so crystalline.

I don't know why this came to mind, when I stood there again at the window of Djuna Cobbetts's bedroom, not knowing precisely why none of the lights in the house up the hill were on as they had been the night before. Still I

sensed there was someone moving around in the rooms. I
hadn't noticed that the cars in the drive were gone, and I
didn't know at what stage in the film Berg and his crew
stood. There was movement in the house, I couldn't see it,
but there was, and whoever was walking around inside
either didn't care about running into furniture, dusty
chairs and the like, or else, like a ghost, knew the place well.
Then I got it. Berg was alone. Of course, he had been left
to his own devices. It felt like a leap of knowing, but, as I
say, I think Bonnet had a point—it was a graduated thing,
this understanding of my brother's abandonment.

Berg was in trouble. He deserved to be in trouble. But
still I wondered hard whether he had made a mistake that
would deserve the kind of punishment he might have set
himself up for. Barely knowing what he had done, or was
in the process of doing, I sensed that he had made no real
mistake. He was lost, is all. I had figured out that the girl
in the orchard was supposed to be me, that Desmond was
the naked boy sent in to make love to me, that the stranger
at the edge, watching, was both the voyeur audience and
the character Berg.

Sex was a fiction in the fact of life that I felt I'd made my
peace with—I could take it or leave it, all it ever had done
for me was either get me into trouble emotionally, or shat-
ter a relationship that I felt was better off before sex entered into it. I had no quarrel with Berg's casting me as
some kind of incestuous nymphomaniac—I knew that I
was and wasn't. Nothing he could invent would ever match
what had happened in my life. Nothing anyone could invent could ever match what happens to any of us. I didn't
care that much about the artistic integrity of his endeavor.
Other than the money, which again I didn't care about
except insofar as it might cripple Faw, none of what he was
doing affected me, did it? I had to admit to myself that
though I only glimpsed his contorted portrait of me, I
understood that it wouldn't finally make much difference
to me one way or another what he thought of our past, and

how he described it to others, who would never perfectly
understand it either, no matter how they tried, no matter
what form the presentation took. What had Berg ever given
as a brother to me, beyond this funhouse-mirror movie
portrait he was proposing to complete?

I could hear my blood beating in my ears, and my breath
coming in and leaving me. The distance between the carriage house and the farm seemed long. Tonight there were
clouds that hazed out the stars and moon overhead, and it
had been quite a lot chillier when I rode across the open
causeways. There was a damp over the island that smelled
of rain. Dressed in my blacks, I had walked across the field
to Mrs. Cobbetts's this time with considerably more courage than the night before. The key had gone into her back
door lock with far greater ease, the staircase though
shrouded in dark I found and ascended without the same
trepidation I had experienced on Tuesday. But now it
seemed that all my confidence had flowed out of me. I could
have gone back downstairs, and across the dying grass to
the house, walked in, and discovered precisely what was
going on over there, and been well within my rights. Instead, I dialed the house.

Berg answered, "What," in a guilelessly nettled voice.

"Berg? It's me, Grace."

He hesitated; I sensed he was working through whether
this boded well for him or not, whether I could be of some
use or not, and as I heard that silence, and divined his
process of thinking about me, I realized that I myself had
reached a moment of profound change toward him, toward
the whole family, such as it was. I didn't have the energy
to wait for him to decide how best to use me—was it energy, or immaturity that empowered such behavior in people? a question with an obvious answer, it seems to me now.
And so I burst in on his silence, "Berg, I know more or less
what you are doing. I know that you're in trouble."

"Where are you?" he asked.

It wasn't the right question. He was buying more time to think.

"Berg. I think you, and maybe Faw, too, are in deeper trouble than you understand. Someone knows."

"Knows what?"

This infuriated me; here he was, so transparent that even I, his sister, had been able to observe his activities at close quarters without being detected, so vulnerable that his extravagant fantasy had been found out even before he had begun to indulge it, and yet so blind to his own plain pretenses that he could even now feel comfortable prattling along to the one person who might stand beside him. Given that, though I didn't know—in some ways may not ever know—how freely he had entangled me in his illegal whimsy, I understood there was more at risk than Berg's or my feelings, I didn't bother to chastise him, or preach. I said, simply, "We've got to get all that stuff away from the house, destroy the film."

"I won't do it."

"You don't do it, and I'm going to have to go to Faw."

There was a kind of shredded laughter, choked, that I heard, before he said something to the effect that he wasn't impressed. "Going to tattle," was in his outburst, and then he said, "Where are you?" and it felt remarkably threatening. I have always had this problem of measuring my own perceptions, trusting the clarity of my hearing and seeing. Impressionable I know I've been in the past, and box-drama tutored; but he was cornered, and sounded it.

"Berg, I'm willing to help you. Let's get the equipment out of the house. Then we'll decide about the film."

"You don't understand, Grace."

"I do."

"You're willing to help, you say, well if you're willing to help just steer clear, all right, just leave me alone."

If there were an empty space between any two beings, what reason would there be for proceeding from the one to the other?

Bonnet hadn't written these words to mean what I then garnered from them. The night yard that stretched beyond the carriage house seemed now to extend in such a way that it became swollen with anger. Maybe I cared more than I thought, at least about that empty space that loomed between me and my brother. Or else, maybe there was a reason for choosing not to proceed toward him. Berg might assume that I wouldn't go to our father, but did he know that I might, in fact, be willing to take him up on his instructions to stay away? A peculiar wave of liberating peace came over me—if only that anger could be reconstrued into some sort of indifference, then maybe I'd find a way to be able to love Berg, as a sister, from a sister's distance.

I must have been crying, because he was telling me not to cry. I didn't understand anything about his project, he was saying, and there were no serious problems with anything he was up to with it. He hadn't meant to be so short with me. Nothing he was doing was intended to cause trouble for anyone, least of all the family. He didn't know what I was talking about when I said that someone knew, someone had something on him—everyone's got something on everyone. It's nothing out of the ordinary. His intentions were good, he said it twice.

I let him finish his monologue without interrupting because what I was searching for was the key to my indifference, which would be the key to my being able actually to hear my brother, even maybe help him, if there was anything that could be done to help him. The insight that came to me, as fallacious as it might have been, helped me to discover, possibly, the beginnings of what it was I thought I wanted from myself in order to survive (I recognize this is abstract, but it is the closest I can come to formulating in words what happened to me, then). You see, it dawned on me there was someone else who might have had a motive in sending me that anonymous letter. Berg himself. Why not? Wouldn't that have given him the perfect means by which he could escape falling alone? I considered asking him, but now I understood that anything he might say would have to be taken with a grain of salt. *Everything is graduated, shaded,* it is true.

When I finally agreed to consider Berg's request that I stay out of his way, and that I keep what I know to myself, I sat on Djuna's pliant bed and noticed how heavy the receiver had gotten in my hand. It seemed I could hardly hold it up. I was trying to remember something that I knew, not something that was pertinent to what Berg and I had been discussing, no; it was a sensation that now spread over me. That Berg had set the phone down, maybe on the counter in the kitchen, maybe on the desk in the library, became faintly clear to me through this apprehension of weight in the dark around me. I hadn't hung up, I knew, because there was no dial tone coming from the handset. My throat was a little sore, and my ears hurt, especially my left ear. When I put down the handset on the bed, quietly, because I just couldn't hold it up anymore, it occurred to me to go to the window and open it, and get some fresh night air. I stood, and made my way to the nearest casement, unlocked it, feeling drugged or dryly drunk, and pulled up, and got down on my knees and rested my head on my forearms on the sill. I breathed in slowly and deep. I remembered Dr. Trudeau once telling me about breathing into a bag, and to stay calm, not to be afraid, not to begin hyperventilating—and though I didn't have the strength to go about searching in the dark through Mrs. Cobbetts's closets and drawers to find a bag, I did tuck my face into the top of my blouse and drew in air that was caught between skin and fabric. The ocean, I thought; my damp skin smelled a bit like the ocean, salty and of apricot.

Several of the lights in the farmhouse had been turned on by the time I recovered my senses. From where I sat against the wall I could hear the tone signal from the telephone, a three-tone scale that strode up, quiveringly, high-pitched. Whether minutes or hours had passed I couldn't tell, but I would guess that it was the former. My petit seizure—this is what must have occurred—had passed, and now my senses were clearer than spring water. I was still moving in a sort of slow motion as I hung up the telephone, and it was an almost (almost) pleasant feeling to swim back to the window. The air was very brisk. Though my clothing was damp from sweat, my skin and mouth were as dry as if they'd been baked.

When I put my fingers to the frame and began to pull down on the window, the light, or lights, up the rise, up in the cherry tree by the house, flickered in the most cheerful way. Pygmyish, bantam lights; and for a second I thought, *megrim*, which would explain my having passed out. But they seemed, and I hope you will understand, *less real* to me than any of my megrim lights, less internal to me, less a part of me: they were out there; and their being out there brought them into an even more frighteningly sharp focus.

What was Berg doing up in the tree? was my first thought, or hope. The light—now it seemed to be just one light, but jostled, perhaps in the hand of whoever was climbing the tree—was white, another indication that it wasn't the flare man out there, who finally had found his way out to Shelter Island, to his old friend, Grace. But then I realized that, of course, no, it wouldn't make sense for Berg to be up there. It had to be the author of that cryptic little message I received the other day, or someone else who was aware of Berg's film or the Trust scam—aware, that is, of the "mistake."

Now, I have never been a brave person. As one gets older the wisdom that one gains, whether by purpose or chance, allows less and less for one to flirt with the impudence of things unknown. "Even paranoiacs have enemies," a poet once said, and he was surely right. Nevertheless, what could I do? There were only a couple of possibilities here. National Council of Churches, I thought—I would have laughed but for the fact that I preferred to maintain my

own cover. Or else it was Neden, or Pannett, or more likely
one of those types—skin trade brethren of Neden and Pannett—that Berg had obviously gotten himself entangled
with and possibly betrayed.

I decided that I couldn't stay here in Djuna Cobbetts's
room any longer. I wanted to do something, anything. It
hardly mattered whether I would walk up the hill and
confront the light in the tree, confront Berg, bring matters
toward some manner of denouement, or else backtrack
along Coecles Inlet toward the causeways on foot, leaving
the bike behind, and just get out of Berg's life like he asked
me to. Up here, hiding as I'd always done in high places,
aeries, looking out onto the world like a raptor but without
so much as the most menial set of claws with which to
address it and bring it under my control, I had no chance
of bringing our scattered lives back into some kind of align-
ment. I felt like a child. I felt like screaming.

Of course I didn't retreat along the lapping inlet toward
that miserable, airless hotel room on the other side of the
island. Retreat just didn't seem an option. My life, such as
it happened to be, was here. What I knew about the world,
such as it happened to have come to me, had come from
here, too. So I climbed, like a possessed woman out of a
late-night movie, say, a zombie, someone beyond the
thaumaturgical good old pale of death that you sometimes
see long about two in the morning on the box, someone
who can no longer be hurt because she's been hurt so much
that there is no more hurting her that will register, and the
direction I was headed was up toward my home. My lost
older brother was there. Someone I had loved as a brother
and in my imagination, as a child, as a lover was there in
spirit. My father, whether he chose it or not, and my
mother as well, idem whether she liked it or not, were
there. And it was where I was going to go.

The light was down out of the tree by the time I got to
the row of arborvitae, and it was almost past me by the time
I knew what hit me. Whoever knocked me over had run

past me, past Djuna Cobbetts's house, and, I supposed, made his escape along the scree and vegetation that lined the water edge. The figure had emerged from behind the corner of the house, where the cherry tree stood, so suddenly, and bore down upon me with such frightening speed, that I had no chance of seeing him in the dark.

"Grace?" said Berg.

He helped me up, and took the sheet of paper that was there on the ground beside me. My head throbbed, not of a megrim pain, but from having been hit—grazed, really—by the escaping figure. Berg put his arm around me, and we went inside. He was as unsteady on his feet as I was on mine, and I could smell the vodka on his breath and clothes.

Of all the unexpected events of the evening, what was typed on the sheet of paper was most unexpected of all. It was the same white paper, the same typeface, and was unsigned, just like that note I had received before. Berg read it first, and his face was drained of color when he finished and handed it to me. "If you want to avoid a certain party's reporting all the activities of that division of Geiger known as the Gulf Stream Trust, and its illegitimate bastard offspring known to the Revenue Service people as the Almanac branch, and if you want to avoid a certain party's putting into the hands of Mr. Charles Brush, who, like the rest of you, will not survive said disclosures, a complete and accurate cataloguing of all 'creative' activities that have been financed through the unfortunate lending services that you his son and daughter have undertaken to facilitate, payment of five hundred thousand dollars . . ." and the note went on to describe details of how the money was to be dropped off in front of a car rental desk at La Guardia Airport—it was just frigging ludicrous!

Berg was yelling something about how all this was my fault, that the only person who could have known about everything was Cutts, and that if I'd shown a little restraint . . .

Incredulous at what I was hearing, I said, "You know

that's all a bunch—look, Berg, what does this mean here about 'his son and *daughter*,' I mean listen, what the hell have you been doing?"

"That's wrong, that business, I don't know what they're talking about. I don't remember—"

"You what? You don't remember what? You used my name in some of this stuff, didn't you?"

"I don't know."

"What kind of junk have you got me involved in?"

"It doesn't even matter. What matters is what are we going to do?"

"We? Leave me out of it."

"Hey, Grace. It's too late. I told you to stay out of it, didn't I? I told you to leave me alone. I told you it wasn't any of your business. Well, you didn't listen to me. You're in it, too, now. I think what we have to do is pay him. He goes through with this and everything falls to pieces."

"Not everything, not me. I haven't done anything."

"We don't know who this is doing this, but as I said it seems to me that Cutts is the only person I can think of—"

"Cutts would never do this. That wasn't him just then."

"How do you know?"

"I don't know for sure, but I'm saying Cutts, this just isn't something he would do, that's all."

Berg paused, and said, the paper quaking in his hand, with as studied a calm as he was able to summon, "Do you have any idea how Faw would react if he knew about you and Cutts?"

"I'm not six years old, Burke. There are limits, all right, there are limits to how much I'm going to be able to care what he or you or anybody else thinks. Whatever right he might have to make a negative judgment of me has got to be offset by what he's doing himself out there, with this church thing, and all the rest. I don't pretend to understand business, and I think he's wise enough not to pretend to understand my personal life. For openers, he'd realize what Cutts and I did is none of his business, so to speak."

"And what about Bea? What about your friend Bea?
How would she feel if she knew?"

"Pretty cowardly thought."

Berg folded the paper, put it in his pocket, and in a
quieter voice said, "What about me and Faw?"

"You actually want to pay this person, is that what I'm
hearing here? Have you lost your mind?"

What would I have done, just then, standing there in the
house where we grew up together, if I had known what I
was to know about a month later? I wonder whether I
would still have turned my back on Berg and walked out
into the night field, returned to the hotel, settled my bill
after waking up the poor innkeeper, and driven back to
New York. Would I still have made the decision to leave
him to his own devices and accept whatever consequences
my refusal to capitulate to his maudlin requests might
bring?

I don't know. I'd love to think I would have had the
clarity of mind to make an even response. There are reasons for me to believe I might have managed, in the face of
Berg's desperate duplicity, to maintain some dignity; to
have found a middle path whereby I wouldn't become his
friend, but nevertheless wouldn't turn into his enemy, either. Even now, I surprise myself. Even now I look at what
a shambles things had become, and I have to pinch myself
to see whether I am awake to all the nuances of what Berg
has accomplished, not only practically and legally, but
emotionally. If I saw Berg how would I react now? Maybe
I overestimate my ability to remain loyal in the face of
cowardice and rejection and betrayal. I look back over these
pages, and I believe that everything I have been able to
puzzle together about us, this family, is truthful, and fair.
It seems, in its perverse way, logical that Berg would have
felt his resorting to a bit of cinematic flimflammery was the
best way to drag himself up out of the depths of his disaster.
What a dramatic piece of work to type up a note that

offered to blackmail us—himself included, indeed himself
above all—and lure me into believing that someone else
was involved. He was never going to be able to finish his
Almanac, so why not turn his own life into some kind of
teeming farce, using me as the straight man and audience
as well.

I have to face the fact that it is possible any equanimity
I have had in light of all this would have self-destructed.
Had I known that night that Berg realized he was in trouble and knew that there was no way out of it but to draw
me into helping him at my own expense I can say, I think
I can say with honesty, I might have tried to kill him. It's
not like I'm not a passionate woman. It's not like I learned
nothing about men and their sometimes nakedly vile re-
sponses to the realities of defeat from reading Shahrazad
and Can Xue, or watching those shows on the box. In
Arabia, back in time, when a king could get it into his skull
that the only way to trust a woman as a wife was to make
love to her and then slit her throat at dawn so that she
would never be unfaithful to him, in Arabia it would have
been nothing for me to have taken a dagger and concealed
it in my robes and stabbed this sad specimen in the neck
and left him for some vultures to devour. In Can Xue, he'd
have been transformed into a blind black fly left to make
its way flying about in a room of spinning spiders.

❖

Things are never so bad as they seem to be in the night. It
is a platitude, that, but platitudes have their value, like
mulch. Because as bad as things are—sometimes they are
even worse than they appear to be at first—resolutions
grow like weeds the next morning. It is inevitable.

When it became clear, a week later, that his sister was not
going to participate in his game of threats, Berg confessed
his authorship of the typewritten notes. He even told her

that he was sorry, that he was cornered, trapped, and that she simply happened to be in the wrong place at the wrong time.

"Real genius," was her comeback, but he was far too involved, by then, in piecing together his relationship with Analise to be offended by such sarcasm; Grace had a right to be angry, after all, and while he knew he couldn't suddenly grow wings, he sensed that if he left her alone, didn't try so hard to act as nemesis or as pal, things might work themselves out over time. Analise was his concern, now. She had developed a sense of guilt, as Berg might have expected after that day when she with the rest of the crew had blown him off. During the weeks that followed their peculiar sojourn on Shelter, she offered to help him get the film finished, but only per Meade's firm instructions, in the city, in the controlled environment of a loft studio, with the standard sets—a bed, a backdrop—and with the understanding that a perfectionist director is worse than a lamp without a bulb, and of course Berg knew better than to turn the offer down. He did allow himself the pleasure of telling Analise what a treacherous harpy she'd shown herself to be, leaving him out there on the island the way she did, but she countered with a statement that ran something like, Given she had decided not to leave him stranded—and she certainly could have, damn it all, in light of what a primadonna he had shown himself to be—there was nothing more to say about the matter; and he knew when to say when.

They were back on the film within a week of Berg's encounter with Grace. As the production wore on he found that the original intensity of keeping things honed in tight to their truths, truths as he had always thought he'd seen them, waned. He cared less and less about holding the film up to the concept of being some kind of portrait of the Brush family. Analise and Meade, in their own persistent ways, became cowriters on the film. It changed. It varied, and varied drastically, from his painstaking script.

It didn't take long to finish. Analise had put a new title on the thing, and her colleague made no protest. There was a moment, as they were editing the film, when Berg determined that it might even be the better part of valor to destroy that script. Analise was convinced that what they had ended up with promised to make them some serious money. "Cannes you can forget," she told Berg, her arm around his shoulder in a small private viewing theater that a friend of Meade's had in the basement of his house out in the grasslands of New Jersey—on a beautiful horse farm there—"but I think that you can expect to get your investment back into the account, and then some."

Berg supposed he was grateful at least for that. But he still wondered what the film would have looked like had he been able to see it through, himself. It occurred to him that the only way for him to find out would be to start from the beginning, maybe rework the script, maybe even rewrite it from top to bottom, and then take his time ferreting out the right producer, all the right colleagues for the project.

They should be just malleable enough, he thought, to go along with his wilder propositions and just strong enough to be able to help him pull off, with discrimination and common sense, his film version of what he knew as the milieu in which he'd lived his life.

It wasn't too much to ask. Of himself, or anyone else. So strong were his hopes that it had even dawned on him it might be easier to take the monies that were going to be made off this first film and loop them right back around into the second and surely purer version. Why go through the hassle of having to thread the eyes of needles with unwieldy camels twice, if what he had in mind could succeed?

Yes; if he was right in his meditation on this subject, which now had become so dear to his heart, there would be no need for miracles. He knew that if he could get another shot at it he'd have camels doing back flips through those needle eyes. And let the eyes be burning bright with fire, at that; it might heighten the effect.

❖

Now that I've managed to make some notes, looking back
as a way of making a map—in the grand Brush tradition of
trusting maps—I have found that the flare man has been on
my mind, more and more. I don't know what I will do next,
so I wouldn't have any idea what map to pull out of my
father's map case. But I did think of doing this. I'm going
to try to find out if the people who live in that house up in
Harlem would mind if I visited my old room. People do
that, I think. Come back to the place where they grew up,
just to see what it looks like now that they are older, and
more experienced, and believe they can see it with mature
eyes—see it more clearly than they had when they were
young. I'm sure the flare man will have nothing to say to
me, now. He's probably playing his fabulous tricks for the
benefit of someone else's imagination.

Can Xue has been on my mind as well. I've even considered going to visit her, as a pilgrim, knowing full well that
she would be difficult to find, knowing moreover that she
is a woman not so much older than I, who might consider
my desire to be in her presence an unnecessary intrusion
on her time. She would probably tell me to go and have my
own dream, like Old Jiang and his wife had had, like Ru-
shu and her old man had. But I would know that there is
always the danger of wanting to dream about beautiful,
aristocratic cranes, and then finding yourself instead
among a tribe of croaking toads, trying to keep up with
them as they cross the long expanses of muddy earth they
prefer to inhabit. China is so far away, too. Oceans and
continents and cultures away. My questions seem so much
nearer.

If you can't trust dreams, you can at least try to trust
time. Time and experience have taught me to believe that
the osprey nest, that stick-cloud, will be there longer than
any Brush will be in the farmhouse within its purview.

Having made it through another winter of salty winds and soft snows, the ospreys will return every year, and add a few more sticks and pieces of our clothing and our tools and toys into its weave, just as it has always done in the past. Desmond, in some manner or form, will be there, too, patient as a raptor's aerie, waiting for me like the mother osprey to come home when the weather has warmed. And I know that I'll go there sometimes to visit them both, even though the osprey doesn't scare me as she used to, and though Desmond is too far on the other side of the death-curtain for me to be able to see him or hear him as I could once. But you go, and pay homage when you can. It's what one does. That saying about how it's hard to come back to a twice-left house may be true—but it is smart to test those sayings, as you know. They're like ghosts and can fade away too.

I wonder what will happen with Faw. Berg has told me that he's got the money back into the Trust (should I bother to believe him or not? the point is moot) and that the branch he had established to use for his own ends has been silently closed. The man from the Council of Churches (point moot) telephoned the other day, and asked me whether I would mind talking with him again. We're supposed to meet tomorrow. Him I know how to handle, him I know how to lead afield. Even though I have come to believe my original notion, that I could somehow play a part in the survival of our family, was misconceived (now I see it's a matter of emotional rather than corporate, or legal, survival, and my own, not others') I still can buy Faw something he can never find no matter what corner of the earth he plunders. Time. I'm not so blind that I can't see who they've targeted—they; that omnipresent governmental they—as the weakest link in the Brush chain, the bastards. I don't even care whether they have a thousand principles that clearly state they're right to be putting together their case against him; if I'm the one who's supposed to be so lame that I'll lead them wherever they want to go, then I'll hobble indeed with a hidden smile. Like Berg, Faw may or may not find his redemption. I think he might, because I think he is capable of finding what simple strength it would take to bring about such a thing. He's a builder, and though held in the thrall of obsessive movement there must be a still center, in his gypsy soul, which will eventually orient him. Meantime, the simplicity and clarity and directness that Erin Brush once showed, when her needs became clear to her, I would hold to myself as a model. Slow learner I am, but at least, I swear, a learner.

I still hope that twists and turns of the past can somehow be straightened out, leaving me free to walk on a different road than the one my feet are used to traveling on. In this way I'm like everyone I've ever met. Not that it would matter if I weren't. Time is a welder; time is a cutter. And time—dream in it as you may of toads or cranes, of church or wealth, of iron or a lover's flesh—is indulgent, for all its nasty side. It will let you do in it whatever you want. From where I sit it looks as if that could be the most subtle and dangerous gift any of us should ever hope to hold in our hands. Anyway, that's what I think.

BRADFORD MORROW is the author of a
previous novel, *Come Sunday*, a book of
fables, *A Bestiary*, and is editor of the
literary magazine *Conjunctions*. A Bard
Center Fellow at Bard College, he lives
in New York City.